**W9-DDL-958**

"A TAUT DRAMA OF SUSPENSE."
—*Newsweek*

"Read it. . . . You won't be disappointed."
—*Chicago Sun Times*

"Full of unusual twists. . . . Excitement carries the reader along to the very last page." —*Library Journal*

"What happens to Anne is chilling and suspenseful. . . . Kate Wilhelm peeks into the not-so-distant possibilities of the medical-scientific world." —*Publishers Weekly*

"A gripping story." —*Boston Herald Advertiser*

THE CLEWISTON TEST
A Nebula Award Nominee

**Books by Kate Wilhelm**

Abyss
City of Cain
The Clewiston Test*
The Downstairs Room
The Infinity Box
The Killer Thing
Let the Fire Fall
More Bitter Than Death
The Nevermore Affair
Where Late the Sweet Birds Sang*

*Published by POCKET BOOKS

# The
# Clewiston Test

## KATE WILHELM

**P** A KANGAROO BOOK
PUBLISHED BY POCKET BOOKS NEW YORK

*This is for Ed, Eula,*
*Ken, Russ, and David*
*With much love always*

## THE CLEWISTON TEST

Farrar, Straus edition published 1976

POCKET BOOK edition published February, 1977

This POCKET BOOK edition includes every word contained in
the original, higher-priced edition. It is printed from brand-
new plates made from completely reset, clear, easy-to-read type.
POCKET BOOK editions are published by
POCKET BOOKS,
a division of Simon & Schuster, Inc.,
A GULF+WESTERN COMPANY
630 Fifth Avenue,
New York, N.Y. 10020.
Trademarks registered in the United States
and other countries.

ISBN: 0-671-80888-5.
Library of Congress Catalog Card Number: 75-31683.
Front cover illustration by Alan Magee.
Back cover illustration by Roger Kastel.

Printed in the U.S.A.

# ONE

THE WATCHMAN made his last round at six in the morning. He left his station at the back entrance of the company and slowly walked the wide corridor to his first checkpoint. The only sound was that of his foam-soled shoes as they made contact with, then pulled away from, the waxed vinyl floor. The sound was a faint, regular squeak. He had been making this round for twenty-nine years, and he no longer heard his own footsteps consciously. He no longer had to consider anything; his feet took him, his hands punched the clocks, and if ever anything was wrong, he trusted his nose to sniff it out, his eyes to focus again to spot the trouble. Like a sleepwalker he made his rounds, not aware of any discomfort, not especially tired, not even bored.

His first check was the animal division. Unhurriedly he selected the right key, opened the door, and entered. The room was dimly lighted in such a way that the walls seemed to recede into distance, and with no personnel cluttering up the aisles between the cages, the room took on proportions that were on an inhuman scale, as if somehow this room had grown larger than the building that housed it.

The squeak, squeak of his shoes as he walked among the cages was part of the routine; no animal stirred. He checked the great double doors at the back wall and then shone his flashlight over the high, useless windows on the same wall. He started up the far side of the room toward the front again, and, midway, he paused.

Something was wrong. Mentally he ticked off the sections of the room: the guinea pigs, all sleeping, curled up, invisible almost. Some of the cats were awake, were always awake no matter when he looked in. The dogs had been quiet, although he knew their sleep was deceptive, that their ears, like antennae, followed his progress through the room. The chimps were quiet, each in its separate cage, sound asleep.

He shook his head and turned back and walked down the aisle, this time looking through each row of cages he passed. Then he saw the chimp, a large one, made gargantuan by the feeble glow of the night lights cast up from below. The chimp was standing up grasping the bars of its cage. It was watching him.

The watchman exhaled softly. He took several steps toward the cage, played his light over the lock to make certain it was secure. "Ugly bastard," he muttered. The feeling of wrongness persisted as he made his rounds, and only gradually faded.

The chimp continued to stand holding the bars. Presently his lips stretched back over his teeth and the hair on the back of his neck began to rise. He gripped the bars tighter and tested them, tried to shake them. After a few more minutes, he left the front of the cage, withdrew to the shadows under the shelf, and sat down on his haunches to stare straight ahead unblinkingly. No other chimp stirred.

Miles away, across from Cherokee Park, a smudge of light appeared on the ground floor of one of the solid old three-story buildings. Drapes were opened and a three-sectioned bay window revealed, with greenery in it, and a warm light streaming from it.

The room behind the windows was large, with space enough for the oversized bed, two comfortable chairs covered with rust-colored velvet, a chaise, a card table with two straight chairs. Pushed to the side, leaving four feet between it and the bed, was an exerciser, parallel metal bars with a green rubber walkway. The house had been built when ten-foot ceilings were not an unacceptable expense, and the high ceiling had been followed by the bay window that made up the southern wall. The doors in the north wall were solid maple, the floor dark and light oak parquet.

The door to the bathroom opened and slowly Anne pushed it wider to give clearance for the wheelchair. Clark had been in to open the drapes. She wondered if he waited until he knew she was in the bathroom to do it every morning. He knew it pained her to be seen heaving herself out of the chair clumsily, fearfully; as graceful as a hippopotamus, she thought, eyeing the bed that sometimes seemed an impossible goal. That morning she felt stronger, she decided determinedly, setting the brake; she began to arrange herself for the pull up from the chair, the shift to the side of the bed. She winced when she lowered her body, and sternly she told herself it had not hurt, and it really had not. It was the thought of pain, the memory of pain that she feared. Then she lay back on her pillow and relaxed again. She was trembling slightly.

It was too early to tell if today the sun would shine. Beyond the bay window the world was dull and gray. She reached for a cigarette and drew back. Not before breakfast. Instead, she studied the bay window. She imagined she could hear Clark moving about in the kitchen getting coffee made, doing eggs and toast. He approached his cooking chores exactly the same way he did his lab experiments, with precision, working to an interior timetable that saw everything finished together with little wasted effort. She wished he would hurry with the coffee. Again she concentrated on the window.

It was made up of six small panes of glass in each section, bordered by smaller irregular bits of stained glass, not in a fruit or flower motif, but simply odd geometrical shapes leaded together randomly. The colors in the stained glass were rich, and when it was sunny, vibrant reds, blues, greens, yellows fixed first here, then there, changing, not always subtly, those objects so lighted. The bay window was ten feet wide, with a window seat painted soft white. There were no curtains, only opaque beige drapes that, when closed, followed the curve of the window, leaving the wide ledge clear. There were cushions on it, hot colors—

bright yellows, oranges, crimson—and a terrarium, a
five-gallon carboy that housed a little world of tropical
lush growth—purple leaves, velvety greens, whites.
The earth in the terrarium was jet black with flecks of
white vermiculite that looked like snow. There were
other plants on the window seat, but they had been
neglected. Leaves had fallen from the African violets,
there were brown-tipped leaves on the philodendron,
and the dieffenbachia had grown toward the light without being turned, so that it seemed to have rejected the
room, and showed the backs of heavily veined leaves—
plant architecture that was stark and functional.

For two weeks Anne had been watching the leaves
twist more each day, until now they were vertical, all
looking out together. No one else had noticed them.
How queer it would be to live in that time frame, she
thought, where that gradual movement would seem
natural and perhaps even swift. Once, as a child, she
had sprouted beans in a glass with a piece of blotter
that reached down into an inch of water on the bottom
and held the beans against the clear side so their every
change could be observed. But the changes had been
impossible to watch, only the difference could be
measured each day.

On either side of the bed were night tables, one of
them a hospital stand with a plastic top and with doors
that concealed a washbasin and bedpan. She no longer
needed the equipment, but the stand was still there,
and a pitcher of water on it sweated and made pud-
dles. On the other table, books were stacked, along
with an ashtray, a notebook and pencils, magazines—
scientific journals and a chess magazine—and a calendar in an elaborate silver frame, deeply carved, rococo,
a gift from Clark's mother. She drew the calendar to
her and with heavy, firm strokes made a red cross
through the date, Monday, February 6. She had started
the crosses in November.

"Hi, honey. Coffee." Clark came into the room with
a tray and put it down on the card table before the bay
window. They had been having their meals in the room

at that table for the past months. He had poached an egg for her, had made bacon and fried eggs for himself, and a pot of coffee. In the mornings she didn't get up to sit at the table. Later, after Ronnie arrived, she would get up again. Clark was unwilling to go to work unless she was safe in bed. He was afraid she might fall. Because, she thought, she had fallen once, and it hurt like hell, but more than that, it had frightened them both terribly. "The tibia is delicate," the doctor had said. "We don't know just why, but often there is trouble getting it to heal properly. You're not unique there, Annie."

Clark propped her up with the chair pillow and then went to the window. A fine rain had started. In January there had been three days when the sun shone all day long. In February, still young, still hopeful, there had been one such day. Anne sighed and started to eat her egg.

"Might be late," Clark said, chewing. "Board-meeting day again."

She nodded. After the board meeting the different departments had their own meetings. "Klugman will manage to remind you gently that I'm still on payroll and my brain belongs to Prather," she said.

Clark grinned at her and said, "That's okay as long as the rest belongs to me." He drank his coffee. He had plenty of time. Clark always woke up before the alarm clock sounded; it was as if the action of setting the clock also set one in his head and it went off first, soundlessly, with greater urgency than the mechanical one. He poured more coffee for both of them.

"And Klugman will also remind me that March 30 is creeping up on us. He'll want reassurance that you'll be there, all well and glowing and smiling."

"But I won't. I'll scowl and look like a mad genius," Anne said, scowling to demonstrate.

Clark laughed and sat on the side of the bed with his cup in his hand, and smoothed her hair back with the other hand. "You don't know how to scowl, and you don't look mad, and you aren't anyone's stereotypical genius. What you look like is a damn sexy blonde in a pretty frilly thing, and if I don't rape you outright in the next few weeks, I'll be a candidate for sainthood." He spoke lightly, but his hand on her hair became too still and when he moved it away his motion was brusque. He returned to the table and lighted a cigarette.

Anne, looking at him, thought how broad he was. What thick arms and legs, deep chest. She always thought of him as a very large man when he wasn't there, but actually it was simply his massive build; he was not tall. She was an inch taller than he, but still he gave the impression, left the impression, of a very large man. He always liked sex in the morning, while she, as she once had whispered, liked to go to sleep wet between the legs. It was because he woke up so thoroughly so suddenly. He awakened in a room that was lighted, heated, everything ready to be used, needing only for the occupant to step inside to start functioning perfectly. And her room was dark when she awakened; she groped around for hours finding the light switches and the furniture, waiting for the heat to spread throughout. But, even if it never would occur to her to initiate sex in the morning, it didn't take much to make her as horny as he was, and looking at his broad back, she wanted him as much as he wanted and needed her.

"Deena will be here in ten minutes," Anne said softly.

"Yeah. Be right back." He moved fast, almost jerkily. His movements were those of a thin nervous person, not one built as solidly as he. In a moment he was back with his corduroy coat and rubbers. No particular dress was required in the lab, although it was understood that all other downstairs departments observed the coat and tie rule. Clark wore faded slacks that were fraying slightly at the bottoms, a short-sleeved shirt with ink stains at the pocket. His pockets all bulged with notes and trivia that he forgot to sort through for weeks at a time, simply transferring the mass from pocket to pocket each morning. His muscular arms were dark with hair; his shirt, unbuttoned at the neck, revealed thick hair on his chest. His belly was hairy, his back; if he let his beard grow, as he had done three years ago, it was bushy and wild-looking. Now and then, when he remembered, he cut his hair, and usually he kept it above his collar, but that Monday morning it was long, and it curled about his ears and over his shirt collar. It was very black and shiny.

A bear person, Anne thought, watching him pat his pockets, feeling for what she didn't know. He carried a pocketknife with a can opener and a corkscrew and a spoon and a screwdriver all built in. He had fingernail clippers, and a comb, cigarettes and a cigarette lighter that didn't work, but that he meant to leave off to be repaired when he thought of it. There were pens and pencils. At least two notebooks, small spiral ones with the pages loose and ragged. There were match folders, receipts, trading stamps, paper money, and coins. Once she had cleaned out his pockets and counted over eight dollars in change. There were keys. The house and car keys, lab keys, keys for his desk and his locker, and her desk and locker at the lab, keys to a car he no longer owned, keys to the suitcases in the apartment basement storage room, and keys to his parents' home. When she had said once how stupid it was to carry every damn key he owned, he had agreed, as he stuffed them back into various pockets.

He left again to get his briefcase, and now he was ready. "I'll call you," he said, pulling on his rubbers.

She nodded, smiling. He would call three or four times.

"Anything I can pick up on the way home?"

She shook her head, still smiling. He left their car for the practical nurse, Ronnie, to use to take Anne for therapy, or shopping, or whatever, and it never would occur to him to ask Deena to stop for an errand.

"Look, why don't you have Harry stay for dinner with you. I'll have a bite when I get home."

Anne laughed. "You always say the same things, did

you know that? And I always answer the same. I'll wait. If Harry can stay, he'll wait too. Ronnie will fix us a casserole or something that will hold for however long it has to."

He came back to the bed then and leaned over to kiss her chastely on the forehead. "Right. Look, ask your doctor about that other little matter. Okay? See you tonight." The horn sounded outside, and he left, waving at the bedroom door. It seemed very still in the apartment as soon as the hallway door opened and closed.

Anne considered the day stretching out before her. Therapy on Mondays at ten. Back home exhausted, lunch, nap. Fifteen minutes with the exerciser at two. She looked at it distastefully. It was only fifteen feet long, but it seemed to her, standing at one end, looking at the other, an impossible distance. Rest after that. At four or so, Harry, her uncle, would come to keep her company, play chess, talk about his students. He taught eighth-grade classes in social science, history, and, it seemed, any other subject where there was a shortage of teachers. One year, he had a girls' gym class.

Leaning on one elbow, she began to work a thick notebook out from under the stack of magazines. Usually the stack started an inexorable slide to the floor at this point; she pulled the notebook free and leaned back with her eyes closed, the notebook in her hand, and listened to the noise the magazines made as they hit the floor. Her pen was clipped to the cover of the notebook; presently she began to write.

Deena talked disconsolately about the weather as she drove, and Clark listened without paying attention. He didn't understand people who gave thought to the weather. He never knew if it would snow or rain before the day was over. He wore his rubbers when it was raining and didn't think about them if the sun was shining. It wasn't that he was surprised by the elements, it was simply that he accepted whatever there was. His gaze was straight ahead, but instead of the rain-obscured traffic, in his mind there was an image of Anne in the bed, her pale wavy hair tight against her head, no makeup, and to him beautiful. It had surprised him once to overhear two of their friends discussing her coolly. One had said she was not very pretty, and the other had agreed, but both had said something about attractiveness. He hadn't understood that either. To him she was beautiful. Her hair was pale brown; she had been a towhead as a child and over the years it had darkened; her skin was warm and glowing without a blemish, her eyes deep blue. She was tall and slender, with broad shoulders, perhaps too broad for a woman, and lovely, long legs that she sometimes said just went on and on without knowing when to stop. She was comfortable in jeans, slung low on her slender hips, but when she dressed up and used makeup, she was model-lovely, and he knew most men envied him. She was quiet with strangers and few people ever realized how intelligent she was. Growing up in a family of mediocrities, she had learned very young that her own brilliance was the oddity, and she had learned not to voice her quips and judgments, not to demonstrate her intelligence in any way.

"I said, Emory wants to see you before the board meeting," Deena said. There was an exasperated tone in her voice, as if she had been talking for a while.

"Sorry." Clark shook himself and looked about to see if they were there yet. They were a few blocks from the plant. "I'll do it first thing. Anything in particular on his mind?"

"The usual thing. How long are we going to have to keep cluttering up our department with your monkeys? He knows as well as I, and you, that we'll keep them until Anne says she's through with them, but he has to ask, so his latest dope is the latest dope. You know."

"Sure." Deena was a psychologist, in the animal lab. Nearly forty, divorced, with a daughter in her early teens, Deena had to prove her own intelligence over and over, he thought. She had become a militant femi-

nist in the past year and consequently most of the
people in both departments tried to avoid her whenever
possible, which made her still more aggressive. She had
no illusions about whose work the Clewiston-Symons
experiments were, really. Her reports to Anne each
week were meticulously detailed and at least once a
week she dropped by to talk with Anne about the
work.

They turned in at the gate and followed a line of
cars to the east lot behind the new research annex.
Anne was the brains behind the idea; it had been hers
from the start, and his name was attached only because
she had insisted that without his encouragement, the
long talks they had had, his role of devil's advocate,
and then his meticulous follow-up work, nothing would
be there to be called anything. All true, he reminded
himself. Together they made a hell of a team. But it
was her baby. And it was going to make her a big
name in their field. Maybe even a prize. There was no
resentment in the thought. He was very proud of his
wife, very proud that she was his wife.

## TWO

BY NINE O'CLOCK the rain was steady and starting to
freeze on the colder surfaces—wires, tree limbs,
bridges. Bob Klugman stood at the window of Edward
Helverson's office and watched the rain. Behind him,
Jack Newell was leafing through pages of a report from
the production department, muttering now and then,
making notes. He had had the report all weekend, but
hadn't found time to digest it. He was frightening, Bob
Klugman thought, unable to watch the young man skim
the meaning from the pages almost as fast as he could
turn them. That speed-reading course had done it, of
course. He should take a course like that. Wouldn't
have to mention it, just do it quietly and let the results

speak for themselves. He sipped black coffee and knew
he wouldn't take any course ever again. The ship's
clock on the wall chimed nine and he checked his
watch. Helverson would be there within thirty seconds.
Never be more than thirty seconds late, was his motto.
Also, make the others be there ten minutes early. Bob
sipped again. He hadn't had breakfast and there was a
sour taste in his mouth; the coffee was bitter. Had to
give up sugar, give up smoking, give up late hours, and
what for? he wondered, watching the water run down
the window. What the hell for? Sixty. Five more years,
then out. And what for? Even knowing his thoughts
were merely Monday-morning thoughts, he couldn't
shake them. It was that damn Newell flipping pages,
trying to prove some damn thing, making a big show
out of it. If he was really efficient he would have done
the homework at home, or in his office, not here.

The door opened and Edward Helverson entered.
He was six feet tall, with prematurely silvered hair,
and he looked like presidential material. He had the
air of confidence, the openness, the friendliness mixed
with reserve, the good health and lean, lithe figure that
could endure the stress of being president of a company, or vice president of a corporation, with his eye on
the chairman's seat in another ten years. At forty-four
he was at the age to start the ascent to the very top.

Jack Newell stood aside while Helverson took Bob
Klugman's plump hand and shook it warmly. Jack
Newell was dark and slim, and unobtrusive, as an
assistant should be. He and Helverson didn't shake
hands. When Helverson turned to him, he nodded almost imperceptibly and Bob Klugman felt uncomfortable, aware a message had been passed.

"Bob, how's it going? What's new?"

Bob shrugged, never quite certain how to answer a
question like that. Did he really want to know what
was going on in R&D, or was he making conversation,
warming up to the real subject that had summoned Bob
to this pre-board meeting?

"Sit down, Bob. More coffee? Is it hot?" Helverson

poured himself a cup of the steaming coffee and sat down with it, not going behind his large, empty desk, but choosing instead one of a pair of leather chairs with a table between them. Bob sat in the other chair, uncomfortable, wanting a cigarette. There was an ashtray on the table, but it was polished onyx and looked as if it never had been used.

"We've had a break, Bob," Helverson said. "A piece of incredible luck. How soon can you get things lined up for the pregnancy tests and the teratology studies on Clewiston's serum?"

Bob blinked rapidly. "The end of March we're holding a meeting, have our plans ready to go as soon as the IND is approved."

"We're getting the IND back this week, Bob," Helverson said, and leaned back, smiling.

"This week?" Bob looked from him to Jack Newell in confusion.

"We'll be going ahead as soon as you can get the stuff ready. This afternoon I'm meeting with Dr. Grove to arrange subjects for the pregnancy studies. He'll have his data ready in a day or two and we'll have a full committee meeting then."

"But our schedule . . . There are problems with computer time. Collecting blood samples, making the analyses . . ."

Helverson stood up and held out his hand. The interview was over. "I know you can handle that end of it, Bob. First priority, all that. Arrange for overtime, whatever you need. This comes first. As it should," he said, frowning slightly now. "Think of the suffering, Bob, all that needless suffering. My God, if we can knock a week off for some poor soul out there, make life worth living again a day sooner, isn't it worth the extra effort it might take here? We can do it, Bob. At the meeting this morning I'm going to announce that we can go ahead by the fifteenth. And we can do it, Bob! We can!"

Bob Klugman was being propelled to the door. Momentarily, he resisted the gentle pressure. "But Anne Clewiston, Mrs. Symons, she's not back yet."

"And I'm counting on you to keep her informed every step of the way. My God, when I think of that brilliant young woman, a genius, Bob. One of God's gifted ones. I stand in awe of her ability, Bob! She's to be on the committee, just as planned from the beginning, and as soon as her recovery permits, she'll be there in person."

Bob Klugman stood outside the door and blinked without understanding. He thought of the bottle in his desk, and he shuddered and started to walk. Nine o'clock and he was thinking of the bottle. Annie would kill him, he thought, work her way through him right up to Helverson and kill him, too. He felt sorry for Clark, who would have to tell her, and again the image of the bottle came to mind, and this time he hurried a bit.

Clark stood in the open doorway of Emory Durand's office and looked at the scene beyond while Emory talked of the lack of consideration everyone showed his department.

The animal laboratory was the biggest single room in the Prather Pharmaceuticals complex. Bigger even than the production departments on the second and third floors. This end of the lab was devoted to small animals, mice, guinea pigs, rats, even some snakes in glass cages. Beyond, out of sight from where Clark stood, were cat and dog cages. He could hear the excited yapping of the dogs as they were being fed, and the occasional howl of a cat. Farther still were the primates, spider monkeys, gibbons, and the chimps that he and Anne had used. At that time of day the lab was abuzz with activity as the animals were fed, specimens of stools and urine collected, blood taken for testing; animals were being taken from the night cages to various communal compounds for daytime study. White-coated figures moved among the animals, pushing carts of food, testing equipment, transport cages. The lab was spotless, and there was practically no odor.

Emory Durand was the supervisor of this department. He was a veterinarian, and it was rumored that he had taken this job only to escape having to sacrifice animals personally. He never attended the sacrificial slaughter or participated in autopsies. The lab people all called him Noah behind his back. The spotlessness of the lab was reflected in his office and his person. His shoes were polished, white. His trousers were creased, white. His lab coat never showed a smudge. They said Noah dusted his chair every time he used it. His hair was sandy, thin, kept short, and his skin was pale and looked unhealthy, although he never missed a day or complained of anything. He was a vegetarian with no vices. Altogether a despicable character whom everyone should automatically hate, Clark thought. But no one hated Emory Durand. He was one of the most popular men in the downstairs section. His own people feared and respected him, and brought him their troubles if necessary, and outside his department he was admired and liked. Anne had said once that it was because he treated people with the same grave courtesy and respect that he showed his animals. Clark had put it more bluntly. You could trust him. That summed up Emory Durand for him.

Emory's voice rose slightly and he knew Emory was trying to force him to pay attention, to be concerned. He listened.

"I fully expect a herd of elephants to show up any day. 'Take care of them,' someone will say and disappear. And I ask you, Clark, how many animals do they really think we can fit into a finite space? How many?"

Noah's Ark was packed, Clark admitted, silently. No one dared encourage him because they all felt some degree of guilt. Emory Durand was probably the most overworked person in the plant. "Is the annex causing the trouble now?" he asked.

"The annex. Your goddamn monkeys. At least the control chimps. Can't we get rid of them?"

Clark shook his head. A white-coated girl passed, pushing a cart loaded with a stack of stainless-steel bowls, a scale, a bucket of malodorous mush that looked like shit. Feeding time for the guinea pigs. Clark wrinkled his nose and stepped backward into the office, closing the door.

"Soy beans and sawdust," Emory said in disgust. The annex people were working on soy-protein products and their offerings seemed more noisome each day. Also, the guinea pigs were wasting away and showing a tendency to die in convulsions.

"Give us a couple more months," Clark said, returning to the subject of the chimps. "Probably three at the most. The IND should be in by then and we'll know if they've approved it."

Emory sighed. "So far, Henry Barrington's the only one to say heave them out. And he has a dozen white mice at stake. A lousy dozen white mice. Okay, Clark. I had to ask. So I'll go to the board and demand more money, an annex of my own, more assistants, more equipment . . ." His voice was toneless now with resignation. "And they'll pat me on the head and say what a fine job . . ."

A hoarse scream followed immediately by the sound of breaking glass penetrated the office. Clark yanked the door open and moved out of the way as Emory dashed past him. They ran to the other end of the room.

One of the lab assistants was sitting on the floor, holding his arm close to his chest. The redness of blood against his white lab coat was shocking. A low moan started, rose, fell and repeated, over and over. A long-haired girl was standing rigidly, staring down the aisle of cages. She was pale, ready to go into hysterics. Clark grabbed her arm and shook her. "What happened?"

Deena appeared, buttoning her lab coat. Emory was kneeling at the side of the injured man now, and others were gathering, getting in the way, asking questions.

Above it all the animals were screeching, chattering, howling in excitement. Clark shook the rigid girl again. "What happened?"

"The monkey bit him! It tried to kill him! I saw it! It tried to kill him!"

"Snap out of it!" Clark said, holding her arm too hard, ready to shake her again. "Where is it now?"

She nodded toward the aisle and he released her. She staggered backward away from him, turned and ran.

Clark glanced toward the injured man. He seemed to be in shock. The moaning continued. Emory was telling someone to get a doctor, a stretcher, call an ambulance. Clark turned toward the aisle. Deena's voice sounded close by, calm, low, soothing.

"Duckmore, come here. Come on." She came from between two cages, looking between the two opposite her. "Come on, Duckmore."

A large male chimp appeared and held out his hand. Deena took it and started to walk back toward the chimp cage with him, speaking in a low voice that somehow seemed to carry over the tumult of the lab. Clark watched while she put the chimp back inside the cage and locked the door. The chimp settled on his haunches and peered out calmly at the cluster of people around the man he had tried to kill.

Deena went to Emory then and knelt. "Can he talk?"

Emory shook his head. He was holding the man's arm to his chest and was supporting his weight now. The assistant's eyes were open, but blind with shock. Even his lips were white.

Deena stood up. "Did anyone see it? What happened?"

The girl who had been pushing the tray of guinea-pig food said, "The chimp's been trying to get him for a week. He told me the chimp hated him. For nothing. No reason at all. He was good to the animals."

Presently the doctor arrived and the first-aid crew,

and the bystanders left. Clark stood by Deena's office as order gradually returned to the animal laboratory.

"Can you tell anything about Duckmore?" Clark asked, when Deena appeared.

"He's as normal as ever, as far as I can tell," she said.

"Did the kid tease him? Hurt him over a period of time?"

She shook her head. "You know we wouldn't tolerate anything like that. No, Pat was good with them. He likes animals. They respond."

"Yeah," Clark said moodily.

"Don't get in a panic," Deena said. "We'll observe Duckmore for a while, run some tests. Maybe he saw Pat fondle one of the young chimps, became jealous. God knows what's going on in their heads."

"Yeah," Clark said again. "Look, can you get some blood tests right away? An EEG? Whatever else you can think of?"

"It's already started," she said crisply. "I'll send results over as soon as they start coming in."

Scowling at the floor, Clark returned to his own office. The animal lab was the entire west portion of the sprawling complex. Separated from it by a wide corridor were the research laboratories: Petro-Chemicals, Dyes, Food Additives, Industrial Compounds, and Pharmaceuticals. The pharmaceutical division was the largest, the original lab space, with wide, high windows and ancient steel lockers, an uneven floor that tended to collect rollable objects in one spot under the water fountain. In Pharmaceuticals the walls had been painted yellow and green back in year one, and the color scheme never had been changed. This lab seemed abnormally quiet after the animal division. A dozen people were working at various pieces of equipment. The others were in their offices.

It was here that old man Prather had mixed up his first liniments, his first aspirins and cough syrups. He had compounded iron tablets as big as quarters and then worked to make them small enough for a gentle-woman to swallow. If ghosts walked, then Prather's must have wandered that lab, unchanged except for modern stainless-steel machines that surely would have puzzled him, and computer terminals that would have puzzled him even more. What would he make of cortisone doses so small that they had to be mixed with starch, just to make them visible? Of timed-release capsules that automatically regulated the doses of whatever was needed? Of radioactive materials in pretty blue and pink capsules that couldn't be handled by the people who filled them, but had to be manipulated through lead doors using waldoes?

Clark shook his head, bringing his thoughts back to now, back to the chimp that had gone berserk. He stared at the wall beyond his desk, almost close enough to reach from where he sat and thought. Duckmore had gone berserk, but maybe the assistant had teased him. Maybe he had a sadistic streak that he had managed to hide but indulged privately with the animals. Maybe inadvertently he had issued a challenge to the chimp. Maybe he had twisted Duckmore's arm unnecessarily in hurrying him from his cage to the compound. Maybe . . . Maybe the *pa* factor they had given Duckmore almost a year ago had personality-altering characteristics that were just beginning to show up. Clark rubbed his eyes, tearing from staring so intently at the blank green wall. Maybe.

## THREE

BOB KLUGMAN looked at Clark obliquely and shook his head. "You can't be serious," he said, for the third time. "We can't back up six months."

"We can't go ahead," Clark said impatiently. "We can't start human testing in two weeks."

"Deena, how's the monkey now?" Bob asked, turning from Clark. He felt a rumble in his stomach and knew that soon it would be burning and gas would be building, pressing against his heart, making him wheeze.

"It's a chimp, as you know," Deena said, looking just above his shoulder as she spoke to him. She had smelled liquor on entering the office; her mouth was tight and hard, her gaze avoided his deliberately. "Duckmore appears normal enough. We don't have any test results yet."

"Well, give it your personal attention. Divert whatever else you can and follow it through." Klugman looked at his watch; the board meeting had been in session for half an hour, too late to contact Helverson, to alert him to the possibility of trouble. He turned to Emory Durand. "How are the other animals in that group? Any more trouble?"

Emory shook his head. "I agree with Clark, however. It would be a mistake to ignore this incident. I'll talk with Pat as soon as he is out of sedation and find out what the hell happened, but even that won't be enough. We need weeks of close observation, followed by autopsy, brain examination, cellular-tissue study, the whole works. It's a setback, Bob. You have to face that and explain to Helverson what it means."

"But chances are that it has nothing to do with the stuff. Isn't that right?"

"Hell, Bob, you know the scene. You were on this side of the desk for twenty years, damn it! Helverson's got a sudden itch to move, let him sweat out whatever's bugging him. You know and I know the FDA won't permit us to go ahead with this kind of situation hanging. We have to investigate it, and that means a setback. Even if nothing comes of the investigation." Emory spoke calmly, but his words were too separate, too distinctly enunciated; they belied the calm.

For a moment Bob Klugman stared at Emory, then his gaze dropped and he watched his pudgy fingers trace circles on his desk top. "Opinions," he said. "Do you believe this incident has anything to do with the *pa* factor? Emory?"

"I don't think so," Emory said, after a pause. "But I don't hold that as a belief. I would be unwilling to go ahead on that basis."

"Deena?"

"No. It's been too long. The *poena albumin* dropped back down to normal in eight hours, and it's remained normal since. There has been no physiological change in the intervening months." She didn't look at him; her voice was crisp and professional and very remote.

"Clark?"

"I don't know. My bias urges me to say no emphatically, but I don't know."

Bob studied him. "I wonder what Anne would say." It wasn't a question. No one answered. "How is Anne?"

"She's making fine progress."

"You'll report this to her?"

Clark shook his head. "Not just yet. It would upset her and we don't have enough facts yet. Let me wait for the lab reports on Duckmore. Let's hear what the kid has to say about the attack. Maybe he really did do something to stir up the chimp, maybe he'll admit to something." Deena shook her head, and Emory frowned. Neither of them believed the lab assistant had been to blame. Clark turned back to Bob Klugman. "I think we should wait for Gus to get back before we do anything. He's been following this from the start. Let's hear what he has to say about it. Besides, Emory is right. The IND won't be approved until we clear up any question about this incident."

"The IND has already been approved," Bob Klugman said then. "Helverson wouldn't have told me to go ahead if he didn't know it had already been approved. He's seeing Grove today, and Wednesday we'll have a full committee meeting to finalize the testing procedures."

There was silence in the office. Clark looked at the window streaming water under the steady rain. In the country the rain was still freezing, but in the city it was only rain. It coated the window, isolated them even more from the real world, changed the real world beyond the windows into a surreal, plastic place with shifting lines and unsteady surfaces. They were waiting for him to say something, he realized. On Anne's behalf he should protest, or comment, or belch, or do something. He continued to watch the water on the window. She would be wild with joy over the approval of the FDA of the investigational drug application, and furious that they were going ahead without her. She was to be one of the principals on the committee to oversee the human experiments; she had been looking forward to that for years. Sometimes he knew she was more knowledgeable about the procedure than he; she could see further ahead than he ever could. She had anticipated some of the problems of human testing along with the original conception of the *pa* factor, while he had been plotting their course on a day-to-day basis.

Deena spoke up suddenly, and she didn't attempt to hide the anger in her voice. "Anne has been planning this part of the experiment for months, and everyone knows it. She's been working on the plans at home, flat on her back. You can't simple take this away from her just because Helverson is antsy."

It wasn't fair, Bob Klugman thought, for them to treat him like this. He was their superior. They should treat him with the same deference he had to show his superiors. He stood up. "We'll go ahead and plan for the tests to begin," he said, trying to force the same firm decision into his voice that Helverson had used with him. "Meanwhile, you'll be getting the lab reports on the monkey. We'll see if the IND comes through. Deena, you and Clark both know Anne's ideas for the human tests. You can represent her." They all stood up and now Deena's gaze did stop on him; he turned away from it. As soon as they were gone, he thought, he'd call Gus, tell him they had an emergency, get him back on the job. It wasn't fair for him to have to decide this alone. Gus knew more about what was going on in the lab than he did. It really was Gus Weinbacher's job to make these decisions, not his.

Sometimes Bob Klugman almost recognized the truth that he didn't like being vice president in charge of research and development. He had wanted to be an organic chemist, had been a damn good chemist, had won top honors in his class, graduated *summa cum laude*. When this promotion had come, he and his wife had celebrated joyously. He was getting the recognition he deserved, he had thought then, and had made trips to several different libraries just to see his name in *Who's Who* and the regional biographies. And then what happened? he sometimes wondered, usually after his third drink and before his fifth. Something had happened, and he couldn't understand what it was. All the arguments he had to settle were petty; the scientists he had to handle were childish, demanding, selfish, each one convinced his work was of top importance, with no regard for anyone else's work. And they demanded Bob Klugman agree with them, each in turn. He didn't know how to stall them, how to soothe them when they were excited, how to encourage them when they were down, and over the years he had lost touch with the specific details of the various departments, so that he could hardly even follow their arguments now. Sometimes he dreamed of the time when he had had his own little office that no one could enter, when he would be engrossed in his own problems for weeks, months, even years at a time, bothering no one, demanding nothing except time to work, space to work in. Those were the days, he thought.

He had been easy to get along with, he knew. He hadn't made impossible demands on his superiors, had respected them, and they in turn respected him. His fellow workers had respected him then. And everything changed. The new breed, he thought bitterly, had only scorn for those who had been around a few years. They thought he was getting old, that he could be treated with contempt because he was getting old and was tired. Because he was ill sometimes. Even his wife was contemptuous of his illness, forcing him into one doctor's hands after another. She would be satisfied only when he could do nothing but sit and stare at a wall. Then she would be quiet. *Drinking won't help!* she'd scream at him. *If you're sick, see a doctor. If you're not sick, stop moaning and acting sick!* Just because there were still illnesses they couldn't diagnose, just because none of them could find his trouble, cure it, she pretended he didn't have a medical problem. *The only problem you have is the bottle!*

He shut his eyes. Not true. He was sick, and nothing helped. Nothing. His back ached and his head ached and there was the threat of a heart attack any time, and his stomach was bad, and he couldn't sleep . . . He felt tears forming and he opened his desk drawer and took out the bottle and poured half a glass of Scotch. Now this, when Gus was gone, and no one was around to take care of it. And they treated him like dirt, less than dirt. He could feel his stomach churning and knew he was going to have another attack.

He lifted his phone and told his secretary to get Gus for him, and when she reported no one answered his room in the hotel on Antigua, he told her to keep trying until she did get him, to have him paged, to leave an urgent message with the desk. But get him.

Anne leaned back on the chaise and waited for Ronnie to bring lunch. She pulled the afghan higher and closed her eyes, going over the doctor's words once more. "You have to get more exercise, young lady. You're getting lazy. We'll measure you for crutches today, and start you walking next week. How about that?"

And her reaction had been both excitement and reluctance. Crutches were ugly, she thought, and a person on crutches was ugly, his body hunched up grotesquely, dangling from the armpits while his legs flailed about in uncoordination. Even as this thought had come to mind, over it she had recalled, from one of the early sessions with the therapist, his proposed treatments. After four to six weeks of the crutches, he had said, you'll be so sick and tired of them you'll heave them out and start walking again on your own. Six weeks! Possibly four weeks! She didn't believe the shorter time; she knew her own strength and didn't believe she could recover enough muscle tone in four weeks to permit her to walk unaided. But six weeks was nothing! Not after the months in bed, in the hated wheelchair. Six weeks!

The therapist had been full of surprises that morning. "Can you swim?" he had asked. "No matter. You'll learn if you can't."

"I swim rather well."

"I've scheduled you for four days a week at the health spa off Cherokee Drive. That's just a few blocks from where you live, isn't it?"

She stared at him. "I don't understand."

"You're getting flabby. Look at your arms. Flab. You'll start with ten minutes, and work up to forty-five to an hour in no time. It's a heated pool."

She had stared, and he had laughed at her. Dr. Federicks was a comfortable man, easy to talk to, easy to confide in. Large, heavy-set, a tease in a pleasant way, like a grandfather, someone else's grandfather.

"Look, Anne, you're not a chronic invalid. You're making a very good recovery now and the rest will follow with an inevitable, even dull, routine. Just don't get pregnant for a while."

"You mean . . . ?"

"Anne, you can do anything now. Have fun. I told you that weeks ago."

"I didn't understand."

"Oh, Lord! Go home and screw! Now you understand?" And he had laughed uproariously until she had been forced to laugh also.

Clark called before Ronnie appeared with the lunch tray. "Tired?" he asked. His voice on the phone was mysterious, low, more seductive than in person; sometimes she felt that she was discussing intimate details of her life with a stranger when she talked by phone to her husband.

"Tired," she admitted. "But there's good news. I got measured for crutches. I'll get them next week."

"Hey! I'll take you walking in the park!" They talked about crutches for a minute or so, and then, curiously reluctant to tell him the rest of her news, she said instead, "Anything new down there?"

At once his voice changed. He knew she was holding back something, she thought, and closed her eyes hard, barely listening to his answer. And now it would sound silly, evasive, to say, oh, by the way, I'm going swimming tomorrow and the doctor said screw. She relaxed her grip on the phone and tried to find her place in his rambling talk. Something about a department meeting, he might not be able to call back later. She nodded. He knew. Then they said goodbye and miserably she hung up and shivered under the afghan. Why hadn't she told him?

To punish him, she realized. To punish him for saying he'd take her for a walk. Show off his crippled wife in the park, hobbling along on crutches, feeling the stares follow her progress.

Suddenly she saw again the car out of control racing toward them on a rain-slicked street, on a day just like this one. Clark had been driving. Clark always drove. Having her drive made him feel superfluous. He swerved and they skidded and the oncoming car smashed into them, on her side. She remembered it remotely, as if it were a scene from a movie only partially recalled. There was no emotional overtone to her memory. Just the facts, she thought. Just the facts. She could remember the sounds of the crash clearer than any other details. The horrifying crash of metal on metal, of screaming wheels, of a human scream that she still didn't identify as hers. For a long time she had been pinned, and there were sounds connected with that. Someone sobbing, screaming with pain, and then again metal on metal as they tore the car apart to free her. Later she learned she had a crushed pelvis, and a

compound fracture of the right tibia. Clark had been
shaken up; he had suffered mild bruises, and con-
tusions. The other driver, whose fault it all was, was
uninjured.

She thought of Mr. Leonard Chelsea, seventy,
drunk, careening about on slippery streets in his Cadil-
lac, and she could almost sympathize with him. His
lawyers were fighting hard to keep the old man out of
jail. This was not the first accident he had caused.

Ronnie entered with the lunch tray and started to
put it on the lap board. "Bet he was happy about the
swimming, wasn't he?" she said. Ronnie was thirty-
eight; she had been married three times and was at
present living with a man who already had a wife. She
was cheerful and philosophical about it, and not a little
obscene sometimes. "Keep on trying to put a square
peg in a round hole," she would say with a wink, when
talking about her marital adventures. "No way it's
going to fit."

"I didn't tell him yet," Anne said. Ronnie looked at
her in surprise. "I . . . I thought I'd surprise him
tonight."

That day Anne worked out for twenty-five minutes
on the exerciser. At the start of the session she cursed
fluently, and toward the end, during the last ten minutes, she simply grunted, but she didn't stop until the
alarm clock sounded. Flabby. He'd said she was getting
flabby. Ronnie helped her back to the wheelchair and
left her to draw the bath. Part of the routine—work,
then bathe and soak in a hot tub for twenty minutes.
And in six weeks, walk again.

Harry arrived before she was finished, and Ronnie
ushered him to the living room to wait. When Anne
was settled once more on the chaise, flushed from the
hot water, fragrant from the back rub Ronnie had
given her, Harry was finally admitted to the bedroom.

He was fifty-seven, her mother's only brother, and
Anne never had known him, not really, until the acci-

dent, when he began visits that had now become as
regular as everything else in her routine. He was tall,
like all her maternal relatives, and like them, when he
started to gain weight, it had all gone into his torso,
leaving his arms and legs as thin as a boy's. His body
was heavy, nearly barrel-shaped; his clothes fit poorly
because he bought ready-mades that were not designed
for anyone with his particular weight distribution. His
trousers were too tight at the waist and through his
hips, and hung too loosely on his thighs that, Anne
imagined, were like broomsticks. She brooded about his
figure, seeing in him and in her mother, who was
shaped like him, a forecast of what she could become if
she didn't exercise and stay fit and watch her diet.

Harry came in carrying his shoes and socks.
"Thought I'd better put them on the radiator," he said
apologetically. "They're soaked."

"You'd better get some of Clark's socks out," Anne
said, eyeing his long, narrow, elegant feet. Clark's feet
were very short and broad, with high insteps; Harry
would have to fold his feet in the middle to get them
into Clark's slippers. But the socks were stretchable.
"The third drawer," she said, pointing to the chest of
drawers.

"You're looking pretty and fit," he said, rummaging
in the drawer, finally pulling out a pair of black socks.
"These?"

"Anything. What's new?"

"Nothing. Same old drudgery day after day, year in
year out. Today I had a lively discussion with a twelve-
year-old girl, in Civics." He looked up at Anne and
grinned. "Shocked her into silence."

"Did you give her a detailed account of the deflow-
ering rites of some esoteric tribe that no one on earth
except you has ever heard of?"

Ronnie came in with a tray loaded with coffee, cups,
crackers, cheese, cookies. "Hi, Harry! Hardly had a
second to greet you before. Good Lord, you were one
wet man! Better now? Dry? Warm?"

"Fine, Ronnie, thanks." He turned back to Anne

and said, "Actually I told the child that there is no such thing as love. It's a habit, that's all. We try to glorify what is essentially a grotesque act by giving it a sublime name."

Ronnie was arranging the tray, and now stood up, looking it over. She nodded to Harry. "How old's the kid?"

"About twelve. They're all twelve or thirteen in that class."

"Time she learned a thing or two. She won't buy it, though. Not at twelve. Too romantic." She strode toward the door. "Got things to do in the kitchen. You want anything, you just yell. Hear?"

"Right, Ronnie," Harry said. He poured coffee for Anne and handed it to her. "What a marvelous girl she is! She's smart, practical, capable, good-looking, not an illusion in her body, no hang-ups. How do you suppose that all happened?"

Anne sipped her coffee and put it down on the arm of the chaise. She felt pleasantly tired now, relaxed and cheerful. It was curious about Harry, she thought, how she had avoided him for years, until now. She had always assumed he was the male counterpart of her mother, but aside from appearances, they were as unlike as it was possible for two people to be. "What *did* you tell that poor kid in your class?" she asked lazily.

"Well, look. You hate people from the time you're born. The doctor who gives you painful shots. Your mother for not feeding you when you're hungry, or not changing you when you're wet. Your father for being too rough, or not being there when you want him. Your brothers and sisters for teasing, for hurting, for being selfish. Then you get beyond the family circle and the hatred goes with you. Everywhere we turn there's someone new to hate for a real cause. Petty things to the big things that never stop hurting. We're all full of hate. So it's reasonable to assume because of our symmetrical selves, because of our love of balance, our trust in opposites of equal strength—black and white, hot and cold, high and low, and so on—we naturally assume there's a balancing emotion to offset the hatred. There really isn't, any more than there's an organ to balance the heart, or the liver. The symmetry is more apparent than real. But, in our need for balance and for equal opposites, and just to rationalize our ability to hate so fiercely, we invent love. At first, with the small child, it's a shield to protect him from the wrath of his parents. If he plays this role, they hurt him less often. Later, when the biological itch starts between the legs, again he rationalizes it as love. He knows the bull feels no love for the cow he mounts; the stallion feels no love for the mare; the dog humps and runs, and so on. But man is above nature, right? He has an immortal soul, and free will, and reason. If he mounts a female, it must be something more than a biological itch. *Violà!* Love!"

Anne laughed and caught her cup before it spilled over. "You maniac! You'll get yourself fired!"

"Oh, I didn't go into all that. I merely said it was a habit. A man and woman live together and each fills a need for the other, and so long as that need is being filled, the habit is maintained. If the need no longer exists, this particular habit also dies." He put cheese on two crackers and passed one to Anne, kept the other and said between bites, "Any arguments with that?"

"Plenty. You're being cynical and cute because it's been raining for years and years, and you're bored with Civics classes. Maybe you're coming down with something. Clark and I love each other and have for seven years, and I don't see an end in sight yet. And it isn't just a biological itch, or filling some unspecified need that anyone else could fill."

Harry nodded. "I would expect anyone to defend, even to the death, the rationalization that permits him to continue an absurd activity that gives him pleasure, and relieves his anxiety."

"Didn't you love Aunt Marya?"

"I thought I did, but now I wonder. I don't know any longer."

With these words the air changed and the conversation was no longer light and amusing. Anne shivered and glanced at the window past the little-world terrarium. The rain was turning to sleet again. It was hitting everything with force that could be heard within the house.

"I don't know how much more of this weather I can take," she said in a subdued voice. "God, how I long for sunshine and heat. As soon as I'm well again, we're going on a vacation. To the Bahamas maybe."

"When does the next stage of your work start?"

"Months and months from now. The government never hurries with the IND. Everything has to be checked and double-checked, and checked against the literature to make certain no one has done it already, with negative results. Things like that take time."

"And someday, when the time's right, you're going to explain to me what it is you've done, remember?"

Anne looked at him steadily and said, "Mother has a high pain threshold, did you know that? So does Hal, and Tres, too, although probably not quite as high as theirs. Wallace, however, has a very low threshold, and mine is probably even lower. When we were all kids they used to call Wallace baby a lot because he cried when he got hurt, the same kinds of hurts that Hal simply shrugged off without noticing. But things hurt me, too, more than they did Tres. I thought Hal and Tres were brave, Wallace and I were cowards. Mother certainly seemed to think we were cowardly. And Dad. But it wasn't that at all. We actually suffered more from pain than they did. Our threshold was lower. How do you think you'd rate yours?"

"Very low," Harry said at once. "I've marveled at your bravery with those multiple injuries, wondering if I'd be able to endure it. I don't think so."

Anne made a waving-away gesture and said, "I puzzled about this when I was very young, and then forgot it until I was a senior in high school. An article in the newspaper brought it all back, and seemed to give me an insight that I've been working on ever since. Eight years," she said. "Eight, long, fucking, hard years."

"The article?"

"It was a human-interest story about a four-year-old child who was dying. One of those heart-wrenching sob stories. It seems that some people have such a high pain threshold they never feel any painful stimulus at all. They simply can't feel pain. And usually they don't survive childhood. You know, the pain of headache that goes with fever. The pain of a broken limb that sends a child screaming for help. The pain of a strep throat or an earache. Acute appendicitis. They don't feel any of those things, and often they die of undiagnosed disease before their parents realize how ill they really are. Or they die from accidental injuries that they never mention. And so on. And I thought to myself, they have something in them that's different from other people. Something that everyone has to a certain extent, but they have in excess. And I started looking for it in a high-school chemistry lab."

She stopped speaking and stared at her coffee, and then quickly drank it down and held out the cup to her uncle.

"You found it then?" he asked, watching her intently, a little awed perhaps, she thought.

She nodded. "I found it. And it works, without side effects. It will be cheap and safe. And no one ever need suffer again from pain. Never again."

## FOUR

"HE WON'T BE ABLE to go through with it," Deena said. "Helverson can't be on that committee, and neither can Bob Klugman. Bad form. Against company policy. We'll outnumber them, won't we?"

Benny Bobson glanced at Clark and shrugged. Benny was a veterinarian, twenty-seven. He looked like a skinny kid, one of those late-maturing people who would look like an adolescent at forty. His head was oversized for his frail body, and he wore his hair fashionably long and full, adding to the bulk of his skull. He looked like a caricature scientist with his great head and stick figure. His hands were never still except when he was with his animals, and then he relaxed and all the superficialities vanished, leaving a competent, very intelligent doctor. In Deena's office he fidgeted and shifted his weight from foot to foot, unable to sit still long enough to take the chair she had offered him.

"We know Gus won't allow any short cuts," Clark said. "He'll carry the weight. Not us."

"Do you know Grove?" Deena asked.

"I've met him, that's all. When Helverson first enlisted his help in setting up the pregnancy tests, I was called to his office; Anne, too; and we met long enough to shake hands and listen to him say what a marvelous thing it was we were doing. He's a politician first, doctor second." He spoke bitterly. Grove was the director of the State Board of Health. He had volunteered women in state prison hospitals.

Deena's nose wrinkled with distaste. "So, there'll be Gus, you, Emory, me, Benny . . ."

Benny cleared his throat and perched nervously on the edge of her desk. "Don't be in such a hurry, Deena," he said. His voice was high-pitched. "Klugman's seen dozens of new drugs go through this. He knows what he's doing."

"Klugman's an ass. And you can report that back to him if you choose," Deena said. "Are you on the fence, or have you jumped?"

"I just said don't rush things." He moved away from the desk. "The tests are coming in now and there's nothing wrong with Duckmore. If he checks out, there's no reason to wait. Clark can keep Anne informed, she'll still have a voice. God knows the tests will go on long enough. She'll be here long before they're through. It isn't as if she's being cut out altogether. No one even knows who'll be on the committee yet."

"You pig!" Deena said. "She's been on this for eight years! If it were Medgars's drug, no one would dream of moving without him. If it were yours, you'd have a screaming fit if anyone suggested a move was to be made when you were gone. But Anne? We can drop her a note from time to time. Is that it?"

Benny slouched to the door. "Look, you're the one who's having a screaming fit. I'll talk to you later." He left.

"That gutless wonder! Clark, don't you see what they're doing?"

"Yeah," Clark said. "I know. Let's go have coffee or something."

"Well? What are you going to do about it?"

"Nothing today. I'm waiting for Gus to get back. It's his department. He won't let anything happen to destroy it, and if they try to go ahead, ignoring this incident, the department could be destroyed. He'll use that argument, not loyalty to Anne. It's the only argument that has any weight."

Deena pulled her purse from a drawer and stood up. "What if they do decide to go ahead, Clark? What will Anne do?"

Clark opened the door and, without looking back at her, said, "Nothing. What could she do? She understood from the start that her discovery is company property. We all understand that. Theoretically she's in charge, but if she's incapacitated . . . She won't do anything."

Deena stared at his broad back and a shudder of rage passed through her, leaving her trembling. "I won't let them do it to her. Not to her!" she whispered, too low for him to hear the words, but the vehemence reached him and he turned to regard her bitterly.

"Let's go for that coffee," he said after a moment.

At four, Bob Klugman told the meeting of the R&D personnel they would be going ahead with the human tests in the middle of the month. "You all understand what that means as far as the computer is concerned, the blood analyzer, everything else as far as equipment goes," he said. "Make your plans now to have completed your runs, or to postpone them. This takes first priority."

Steve Ryman from the soybean annex stood up. "What about our priority? Our tests are scheduled to run through June."

"You'll have the facilities, but on a shared basis. I want schedules, projections for the next six months, you all know the sort of thing. Gus Weinbacher will be back tomorrow. Work it out with him."

Clark watched him in silence. Bob Klugman had been drinking all day. His face was flushed and his words slurred just enough to be a giveaway. Six months, he thought, would be too long for Klugman. He'd bitch up something long before six months ended, and he'd get the can. Early retirement for health reasons. Then, if all went well, Gus would be promoted from supervisor of Pharmaceuticals to vice president in charge of research and development. But maybe not. Gus was a maverick. Prather, the old man, would have promoted him in a flash, before now even. Old man Prather would not have tolerated Bob Klugman. But old man Prather was out of the picture, and because young Master Prather didn't give a shit, it was Helverson's show. And Helverson was bucking for merger or incorporation, or submersion with one of the giants. For two years he had been working quietly behind the scenes to bring about the sell-out, and now he was working more openly, and even harder. And he was using Anne's discovery to help along the coming consolidation. Prather Pharmaceuticals was a medium-sized company with enormous prestige, and Anne's find was whipped cream on the cake for Helverson. He was a businessman, not a scientist. A setback at this particular time might make the cream appear curdled a bit. He'd have to push, not let a mere technicality slow anything down. Even if they went ahead today, it would be a year before the pregnancy tests and the following teratology tests could be completed. He would be able then to name his terms, if they had the *pa* factor secure, with the human tests behind them. Whatever he wanted that the parent company or corporation could furnish would be his. Chairman of the board? President of a giant corporation? Stock? Whatever.

He would take home the glory, Clark knew, but if there was no glory yet, if the incident with the chimp that morning was simply the first of a series of such incidents, or if something showed up in the blood, or in the brain or nervous system, then Helverson would be home free anyway. A drunken vice president who let the experiment proceed would be the goat. And the scientists who initiated the tests knowing there were possible hazards. Klugman and Anne, and probably Gus Weinbacher.

He realized with a start that people were milling about, talking in tones of frustration or anger or resignation. Everything changed in a flash, everything rescheduled. There would be lights burning late into the night as the various groups replanned the spring.

In Pharmaceuticals, each scientist had a cubicle of an office, not big enough to pace, but offering privacy. When the office door was closed, no key was needed. No one ever interrupted another who had closed his door. Clark avoided the others from his section and went to his office and shut the door hard. Call Anne, he thought, and then . . . He couldn't get beyond the "call Anne" step, and he sat down and put the call through the board.

She had been laughing, he thought, when she answered. Harry was telling her funny stories about his students, or Ronnie was giving her the latest chapter of her sex life. He smiled at the wall and listened to her summarize Harry's argument against love. As she spoke, he realized there was an undercurrent in her voice that was not totally masked by the amusement. There was a tension she was trying to hide, play-acting for his sake, for Harry's, possibly for her own. He

gripped the phone harder and visualized her on the
chaise, dressed in a long, soft, brown robe of some sort,
a drink or coffee in her hand, cigarette smoking itself
away in the ashtray. She seldom smoked one all the
way, but put it down and let it send its ribbon of smoke
into the air until the filter burned, when she stubbed it
out. She would be smiling. He wondered if she was
grasping the telephone as hard as he was, and he
relaxed his hand slightly.

When she finished her story, he told her he'd be
home by seven or seven-thirty.

"Anything special going on?" she asked.

He couldn't tell if her voice had been too light, if
there had been a hidden question. "The usual," he
said. "Klugman's hitting the bottle. He's unhappy
about the scheduled computer time, and the analyzer
being tied up by the soybean boys, stuff like that."

"Ass," she said cheerfully. "Is it still raining there?"
When he said yes, she said, "I sent Ronnie home a
while ago. Everything's getting coated with ice again.
Who's going to bring you home?"

"D . . . don't know yet," he said. He closed his eyes.
Deena never worked overtime. She refused to stay
after five unless there was an emergency that involved
her. Her daughter was not to be left alone after dark,
she said emphatically. Tonight, Deena would be working overtime.

"Well, try to get away as early as you can. Driving
will be bad. I'm going to talk Harry into staying the
night."

They chatted another minute or two and Clark hung
up. He felt uneasy, resentful of the need to deceive
her, and he knew she had sensed his deception. It
would be hard when the time came to justify it. He
wondered if she ever would forgive him, in fact, if the
plan did go on without her, without her knowledge that
they were proceeding. What he ought to do, he
thought, was saunter over to Klugman's office casually
and hang around until Bob Klugman offered him a
drink. Instead, he opened his door and almost immedi-

ately Wilmar Diedricks appeared, with Janet Stacey and Ernest James in tow.

"We've been assigned to you," Wilmar said. "Do with us what you will." Janet Stacey giggled and Ernest James rolled his eyes in exasperation.

Janet and Ernest were laboratory assistants; Wilmar was a hematologist. Clark nodded. "Okay, let's get to work. We'll start the separation process immediately, tomorrow, first thing. We'll need . . ." He figured rapidly and said, "Fourteen hundred milliliters by the fifteenth. Okay?"

Wilmar put his hands behind his head, sprawling out in the only visitor chair in the office. "Not okay," he said. "At least two shifts. We'll have to process six liters of blood for every milliliter we extract. Might need three shifts."

"Go to however many shifts you need," Clark said. "You heard Klugman. Helverson says go."

"Can't run the processor and do the syringes, too," Ernest said softly. "Need an extra guy on each shift for that."

"Get someone," Clark said. "Look, Wilmar, I know everyone has to drop what he's doing. I didn't order this. If we can stop it, we're going to, but meanwhile we have to assume the order's good. Now get to it."

Wilmar stood up. "I don't like having to run when a walk's good enough," he said. "It smells, Clark. Do you know why the sudden rush?"

"No. No one tells me anything."

For a moment they stared at one another, then Wilmar shrugged. "It still smells. Come on, children. Let's plan to get rich in the next two weeks. Hey, Ernest, your woman let you stay out past midnight? You want a night-owl shift?"

Ernest chuckled. "Double time?"

"You betcha."

"You're on."

"Christ," Clark said. "Hold it a minute, Wilmar. You can't fill the syringes yet. Not until we get the blood analyses of the test subjects. It's a variable dose, remember?"

Wilmar paused at the door and shook his head. He motioned the two assistants to leave and closed the door after them. "Clark," he said again, "it really smells. Doesn't it? When Gus gets back, I'm asking for a waiver of responsibility, or something."

"Serious?" Clark asked, joining him at the door.

Wilmar nodded. "Serious."

"See if Gus can get you in that committee meeting, on the committee would be better."

"Someone should bring out the thalidomide file and shove it under Helverson's nose," Wilmar said.

"Be at the committee meeting," Clark repeated.

Wilmar nodded and left, closing the door after him.

Harry was doing mysterious things in the kitchen; the heavy drapes were closed now, hiding the world that was being coated with ice, and with the closing of the drapes, the noise had faded, leaving the room as isolated as a space capsule in orbit. Anything might take place in such a room, Anne thought. The apartment was insulated, sound-proof almost, to the extent that no sounds from the kitchen or the living room penetrated this far. Restlessly she glanced about her space capsule: an Indian elephant, two feet high, adorned with blazing diamonds and rubies and emeralds (or possibly bits of colored glass); a shiny telescope on a stand, all black and silver and phallic as hell; everywhere books and bookcases; a small Sony television; a print of a Turner seascape; a woven wall hanging from Venezuela, geometric and garish and lovely; a radio-stereo combination with a plastic cover that from where she sat looked like a dome of smoky quartz. The control panel, she decided, where she could guide the ship, compute their course, decelerate to land, punch button *A* for food . . .

She closed her eyes. Space capsule: prison. Lovely young woman held captive for seven years, chained to bed, her frail body covered with old scars, whip marks.

She should write in her diary now while Harry was busy. He was making dinner, probably. Something fancy, gourmet cook that he was, living on Campbell's soup and graham crackers and cheese spreads. And vitamins. Six a day of this, three of that, two of something else. And ice cream. He had a weakness for ice cream. Breyers all natural flavors only. Nothing artificial, except his vitamins and the additives in his soups and cheeses . . .

She wrote in a scrawl that few others could read: *My sex drive is undiminished.* A biographer would play hell trying to piece together her inner life from her diaries, she thought, looking at the words. Only her professional notes were detailed and legible. Probably she deliberately reverted to the scrawl when she touched on her personal life, and then she wrote in cryptic one-liners. *My sex drive is undiminished.*

She was reluctant to write in the diary, she realized, because she didn't want to put down in black and white what she had withheld from Clark. Although sometimes she lied in the diary, and in person, she added, she was reluctant to write that, because if he saw it, he would be hurt and confused by her silence about what had to be a tremendous step forward. Or at least breaststroke forward. Of course he never looked in her diary. If he kept one, she knew she would sneak it out at every chance and read every word. And that was one of the great differences between them: he was willing to allow her to be her own person, separate from him, and she insisted on that; but she, on the other hand, could not bear for him to have a life apart from hers. What are you thinking? was her question, never his. What are you feeling, what's happening in your head, are you happy, unhappy, neutral? Check one. If only she could creep under his skin, just one time, and know.

"You should see this," Harry said at the door; he crossed the room in a loose-jointed, almost awkward walk, as if his legs were as tricky under him, as unreliable, as hers. "Watch," he said, and opened the drapes again.

Anne slipped the diary back into the pocket of the wheelchair and pulled herself upright on the chaise. Laboriously she worked herself out of it and onto the chair. Harry didn't offer to help, and seemed almost impatient for her to finish and join him at the window seat. Beyond the window the street lights shone through the bare tree branches and were reflected in a million prisms of ice.

The building was fifteen feet above a winding road that skirted Cherokee Park, her apartment another ten feet above the terrace. A low-spreading wisteria tree, planted at street level, was outside the windows; its topmost branches came only to the windowsill. In summer it was the curve of a canopy of feathery leaves that moved when there was no discernible breeze, in winter a tracery of spiderweb twigs. It seemed too delicate to withstand weather of any sort. Now with the street light showing through the branches, each twig, each branch, every part of the tree sparkled and shone and gleamed in a sheath of ice that took on colors the source of which was not apparent. Surely not the drab yellow street light. A million prisms broke up the light and changed it—transcendent light of pure prismatic colors.

"Fairyland," Harry said.

Anne nodded, gazing at the tree.

"Thought it a shame for you to miss it," Harry said, and went back to the door. "Busy. Be back in a couple of minutes."

Ice sculpture. Ice pruning. Everything familiar became different and unreal, fairyland world. A face of reality that was mockery, as if taunting her that what she had thought real only moments earlier was subject to change without warning. The strangeness exists, she thought, and only by concentrating on what we need to have real can we keep the change from becoming visible. But it's there all the time. And now, as if freed by her acknowledgment of it, the strangeness seemed to flow through the tree limbs, along the twig ends that were invisible under the ice, and jump through the air to rest momentarily on the panes of glass, and then flow through, to the room, her prison, her space capsule, her sanctum, and the strangeness was all about her. For a moment she could sense the room changing behind her, changing to something she would not recognize, something alarming, threatening. She closed her eyes, refusing it, concentrating on the familiar. Elephant gleaming with colored glass, telescope, television, exerciser, bed . . .

She opened her eyes wide and she felt for the first time, she understood. The strangeness was the reality; it was that which no one could face, and so they constructed and constructed and firmed everything and called it real. And it was ephemeral. All of it. Only the strangeness was real and would endure.

The slam of a car door roused her. She looked out and down across the narrow terrace of grass, down the stone steps to the street level, and there at the curb was a little yellow automobile, Deena's VW. Leaning over, speaking to Deena through the window, was Clark, oblivious of the freezing rain on his back.

Anne didn't know how long the car had been there. She hadn't heard it arrive, and she hadn't looked down before. It might have been there from the time Harry opened the drapes, from long before he opened them even.

Deena, she thought. Deena. It was almost eight. She turned from the window and when she looked about the room, it was familiar, known to the last detail, but the strangeness was still there, waiting to surge back in. Behind the façade of normalcy, she could sense the strangeness.

# FIVE

"ANNE, I'm home!" Clark called from the doorway to the bedroom. "Anne!"

"In here," she answered, her voice muffled by the heavy bathroom door.

"Hi. I'm dripping wet. I'll get a quick shower and be right back."

He crossed the hallway to the guest room–study that had become his room during her convalescence. Harry appeared almost immediately with a drink in his hand.

"Bourbon on the rocks, right?"

"Couldn't be righter," Clark said, taking it, stripping off his shoes and socks with one hand. "Glad you could stay, Harry. How is she?"

"Fine, fine. She's really coming along now. Every week I can see great improvement. Couldn't for a long time."

Clark finished undressing, upended the glass, and went into the shower. For several minutes he let the hot water sting him into feeling alive and human again. His feet and hands tingled from the cold. Twice on the way home he had had to get out of the tiny car and turn it right on icy roads. All the side streets and the county roads were getting impassable fast. Here in the city, the main streets were merely sloppy wet.

When he finished his shower, there was another drink on the desk. Gratefully he sipped at it, and dressed, feeling tired and hungry now.

Harry was in Anne's room when Clark got there. Anne was drinking a daiquiri, and Harry had coffee, he was an ex-alcoholic.

Clark kissed Anne. "Sorry I'm so late. Took almost an hour and a half to get here."

"I was afraid the streets would be completely closed by now." She looked tense.

"They will be by morning."

"Dinner in ten minutes," Harry said. Anne looked at the card table, cluttered with magazines. "Not in here," Harry said happily. "In a tiny, very romantic little restaurant I've found. Intimate, quiet. You'll like it." He left them.

"Tell me what the doctor said." Clark sat on the edge of the window seat, with the strange lights behind him.

"I'm getting flabby, need more exercise. I should stay out of the bed most of the time by now. There was a funny little man in the waiting room today . . ." She began to tell the story, making it up as she went.

"Dinner is served," Harry announced from the doorway, a towel folded neatly over his arm.

Anne laughed and Clark pushed her chair across the room, through the doorway, and down the hall. At the end, where the hall turned left for the kitchen and dining room, Harry motioned them to go right, into the living room. Inside, Anne drew in her breath. The large cheerful room had been transformed. There was a fire burning in the fireplace. A table was set in front of it, with candles; the only other light in the room was a lamp at the far end, and Harry had thrown something red over the shade.

"It's beautiful," Anne said. "It's really beautiful."

"Change of lighting works magic, doesn't it?" Harry said, nodding. "Now, the soup."

"You said you lived out of cans," Anne exclaimed after her first taste of the thick, creamy soup.

"So I lied. More, Clark?"

Later Clark would remember that night with puzzlement, aware of something different about Anne, something different in the air perhaps. She tightened up too much when Harry said he lied, and her quick glance at Clark had been too revealing. From too tense to talkative back to a strained tautness when there was a pause in the conversation, she changed without any apparent awareness of her shifts. Several times he caught her looking about the room as if seeing it for the first time, or as if searching for something she had misplaced. Clark took little part in the conversation, content to eat the delicious food Harry had prepared, to let the waves of fatigue and tension flow from him like an outgoing tide, feeling a lassitude creep up his legs, into his body, so that by the time Harry suggested ice cream and cookies, he could only shake his head and sigh.

"You used to bring gallons of ice cream to our house when we were kids, remember?" Anne said, too gaily.

"Always chocolate, and something fancy for me. Pistachio nut-maple cream, or mint flake—raspberry. Something you dumb kids wouldn't touch with a ten-foot pole."

"I was afraid of you, I think. You'd sit there and watch us like a gargoyle, brooding, analyzing. I didn't know what you were doing and it bothered me."

"I can't remember that," Harry said, frowning. His face lightened. "I know one of the things that might have worried me. You see, your mother is a damn smart woman. You didn't know that?"

Anne shook her head, and looked at her plate.

"Anne, don't be ridiculous! Of course, she's very intelligent. She never used it, never trained herself, but it's there. I was looking for a trace of it in one of the kids from time to time. Never found it. I was looking in the wrong place. I thought it would pop up in one of the boys. A great physicist, or composer, or something."

"What would you have done, if you had found what you were looking for?" Clark asked. He never had thought of Anne's mother as intelligent, rather dull in fact, with piercing eyes and a caustic tongue that he had attributed to malice. Anne's mother was clearly jealous of Anne, resentful of her successes.

"I don't know. I really don't know. At the time I thought I did. I'd take the kid in hand, try to infuse him with some sense of destiny, with ambition. That's been our curse, you see. We have the brains, but no ambition to go with them. Until Anne came along."

Anne laughed, too quickly, too loudly. "What nonsense we're talking tonight. Harry, speaking of nonsense, do you remember the upstairs of our house on Dewitt Street? There was a long, narrow closet that connected two of the upstairs bedrooms. I used to go in there and pretend it was my door to somewhere else. I wonder if all kids have a door to somewhere else."

"Not just kids," Harry said. "I still do. At school in the teacher's lounge there's a door that's locked shut, always has been, far as I know. It goes to the broom closet or something that has another entry in the back of the building. I pass through that door like smoke through a screen."

"To somewhere else," Anne repeated. She thought of the little-world terrarium, where she could be the size of a microscopic spore, or where she could swing through the tropical leaves Jane-like, fighting off dragons, or ape men, or Martians. Like smoke through a screen, she thought.

Clark yawned and tried to stifle it. It was almost ten-thirty. He felt Anne's gaze and turned to her, but she shifted and looked at the window at the far end of the room. The wind was driving the sleet against the windows. "Honey, I'll help Harry pick up and then get you tucked in. Okay? I'm really beat."

Harry refused help, shooed them both out of the way, and Clark pushed Anne's chair back to her room. Later, in bed, aware that Anne was awake still, not yet in her own bed, he tried to sort out impressions of the evening, but they were jumbled and unorderly. She had avoided seeing him, he decided, at least directly. But how many times had he looked up only to find her just then shifting her gaze? And her brightness and gaiety had been faked, at least much of it had been faked, but he couldn't tell which half had been real, which part had been acting. You don't usually think of people with such mobile faces as being able to conceal themselves, but she could, and did. He had watched her do it with others, a sudden change that he couldn't identify, a change in direction when she had seemed immobile, a change of attitude, something, and the new Anne would rise and take over. But never, he thought, had he had the feeling that she was doing it with him, as she certainly had done it that night.

Again Clark felt a rush of gratitude for Harry's presence. And he realized he didn't really want to be alone with Anne until he could tell her what was happening at the lab. He sighed and rolled over to his stomach and in a few minutes he was asleep.

Anne had always known she would be famous by the time she was thirty. When she first thought of a date, a deadline, it had been misty with temporal distance, twelve years. Anything could happen in twelve years. But now thirty was coming at a rate that seemed to be accelerating. Two years, three months. There was still time, but just barely, and no time to spare. She had had the drive, the ambition, the vision, the talent. From that first day when she had recognized what the problem was, and found a way to circumvent it, she had wasted no time. No time at all.

She sat at the fairyland window and stared at the mystical tree, her diary on her lap, alone for the night. Slowly she began to write:

> Look at all the time
> 　　　I've saved—
> Bits and pieces, odds and ends—
> Crammed into boxes,
> Put away neatly on shelves,
> 　　　Saved for the day
> I shall be old
> And the only goal
> 　　　Will be time.

What form, she wondered, would the interest take to be paid on saved time? Abruptly, angrily, she snapped the notebook shut and jammed it back into the chair pocket. Abstractions, she was worrying with abstracttions. Harry's fault, talking about love as if it were something that could be destroyed by an act of reason.

She remembered one of her early teachers, also bored, misplaced in a high school where only one or two in each class of forty wanted to hear what he had to say, and of them, perhaps one would remember, perhaps neither. Custer, she thought. That had been his name. Mr. Custer. "We attack reality on the fringes," he had said. "It's all we can do. The hard core of reality is impenetrable." Abstractions again.

We tell ourselves stories, she thought, and the stories are real, even if they don't touch objective reality anywhere. The story she had told Clark about the old man was real; the story amused him, it had allowed her to talk about her visit to the doctor without having to lie. It had a function in reality, then; it served reality in a way that lying about the therapy would never serve. For a brief moment, she thought, I added something to the dimension of reality.

She visualized Clark sleeping, on his stomach, one arm under his pillow, the other at his side, not snoring. He slept like a child, totally still for a long period of time, then an abrupt change of position, back into the stillness that was almost absolute. Anne was a restless sleeper, awakened by any noise; thoughts, plans, details of work never far from the surface of her mind, ready to flood in, to rouse her to complete wakefulness off and on during the night.

She began to think again of the final human tests. Five hundred women in the first trimester of pregnancy, five hundred in the last trimester. She remembered reading that a woman in the last trimester should turn to her side, permit her husband to enter from behind in order to relieve his sexual needs. She had read the article through twice, trying to find a hint that the author had a clue about the woman's sexual needs. Cattle, she thought. They were treated like cattle. But not the women in her study. She and Deena had

worked it out in detail. They would interview each and
every woman. Not Africans, not South American Indi-
ans, not Mexican peons. American women who could
understand what a double-blind experiment was, how
it was conducted, what the injections were expected to
do, what the possible consequences were. Only women
with medical complications that would warrant their
taking the *poena albumin* in the first place. Immacu-
late, impeccable work, that's what they would have to
say.

Clark had argued that she personally didn't have to
interview each applicant for the experiment, but she
knew she did. And afterward, one of the big universities would make her an offer, a grant, facilities, everything. And the company would make a counteroffer.
But she would go with the university, get out from
under the machinery that let people like Klugman be
over her. Clark would go, too. She would make them
understand from the start: where she went, he went.
They would consider her eccentric, but that was all
right. Genius could afford eccentricity that would crip-
ple a more ordinary being. She would flaunt her eccentricity, in fact.

She remembered one of the sex manuals she and
Clark had read together, giggling at the sketches, trying
them out, giggling even more, finding a few of them
amazingly effective.

Her hands were clenching the arms of her chair too
hard, hurting. Waking, dazed with sleep, to find his
penis hard against her back, his hands caressing her
with greater and greater urgency. His hand at her
breast, hand gliding over her belly, down to her pubis,
the hot, rising, painful need snapping her to full wakefulness . . .

She bowed her head and waited for the moment to
pass, and slowly she loosened her hands from the chair
arms, but she was afraid now to let either hand touch
her body; she let them dangle over the sides of the
chair and raised her eyes finally to stare at the glistening wisteria tree beyond her window.

Harry, she would say, people can and do love each other terribly. It isn't just need, she would say, although that plays a very large part, of course. Naturally. It came as a surprise to me, too, she would say. In my family, she would say, if you were a boy you had to be big, muscular, and make the team, and nothing else mattered very much at all. If you were a girl, you had to be small, petite even, doll-like pretty, and nice. God, *nice!* And I grew up ungainly, with legs that just kept going on, and too smart-assed most of the time, and scornful of the things that mattered—things like making the team, and curling hair, and telling Daddy he was strong and brave and I loved him most of all, because he wasn't, and I didn't. And, of course, I lied, and this made my mother fear for my soul. As if she didn't have enough on her mind without that.

So, she would say, you see, I started at the point you have only now reached; that is, not believing in love. When the day came that I found myself thinking I would rather die than live without Clark, I realized how terribly a person can love another person. Because I truly meant it, even if I was very young at the time. And it is a terrible thing to love so passionately that the self is eclipsed. Whatever he wants me to do, she would say emphatically, *whatever* he wants, I do gladly, happy there is something above the call of duty that I can do.

Harry, she would say quite calmly, without shame or hesitancy, we, Clark and I, engage in all sorts of sexual perversions. Things that are quite against the law in most states, certainly against the law in this state. I welcome each new perversion as a new test of my love, she would say. And, she would say, when we do those things, they are no longer perversions, they become holy almost, and our love deepens.

But she wasn't ready yet, and she knew it. Not yet. In spite of her great love for her husband, and her great need of his love, she was not yet ready to be a receiver only, to be a passive container into which he could pour his fluids. That would only start resentments that had no place in a happy marriage. She hadn't told him, hadn't mentioned it to anyone. Thank God, she hadn't mentioned it to Ronnie, didn't have to face her knowing looks and winks. If only she had been able to withhold the swimming prescription from her, but Ronnie was necessary to get her there and back. There was no way for her not to know.

If she sent Ronnie home by five every afternoon, it would be possible to keep her from seeing Clark altogether. And she would tell Clark when the time was right, when she had tried it out for several days and knew it was working. Not now while there was a problem at the lab.

Poor Clark, she thought, so worried about schedules and computer time, and that ass Klugman and his mini-crisis of the month. There was simply no need to burden him with anything else right now. She thought of him tenderly, exhausted, inert until his body demanded a change in position, then a sudden burst of activity, back to inertness again. He didn't need anything new to worry about just now.

A snapping noise roused her and she started in confusion. The ice had broken a twig, she decided. It had grown thicker while she had been sitting before the window. There would be branches and limbs all over the streets by morning.

She wheeled herself to the side of the window and closed the drapes, and then got ready for bed. Throughout the night she heard the snapping of branches, punctuation marks for her dreams.

## SIX

"WHAT YOU NEED is confidence!" Miss Westchester said merrily. "Dr. Federicks sends us a lot of patients. Broken backs, broken everything, and the swimming does wonders for them! Confidence!"

Anne had hated her on sight. Pretty, dimpled, compact, she looked like a smiling gymnast, all smooth muscles and hard high breasts, eighteen-inch waist, long golden braids down her back, like a transplanted Heidi. She glowed with health and the brainless gaiety of childhood.

"Now, can you walk at all?" Miss Westchester asked. "Is your nurse going to go into the water? Can you swim?"

"I can swim," Anne said. She looked at Ronnie, who shook her head emphatically.

"Water's for drinking if you've got nothing better. And for taking a bath with, and putting in with the beans. And that's about it," Ronnie said. "I'll watch."

"Sorry," Miss Westchester said, dimpling again. "We don't allow spectators at all. There is a competent staff," she added. "We are trained, you understand, to handle crippled people."

Anne felt her jaw tightening. "Can we just get to it?"

"Oh, my, yes! I'll take you to the dressing room. Do you need a handler?" Anne looked at her until she said, "Someone to lift you from your chair, dress you, things like that?"

"No."

"Good! That's fine!"

"I'll stay with her until she's ready to get into the water," Ronnie said then. "You just lead the way." She winked at Anne as she elbowed the pretty girl away from the chair.

The water was soft and lovely, and Anne could swim almost normally, in a lazy, effortless way, on her side, moving her legs only enough to keep them horizontal. She was sorry when the ten minutes were over.

"Now, wasn't that nice!" exclaimed Miss Westchester from the far side of the pool, beaming across at Anne. "Time's up!"

For a moment Anne visualized that pretty face under her hands, below the water, mouth open, eyes bugging out with terror. It was such a real image it frightened her, and she turned away from the girl quickly and swam to the chair lift that would take her from the water.

There was a sauna bath and a sun-lamp treatment, and then she was in the car with Ronnie, heading home through the slushy streets. She felt relaxed, tired, content, the way she always felt after swimming. Ronnie's voice droned on without pause.

She had wanted to kill that girl, Anne thought, but distantly. Probably everyone wanted to kill her. Probably one day they would find her on the bottom of the pool, finger marks on her throat. She shook her head, not good enough. Not good enough just to have someone do it, she wanted to do it herself. Ronnie turned into the alley behind the apartment house and muddy water flew through the air, spattering the car's windows.

"Filthy weather," Ronnie said. "Your chair's a real mess. Soon's you get inside, I'll take it out to the porch and clean it."

Anne nodded. She never had hated anyone like that before, she thought. Instant hatred that wanted an outlet, in violence. It disturbed her that she had reacted so harshly to the girl, who was, after all, simply stupid, not malicious. She was overreacting to situations that used to amuse her, if she had noticed them at all. A few months ago that girl wouldn't have been able to get anywhere near her, she thought with a sense of disquiet. Being locked up in her prison so long had done something to her armor; her insulation from the world had been pierced.

Ronnie parked under the canopy of the parking area and got the chair out of the back, and Anne began to work her way up from the car seat. Ronnie knew when to help, and when to stand clear and wait. Now she waited, always watchful, but not offensively so, not as if she didn't trust Anne to behave responsibly. She waited with the same good humor and patience that she always showed. Anne got into the chair and took a deep breath.

"Made it," Ronnie said, and pushed her toward the back entrance and the ramp Clark had had installed at their back porch. "I'll give that kid a shove into the pool next time. Okay?"

"If you don't, I will," Anne said, and they both laughed.

Gus Weinbacher gazed moodily at the group assembled in his office. Gus was five feet five inches, deeply tanned from his week on Antigua, but ugly. His face was prematurely aged with a thousand etch marks, and his slender body was frail-looking, deceptively so, for he had good muscles, but his appearance was of frailty and old age, contradicted by his gleaming teeth, and his thick hair, dark brown, luxuriant, and his energy when he chose to use it. He could move faster than most people, get more done in a shorter time than anyone else in the pharmaceutical division, endure longer hours for longer periods. He had a knack for cutting straight through all the fluff to get to the core of a problem, and his sharp blue eyes seemed to deride those who hadn't already seen what he then could demonstrate.

Unwilling to believe Bob Klugman, who saw catastrophe every time the wind changed, he had called Emory Durand the previous night, and afterward had taken the first flight back. He had left his wife, Elaine, to rest for the next two weeks in the golden sun, with the promise to straighten things out as soon as possible and rejoin her. It had been a bad winter for them, he thought, what with Rickie getting married at twenty, and Jud dropping out of pre-med school, and Elaine's asthma and allergies triggered by a series of emotional blows. He didn't want to be in his office that bleak morning. He didn't want to confront a problem with Anne's discovery. Most of all, he didn't want Helverson pushing too hard too fast.

He understood Helverson, who was of the school

that said it was better to make a decision, any decision, quickly than let matters drift. A gambler. For Helverson it had worked. As long as his decisions dealt with figures, with paper work, probably it would continue to work, at least long enough to get him to where he wanted to be. When his decisions had to do with premature human experimentation, Gus knew, he had to be stopped. Bob Klugman was out of it. He never made a decision in his life that he could delegate to someone else. His present position was the result of longevity, and the fact that he had very good people under him. Today Bob was home nursing a sore throat, possibly flu, he had said by phone earlier. He would remain out until matters were settled.

That left him, Gus knew. He was afraid it couldn't be wrapped up in a day or two. Yesterday he had been scuba diving among coral reefs; today slush, icy spots on the roads, and now a hospital visit to pay.

"The four of us will go see Pat," he said. "Clark, you want to drive along with me?"

Clark nodded, and Gus went on: "Deena, sometime, as soon as you can get to it, I'll want a summary of your behavior charts. Make a note of anything at all unusual, even if you tend to discount it. Okay? And, Emory, the same with a chart of the physical examinations. Just a summary for now. We might have to go back over it all day by day, but not yet. How are the other chimps? How's Duckmore this morning?"

"Normal, apparently," Emory said. "I decided not to vary their routine, but to use transport cages for them all, not allow a situation that might make another attack possible."

Gus nodded. "Right. Let's go."

Gus drove, efficiently, a touch too fast, the way he did everything. "If we have to check Helverson," he said to Clark, "I'll need you. I wish to God Anne were here. You haven't told her yet?"

"Not yet. No real point in it until we know something."

"Right. Anyway, if I have to beard Helverson, I'll

want you along. If you protest premature testing, with your name on the factor, he will have to accept it. Now you and I both know that, but I doubt if Helverson knows it. We'll have to convince him. He could make things uncomfortable."

Clark nodded. "I don't understand how he could consider going ahead with any doubt about its safety," he said.

"He's a gambler. Probably he'd be right in this instance. This isn't the usual reaction—wrong timing, wrong kind of reaction. Everything so far says it's still okay to go on. Probably he'd be able in a year or two to point to a success and laugh at us for worrying."

"Probably. What odds?"

"God knows. Hundred to one. I don't know. I think it's unrelated."

"You know Grove's volunteered women prisoners?"

"I know. But first things first. Where is that goddamn hospital?"

He had passed the street he should have turned onto, and he made a U-turn and swerved, cutting into the slow-moving traffic in the right lane of the highway.

They arrived at the hospital before the others, and after Gus cleared their visit with the head nurse, he and Clark waited. "No point in making the boy go through it twice," Gus said, pacing the tiny, vinyl-furnished room. "He's twenty, night student studying to be a vet. Next year he plans to go full-time and his brother will start nights, working days. There are three boys, mother with a bad heart. They've got it all planned to get them all educated, keep her, keep the youngest one in school, the works. Hired him myself, a surprise for Emory."

Clark nodded. Gus knew everyone in the animal and pharmaceutical divisions personally, almost intimately. It was like him to have hired someone for two years, put in the time and money training him, knowing he'd be gone long before the investment paid off. Not business-like; human.

Deena and Emory joined them and they all went to Pat's room together. The boy was pale, he had the withdrawn look of one who is sedated, not sleeping, not fully conscious either.

"Pat, just tell us what happened. Okay?" Gus said after touching the boy's forehead in a way that was almost a caress. Pat had one arm in a cast, the other heavily bandaged from the shoulder to the tips of his fingers.

"I've gone over it," he said, his voice faint. He cleared his throat and started over. "I've gone over it so I'd be ready. I had already taken Soupy and Chum to the communal cage, and when I opened Duckmore's cage, he didn't come out. I thought he was playing with me. I called him again, and still he didn't move. So I reached my hand inside, not trying to yank him or anything like that. It's a gesture you make with them. I think they see you don't have a weapon, something like that, and usually they'll just take your hand and come along. Duckmore always walked with me to the communal cage like that. You know, hand in hand. But yesterday . . ." He closed his eyes and swallowed, but his voice was unchanged when he spoke again. ". . . He grabbed my arm, at the wrist, and he jumped out of the cage and twisted my arm at the same time. It was too fast. There wasn't anything I could do. I yelled, I guess. And I saw him baring his teeth, coming at my face, or my throat. I'm not sure now. I put up my other arm to ward him off and he bit it. I think I fell down and broke something. I had a cut on my back from something. Not sure what. I can't remember anything else. I don't know if he left me then, or what he did. Nothing else."

The sedation kept the horror out of his voice, made him calm enough to relate it in a matter-of-fact manner, but listening to him, Clark felt a chill that raised the hairs on his arms, at the back of his scalp.

"Good, good," Gus said, and he stood up and began

to move about the small room, stepping over feet, detouring around the chairs the others had drawn up. "Now, Pat, someone said one of the girls mentioned that you'd noticed a change in Duckmore recently. Anything to that?"

"I'm not sure," Pat said. "It wasn't anything really noticeable. You know he's always been friendly, curious, calm. You know. Very stable, dependable. But recently I've had a feeling that he was watching me in a different way. I was going to tell Dr. Wells, but no one else noticed it, and I watched him from behind a cage, or out of sight, and he didn't act like that with anyone else, so I decided he had just turned against me for some reason. And not always. I can't really explain it better. Sometimes he seemed hostile and watchful with me, but usually not. Yesterday morning . . . there was no warning. Nothing."

"You're doing fine," Gus said, and patted the boy's head again. "You're not to worry about anything while you're in here. You know experimental workers who are injured during the course of the experiment are on full salary until they recover. So just take it easy." He stood at the side of the bed, frowning into space. "How about the other chimps? Anything out of the ordinary with any of them?"

"I don't think so, nothing definitely, anyway. After I began to watch Duckmore more closely, I began to think that maybe Fannie was behaving strangely too, but I'm not sure." His eyes were starting to look glassy and his words were being spaced as if with effort. "I don't know," he said. "Something . . . I can't remember."

"Okay. You rest now. We'll all be back to see you from time to time, see how you're doing. If anything comes to mind, have one of the nurses give me a call. Okay?"

"Yeah. Okay," Pat said.

Gus realized it wasn't medication glazing his eyes, but pain: the medication, sedation, whatever they were giving him was wearing off and the pain was weakening his voice, intensifying his pallor. "We'll get the hell out of here. I'll tell your nurse to stop in and see how you're doing, son," he said. For a moment it seemed he was going to bend to kiss the boy, but he merely touched his hair again, and they all turned and left.

"He should have told me," Deena fumed as they waited for the elevator. "That idiot should have told me!"

"Should have," Gus agreed. "But I can see why he'd be reluctant. Too indefinite. You look for more overt behavior than Duckmore showed."

"He should have told me," Deena muttered again.

None of them mentioned Fannie, whose behavior also might be strange. None of them mentioned that if they had trouble with another of the test chimps, they had to assume trouble with the *poena albumin*.

Anne dozed after lunch. She was in the little world of the terrarium where the leaves were as large as roofs, the light under them a soft green, the air fragrant and rich with the scent of fertile earth and growing things. She ran along a mossy path and came to a place she never had seen before. A deep pool of water stretched before her, its surface unmarred, reflecting back the leaves, and pale orchids that clung to the trees that edged the pool. She stripped and slid into the water. She swam underwater, through swaths of jade, into midnight blue, from that to a pale, milky-blue stream, back into jade. With delight she saw that her body had changed; she was an iridescent mermaid, gleaming, glistening golden tail flicking the water easily, propelling her faster and faster through the magic water.

A sound vibrated through the water and she knew it was Clark, trying to catch her, clumsy, awkward Clark stirring up clouds of silt that blinded her. She swam faster, streaking away from him. The sound was felt noise that touched her again, and she woke up abruptly, all at once out of the dream, and disoriented. She reached for the telephone, then drew back her hand

and put it under the blanket. The muted ringing stopped. Moments later, when Ronnie looked into the room, Anne kept her eyes closed, and Ronnie withdrew.

Anne tried to fall asleep again, to return to the dream, and could not. Later, if Clark said, "Ronnie told me you were exhausted from swimming," she would say, "She was lying. Or teasing. You never can tell with Ronnie which it is."

She should get rid of Ronnie, she thought. She had become too familiar, taking it on herself to act almost as mediator between Anne and Clark, passing messages back and forth, giving unwanted advice.

## SEVEN

DEENA sat with her notebook on her knees, eating a tuna sandwich mechanically, concentrating on the female chimp, Fannie. The communal cage was large, easily containing the twenty-three test animals and eight infants. There was an identical cage for the control chimps. Deena was hidden from view by a one-way glass partition that allowed her to see into the cage, through it to the rest of the lab, nearly empty now during lunchtime. Chimps were grouped on high ledges, on a bench along one wall; several were swinging lazily on tire swings; infants tumbled with one another on the floor. Fannie sat alone with her infant, a mischievous three-month-old male. Fannie was scrawny and ugly and a devoted mother. As the infant suckled, she kept a sharp watch on the other chimps. Nothing erratic here, Deena thought, and realized she had finished her sandwich. Her coffee was tepid, but she drank it, and began to nibble on a candy bar.

She was almost ready to return to her office and the charts spread across her desk, when she stiffened with interest and looked beyond Fannie into the lab. Fannie was baring her teeth, clutching the infant harder against her, so hard she made it squeal in protest. She was looking intently beyond the bars of the cage. Several of the assistants had returned from lunch—three women, one of the young men.

Fannie leaped to her feet and ran up the series of shelves to the highest one, where several other females perched, grooming one another. Fannie paid no more attention to the arriving workers.

Deena made a note of their names. Eddie and Helen never tended the chimps, she was certain. They worked with the annex people. Thelma Pendleton sometimes worked with the chimps, and Jane Lyndstrom was a regular with them. Deena left her high chair and walked around the rear of the cages, out of sight, and returned to her office.

The first name plate they had put on Deena's door had said: "Edwina Wells." She had sent it back and now it read: "Dr. Edwina Wells." She seldom saw it any longer, but it had been very important then, and still was, that the name plate be right. Her office was neat and impersonal. The only non-functional object in it was a picture of her daughter, taken the previous year at her graduation from elementary school. The child was sober, with large dark eyes, long straight hair, and her mouth tightly closed to conceal braces. She would be beautiful when the chubbiness left her face and the braces were a memory. Sometimes Deena found herself studying the picture, wondering about her child, her future. And she thought with a touch of fear how little she saw her own mother.

Her mother had been different, she knew. Her permissiveness had been so tangled with neglect and indifference that it had been like growing up without a mother at all. She would never be like that with Marcie. She knew every intimate detail of her daughter's life; she was always interested in hearing more and Marcie knew that, knew she could trust her mother.

She withheld nothing. Deena would know what to watch for, the signs to be read as certainly as a book. And if Marcie ever showed the first indication of the kind of wildness that had marked Deena's late teen years, she would know what to do about that. She remembered her own adolescence with disgust now. The school advisor had called her a nymphomaniac, had warned her mother to have her counseled, or analyzed, or something.

Idiot, she thought. Completely ignorant. Tying her up in Freudian knots, driving her further from her mother, straight into Roger's arms. And when it failed with Roger, as it had failed with everyone else, she had gone into psychology herself, knowing there were answers to be found, certain she had enough brains to find them without help from stupid psychiatrists who believed Freud was God. Her father had died when she was twelve, and her mother had neglected her; naturally, she had sought reassurance elsewhere. She never had found it, until she had her own daughter, who loved her without question, wholly, selflessly. And Deena had been able to stop searching and for years had been content living with her daughter, having her work, the recognition of her peers. That she had a Ph.D. in psychology and chose to work with animals instead of people never puzzled her at all. She didn't like people very much.

She especially didn't like the oversexed girls who worked in the lab, twitching their hips at the male assistants. She had spoken of them in her own group, and the leader, Sheila Warren, had been sharp with her. It was her duty to educate them, not denigrate them. But they wouldn't listen to her. One had even complained to Emory about her, and she had stopped trying with them. They'd find out, the hard way as she had done, that no male could fulfill them. They had to fulfill themselves, alone, and then just maybe they would find a meaningful relationship with a man. Maybe. She didn't believe it, but she was fair-minded enough to admit the possibility existed, theoretically anyway. She had yet to see it in practice. Marcie at least would not grow up with any illusions.

Deena sat at her desk, and looked at Marcie's picture without seeing it. She began to make notes after a moment, and a few seconds later, without thinking about it at all, she reached out and turned the photograph slightly, so that the wide questioning eyes were not directed at her. There were scratch marks on the desk where the photograph rubbed it, for every time she noticed that someone had turned it away, she turned it right again, and throughout the day the picture faced the wall, then her, then the window, over and over.

When she finished her notes she called Jane Lyndstrom and Thelma Pendleton to her office.

At four, Gus and Clark went over the charts supplied by Emory Durand. "No variation in enzyme induction," Gus said, "and no variation in red or white blood counts. Only this little wave on the *pa* count. What do you think, Clark?"

"Too insignificant to mean anything," Clark said. "It varies with the control animals, too."

"I'll have Jay put it through the computer with the rest of the data, see if there is a significant difference." Gus sighed and tilted his chair back. His office was a shambles, a file drawer partly opened, untidy files at angles; his desk was covered with reports and charts; his bulletin board held current work programs as well as those long out of date; in the center of the bulletin board was a target with darts sticking out, clustered about the bull's-eye. Gus had thrown paper airplanes for years, until his secretary had bought him the dart board for a Christmas present one year.

"If there is a correlation between those waves and the waves on the behavior charts, we'll have to go back to the start with the animal tests, won't we?" Clark asked. He had seen it happen to others.

"It'll be rough on Anne," Gus said, looking at the

ceiling, his chair at a dangerous angle. He'd break his back one day doing that.

"How long can we hold off the autopsies?"

"Don't know. I'll see Helverson in the morning. He wants a staff meeting with Bob and me, for openers. I'll call you if I can."

"Bob will be sick."

"I know."

"If we can hold up the sacrifice just three weeks, Anne can be here. She'll have crutches next week. A couple more weeks to get used to them, get some strength back. She should be here, Gus."

"I know. I don't think anyone else really has the feel for it. She'd know what to look for. She's good, Clark. You know that."

"I know."

"I'll do my best."

Clark nodded and stood up. There was a tap on the door, and Jay Ullman came in. He was the computer specialist. Clark left while Gus was explaining what they wanted, what comparisons they needed.

Clark found Deena perched on the high chair behind the chimp communal cage. "I don't know yet," she said in reply to his unasked question. "I'm trying something."

They were putting the chimps back in their overnight cages. Clark watched as a lab assistant wheeled the transport cage to the door of the communal cage and opened both doors. The girl put a bunch of grapes inside the small-wheeled cage, and then called out, "Soupy! Come on. Soupy!" One of the female chimps ambled over to the cage and shuffled inside, squatted, and began to pick the grapes and eat them. A second girl wheeled another cage into place and repeated the routine. She called Chum, who was as docile and willing as Soupy had been. Clark started to speak, but Deena shushed him. "Wait."

The first girl was back. This time she called Fannie. The chimp didn't move, but stared at the girl and clutched her infant to her chest. "Come on, Fannie.

Come on." Fannie sat motionless. She might have been deaf. Only her unblinking stare betrayed her; she knew she was being called. Clark felt a stir of excitement as he watched the chimp, not openly hostile, but not normal either. The girl said, "Okay, Fannie, you wait. Come on, Finch. Here, Finch." A young male that had been hanging about the door scrambled inside the cage and ate the grapes greedily. The other girl called Fannie and she got up and went without a moment's hesitation.

"She's all right with everyone except Jane," Deena said. "You saw Jane, how well she handled them all. She's good with them." She slipped from the chair and started toward her office with Clark following. "I'll keep a close watch on her and Duckmore," she said over her shoulder. "It's like Pat said, not quite normal, but not enough out of line to make you want to yell cop."

"Are you going to come over to see Anne tonight?"

"I don't know," Deena said. "When are you planning to tell her?" They entered her office, only fractionally larger than Clark's.

"Not until after tomorrow's staff meeting." Clark sat down and lighted a cigarette. "It's a hell of a mess, Deena. I think she suspects something. Maybe it would be best just to level with her."

"Thinking of her, or yourself?" Deena asked sharply.

"I don't know."

"Well, think of her then. There's not a damn thing she can do. Everything's being done that can be done. You and Gus will have to handle Helverson. You know how it would affect her to know it's all up in the air again, especially while she's helpless. If you think she suspects because of your glum face, lie about it. Tell her you've got a severe case of hemorrhoids or something. Tell her Bob's been drunk on the job for a week and fouled up everyone's records. Tell her anything, except the truth for this one time."

"Treat her like a child for her own good, is that it?"

"Exactly. Look, Clark, I'm speaking to you now as a professional psychologist. I know Anne. I know her impatience. I know her scorn for nearly everyone else in the lab. It's okay, she's better than most, she can afford a certain degree of egocentricity. But right now, helpless as she is, that egocentricity could become something else again. Don't you see how she would be certain you were all screwing up her work? The germ of every new idea, every great idea, is intuitive. She knows that. And she would know that no two people can have the same intuitive flashes. They are as individual as fingerprints. All anyone can do is the tedious, plodding, follow-through work now, and it would worry her back to the hospital if she thought there was any danger of lousing it up because she was absent during an emergency. Let's do that plodding follow-up work, and then, when she's able to contribute again, when there's no danger of another relapse, then tell her what happened. She'll blow, you'd better believe! But better then than now. Now, if she blows, it could damage her. Later it will be a relief valve. In either case, you're going to be the goat. Do you understand that?"

"Yeah," Clark said. "You're not coming out then?"

"No. It's bad enough that she's suspicious of you. If I show up and fudge it, she'll know something's up. I'll call her and tell her Marcie's got the flu or something. Maybe after tomorrow's meeting I'll come over. I'll call her right away."

Anne hung up thoughtfully after Deena's call. Clark had said he would be late again, probably all this week they'd be working late. Deena and Clark? She shook her head. Not that. Clark might, he was certainly desperate enough, but Deena never. Anne didn't bother going over all the reasons for knowing this. Not an affair then. Something at work. She had known last night, she realized, and had refused to think about it.

Deena working late? A real emergency, then. Something to do with her work, obviously, or they would have told her what the emergency was.

"Are you all right?"

Ronnie was standing a few feet from her; she looked alarmed. Anne nodded. "Why?"

"I spoke a couple of times and you just sat there."

"Sorry. Look, Ronnie, all week Clark's going to be tied up. How about just fixing me something light, a sandwich or something and coffee, and then you can leave at five. Okay?"

"I don't mind staying, honey. You know that."

"I know, Ronnie. You've been a doll. But there's no need. And I have work to do anyway."

Ronnie was reluctant, but in the end agreed, and shortly before five she brought a tray and plugged in the automatic coffee maker. "Milk in the thermos," she said. "Are you sure?"

Anne smiled at her, all thoughts of the animosity she had felt earlier vanished now. "Go on home to that horny man of yours." She glanced at the table and said, "Oh, just one thing. Can you clear all that stuff out of here and bring those notebooks from the night table?"

It took Ronnie a minute or so, then she was gone, and silence filled the apartment. Anne sat in the chaise for a long time seeing nothing, going over her notes in her mind. For now it didn't matter that she couldn't observe the chimps. The records were better than direct observation. Hormonal levels. Blood counts. Basal-metabolism records. Enzyme induction records. The fluctuation in the *pa* levels. She could almost visualize her own words, written a month ago, sometime in January: *Check: stress decreases* pa *in blood. Is it suppressed, or present somewhere else?* Somewhere else would be the brain, she thought. The theory was that the albumin clumped in the brain, attaching itself to various receptors so that pain stimuli failed to register. During stress, pain symptoms were decreased, suggesting an increase in the clumping.

There had been variation in the albumin levels, she knew, but there had been in the control chimps also, and it was assumed that variation was the norm. She blinked and rubbed her eyes hard. No good. She had to know exactly what had happened. Maybe the FDA had asked for more data. Maybe there was a conflict with another researcher somewhere, working on the same process. Maybe Bob Klugman had burned down the lab with all the records in it. Maybe . . .

Maybe it had nothing to do with her work. Maybe it was the soybean annex causing trouble. Everyone had predicted trouble from them. Each department thought its own was the only one worth financing, understandably, but the annex had demanded ever increasing amounts of money, computer time, equipment, personnel. Maybe they had given a party and poisoned everyone.

She worked her way out of the chaise, onto the wheelchair, and went to the table. Her records were complete, her graphs and charts exactly as she would have done them had she been at the office these past few months. She had every bit as much data here as she could have there—copies of everything from Deena's department of behavior, Emory's department of physical data, and there was nothing wrong. Up to a week ago, nothing had been wrong. Nothing!

She picked at the sandwich Ronnie had made, and ate the salad, and the cake. She still hadn't opened the many notebooks, and she realized she was too tired to want to get into any of it then. Swimming had done it. Ten minutes of unaccustomed activity and she was sitting like a bump, unable to keep her mind on any one thing for more than a minute or two. And now they were messing up her work.

The thought frightened her. She rejected it. She poured coffee and wheeled herself around the table to where she could look out the window. The ice was gone, it was already dark, little traffic passed by the house. If she looked straight out, across the top of the wisteria tree, there was nothing at all to see, blackness of the park, deeper blackness of the dense evergreen trees that were thick at this end of the park. No stars in the sullen sky, a glow here and there from street lights that were invisible, casting lights that were swallowed almost completely, leaving only pale holes in the darkness, as if there were weak spots where one could penetrate, to emerge on the other side of the darkness into somewhere else.

*Captain! We're heading toward a black hole, from which no man, or woman, has ever returned. —Have courage, have courage! There must be a way to turn a ship streaking at the speed of light toward certain doom. Have courage! Go back to your cryonic sleep while, I, your Captain, struggle with the forces of blackness that irresistibly pull us forever on toward that final maelstrom.*

She wondered if the men who walked the moon felt as naked as she imagined them, so much nearer those black holes that drew everything in to themselves, or were they too preoccupied with their hardware, their records, the mechanics of staying alive to worry about them?

Resolutely she turned from the window back to the burdened table and opened her notebook. She wrote: "I have been thinking strange thoughts for days, but that is a symptom of my accelerating recovery. I am impatient to return to work. My brain is stimulated while my body is still weak and unable to perform. I predict the strangeness of my thoughts will increase until I am able to go to the lab every day."

And soon, she thought, she would have to have a real talk with Clark, find out how and why he had changed so much during the past weeks. She felt she could almost see the changes happening. He was getting heavier somehow, more clumsy, with a tendency toward sluggishness. Things he should have grasped instantly he fumbled with and didn't understand until she explained them, step by step. He hadn't been like that when they met, hadn't been like that a year ago. She was afraid some sort of middle-age decline in his mental abilities was already taking place, and he was only thirty-one.

Maybe Clark was in trouble at work, she thought. And she could believe it. They must have noticed the change in him also. Gus was perceptive enough to recognize even a slight decrease in his abilities. They would realize she had supplied the real initiative, the drive, the direction, that Clark had merely been a follower, her follower. He couldn't expect her to drag him along forever. He had to be able to keep up, or be left behind. The rule of the jungle, or the desert, or something. The rule of the little world anyway.

She remembered the clear pool of changing colors in the little world and regretted not being able to recapture that particular dream. But her life was full of dreams, of events never to be recaptured. The year she and Clark had decided to marry, they had taken a motorcycle tour of the Southwest, sleeping in a tent by night, the wind strong and wild in their faces by day. Sometimes they had sought out wild places by strange rock formations, or by springs, or streams, just to be able to make love in a new wilderness. Gone. Down one of the black holes, leaving only trace memories that stirred something in the pit of her stomach, in her vagina, something that was wholly sexual and had nothing to do with the reality of here and now. Here and now Clark seemed undesirable; it was only the memory of their love-making that could arouse her.

She thought of his thick hands on her body and could understand how some people equated sex with bestiality. Suddenly she began to weep and couldn't think why she was weeping.

This room, she thought, when the storm passed. This room, this prison is driving me bananas! She wheeled herself to the bathroom and washed her face, and now she could think clearly of the experiment she wanted to describe to Clark. She went back to the table and began to write in a fine, neat script, detailing the work step by step, with her predictions at the end. Clark came in while she was working on it.

"Darling," she said, "you look awful. My God, it's nine o'clock! No wonder. Have you eaten?"

He had, at the cafeteria. Anne made a face. "Ronnie left some awfully good roast beef for sandwiches, and a salad, with dressing in a jar. Shake it first. I have coffee in here."

"Be right back," Clark said. He kissed her, lingering a moment, and for that moment she clung to him. As soon as he came back, she thought, as soon as he had his drink, and something to eat, she would say, Let's go to bed. The doctor says I should. And I want you, Clark. My God, I want you.

When he came back with his plate, the moment had passed and she began to tell him about the experiment she wanted him to conduct for her.

## EIGHT

"THE DIFFERENCE this time will be stress," Anne said. "Give them the *pa* factor and elevate the blood pressure, and then induce stress. We know the drug and *pa* together are harmless, no interaction showed up at all, but adding stress might make a difference."

Clark looked over her notes. "I'd like to add just one bit to it," he said. "I'd like to include one of the chimps from the test group, not give it additional *pa,* simply elevate its blood pressure and subject it to stress."

Anne thought about it a moment. "That's good. I should have seen it. I think my brain was fractured too sometimes."

"No one else thought of this particular experiment in the first place," Clark said.

"Lola would be good," Anne said. "And in the control group, Hermione. They gave birth within days of each other, the *pa* levels are about the same. Which one for the other test chimp? Do you have time to work this in, Clark?"

He nodded. "I'll get it going first thing in the morning."

He looked over the records of the two chimps she had selected. Lola had been given the factor three times during the last weeks of her pregnancy; the control chimp, of course, had had none. The births were normal, seven months ago, two male infants. Everything to date with both chimps had appeared normal. He was glad she hadn't chosen Fannie. But seven-month-old infants weren't as likely to be damaged by the separation as a three-month-old. They didn't demand as much nursing time; they were feeding themselves by now, and they would be company to one another during the experiment.

"Lilith," he said finally. "Her infant's only six months, but she's the closest we have. If you're right about the results," he said, "you realize it might be a contraindication for people with stress diseases—high blood pressure, atherosclerosis, the like?"

"I know. I suspect that will be the case."

"Okay." He glanced up from the notes to find Anne studying him. She looked away and yawned. "Honey, you're tired. You should get to bed."

Not looking at him, Anne asked, "What's Klugman up to? What's the problem this time?"

The trouble was, Clark knew, there was no way he could tell her only part of it. If he told her about the approval of the IND, she would link that with his late hours, and conclude they were going on. As for the human tests, that was the most important part of the work remaining to be done. And she had fought for and won the right to supervise that phase from start to finish. Deena was right; Anne couldn't stand knowing any of it until she was able to deal with it herself. He was glad she had thought up the stress experiment. He could use this to explain his long hours; they could discuss it. He wouldn't be compelled to live a total lie.

This passed through his mind as he lighted a cigarette and finished his coffee. Then he said, "Oh, Bob's got the flu. Several others are out with sore throats, stuff like that. A couple of accidents, that sort of thing. Routine." He waved it away. "The guinea pigs are dying at a faster rate, the soybean-sawdust diet is a real killer."

Now she smiled. "Still smelling up everything?"

"Worse than ever. They need the computer twenty-six hours a day, as usual."

She laughed and said, "You know what'll happen. Gradually they'll take over everything and the company will become a super-cereal factory."

"They left a tray of gift cookies at the end of the cafeteria line Monday, and nobody touched them. Nobody."

She wrinkled her nose. "The great white hope of the world. Ugh."

Clark stood and picked up the newspaper from the end table by the chaise. "Be back in a minute," he said.

He would be in the bathroom for fifteen to twenty minutes and it would be eleven by then. He would yawn a couple of times, and carry stuff back to the kitchen, and then go to bed, and she would sit there. Visiting hour over, everyone back to the cell block. March! Or roll!

She closed the notebooks and folded her charts. The coffee pot was still half full. She poured another cup and opened a book that she then ignored.

This was the life most women led, those who didn't work anyway. Wait at home for the man, be ready for whatever he proposed, then unprotestingly withdraw when he was finished. Even this prison term she was serving was better than what most women had, she thought. At least once in a while she and Clark could still communicate something to one another. Like tonight, taking an hour to detail her experiment. It had drawn them together briefly, let them touch in the way that was even more important than the physical touch she no longer wanted. He had listened with concentration, had studied her plans, for a short time their minds had been one, and then it ended and he was now sitting on the john reading the newspaper, thinking tired thoughts, wanting the release of love, probably resentful that she wouldn't or couldn't offer it.

How long, she wondered, before he found someone who would fuck? Another week? A month? Oh, good and faithful husband, find thyself a whore, she thought bitterly. Sooner or later it would happen, it might as well be sooner.

It took Clark a long time to fall asleep that night. He thought of her body, first cool and smooth under his hands, against his thighs, her cool firm breasts gradually becoming warmer, then hot, shiny with sweat, the bed wet under them. He dozed and dreamed she kept opening her legs for him, opening her arms to embrace him, opening her mouth . . . Always before he could reach her, a door slammed, and he was on the outside in a cold wind, standing before a featureless wall. He awakened and tossed, and remembered how soft and smooth her inner thighs were, and the underside of her breasts. They were in a motel room, garish, plush, with a panel of controls for air-conditioning, service, lights, radio, everything they could think of. The bed had a machine to vibrate it. All night, at least for hours, they had fed it quarters and made love on the quivering bed. And in the shower. And under the stars in the desert where the air temperature had dropped five degrees every twenty minutes, and they hadn't noticed until later when their breaths were frosty.

He dreamed she was there in his room, gliding toward him like a cloud, making no sound, her eyes shiny with love, her arms widespread for his embrace. She stopped and this time no door slammed. He struggled to waken himself thoroughly, breathing in her faint scent, certain she was waiting for him this time, really there this time. When he opened his eyes, sitting up in the dark room, it was empty.

Clark explained the experiment to his two assistants. "We'll keep the mothers in isolation today and once an hour play the tape of the infants' cries. After four hours, and again after eight hours we'll get blood samples and test the *pa* level. After the four-hour period the babies will be returned briefly, only long enough to nurse. The babies will be returned at the end of the day. Tomorrow we'll repeat it, but keep the infants separated from them overnight and throughout Friday. Okay?"

"And you'll want constant observation?"

"Yes. I'll take the blood samples myself. You two are to keep watch during the day. Take turns, spell each other."

Virginia Sudsbury and Phil Rudolf were two of the brightest of the lab assistants. They had worked closely with Clark and Anne from the start of the primate tests. At the prospect of the tedious job before them, both looked resigned, but unprotesting. Phil had been a laboratory assistant for twenty-two years. He had worked with old man Prather and had been the best then, and was still the best for the detailed, laborious observations that most experiments relied on. He was fifty, infinitely patient, and had never been known to speak unless asked a direct question. Virginia was twenty-one, plump, with black hair that reached midway down her back. She kept it tied with a scarf, or ribbon, or even a string at work, but as soon as her day ended, the hair came down, and it was like a dark river alive with gleaming highlights. Anne had said once that she must wash it every ~~night for it~~ to shine like that. She had said also, mischievously, that if a poll were taken she would bet every man in the building had a longing to run his hands through that cascade of hair. Virginia wore gold-rimmed glasses, perfectly round, like her pleasant face. Her eyes were round, too, Clark noticed, round and very quick to show understanding of what was required.

"Tomorrow we'll put them in the compounds for a few hours," Clark said. "That might liven it up a little."

—          *          *          *

The infants played and showed no signs of alarm at the separation. At first the female chimps accepted the separation also, without alarm, or apparent awareness even. But when the tape was played and they heard their infants' distress cries, all three became agitated. Lola, the test chimp that had received the *pa* factor that morning, tried to shake the bars down, then tried to reach the lock, and when all else failed, sat on her haunches and stared at the section of the lab she could see and bared her teeth from time to time. The other test chimp and the control chimp reacted much the same but tired of their vigil sooner and resumed feeding and explorations of their new cages.

Gus found Clark at the confinement cage and reported on his meeting with Helverson. "We've got a week to prove something, or forget it and go ahead as planned," Gus said. "Anything here?"

"I don't know. Lola's more excited than Hermione and Lilith, but that could be natural temperament. I'll extract blood in an hour."

"Does Anne know then?"

"I don't know. She suspects something. But she's been worrying with this for a month or more. I saw her notes. Something about the way the levels of *pa* fluctuate alerted her to the possibility the cause is stress-connected."

"She's good," Gus said, as he had the day before. "Wish to God she were here."

"How did it go with Helverson?"

"He wants to forge ahead, naturally. He can't believe we'd get a reaction after this length of time. Find it hard to believe myself. But . . . I convinced him it could be dangerous without further exploration. I think I convinced him. Enough to give us a week, and then I'll try to convince him again."

Clark shook his head. "That's not the way," he said moodily.

"In this, the best of all possible worlds, it is the way, though," Gus said. He put his hand on Clark's shoulder for a moment, and then slouched away.

After the incident with Duckmore, they would take no chances with any of the chimps. The transport cages would be used to take the animals to the examination table, where restraints would hold them securely long enough to extract the blood samples, and they would be returned to the isolation cages. They would have to be treated exactly alike, each subjected to the same amounts of stress. Clark left the lab assistants and returned to his office, where preliminary reports on Duckmore and Fannie were starting to accumulate.

At one, Deena collected him for lunch. He had forgotten. By three, Lola was showing signs of great distress, and he went to observe her when the tape was played. She cringed and looked about desperately and rattled the bars, and now she couldn't be still even after the crying stopped. She ran about the small cage, pulled at the ledge, flung herself off the far wall. She hurled a banana, smashing it against the wall, and continued around and around. Lilith's anxiety was acute also, as was the control chimp's, but they merely sat at the bars, clutching them, looking out at the lab and now and again making plaintive mewing sounds.

There was a meeting in Gus's office at four-thirty. "Can we learn enough in a week to know for certain?" Gus asked generally. All day he had been doing his job and Bob Klugman's. There had been a fight over computer time. Cosmetics had been scheduled for that afternoon and he had canceled that and had faced down Sarah Zeller over it. Twice the blood analyzer had stopped functioning and a service call had been delayed. He had fought with the treasurer and the payroll superintendent over keeping Pat on full pay during his sick leave. He had a headache, and more than ever he wanted to lie on a golden beach and listen to the waves murmur, and his wife murmur, and drink tall smooth drinks with fruit salad floating on them, and eat exotic food in exotic settings.

"I think there's a pattern," Deena said crisply. "I charted Duckmore's deviation from the norm from the first time it was noted by Pat. He kept very good notes, by the way. You can see how it grew, up here, then again here. And finally the attack." She pointed to a line she had drawn—all steep climbs and plateaus, always upward. "Now here is Fannie's chart. Almost identical," she said, putting the stiff papers aside. "None of the others show just that kind of behavior line. Some of them seem to have steeper climbs than others, but not just like that. If this is right, then Fannie will erupt into violent behavior after two more minor incidents."

Emory nodded. He and Deena had worked together for eleven years. He had as much trust in her charts as she did. Gus frowned. "How far have you carried the same kinds of charts for the other animals, the control animals?"

"Obviously I haven't had time to do it thoroughly for more than these two," Deena said, almost snapping at him. "I expect to work on it for the next week at least."

"What do you label minor incidents?" Gus asked, ignoring her sharpness.

"The same sort of thing that happened today. Fannie showed hostility for no apparent reason. Completely unprovoked hostility toward a lab worker."

"Okay. Stick with it. We're going ahead with the blood processing, as planned. If we don't get to use it in the coming weeks, we'll be up to our asses in the stuff. Clark, how long will it remain potent, under what conditions?"

"We think room temperature is fine, but we've kept it refrigerated until we run the temperature control tests. The frozen protein is stable for months, no outer limits were found, but the tests haven't been concluded."

"We'll have to do them now." Gus sighed. "Damn all people in a hurry," he said quietly. "Who can start it?"

"I'll find someone," Clark said, "or start it myself."

"Not you. Goddamn, you're needed for other things right now. How about Virginia? Is she good enough?"

"Yes. I have her observing Lola, but I can bring in someone else for that. I'll need two more people. This is an around-the-clock test, you know."

"Take whoever you want," Gus said.

Deena stood up. "Gus, one more thing, and then I'm leaving. I can do my work at home as well as here for the time being. I don't like to leave Marcie any more than I have to." She took a breath. "If Fannie does continue to show the same line as Duckmore, she'll attack someone, and if no one is available, the violence will be directed at one of the other chimps."

"You think she should be confined then?"

"No! Then she'll have to attack the infant. Don't you see? There's an inevitability about it that's frightening. If I'm right."

"Okay," Gus said. "We all know there's really insufficient data yet to call anything inevitable, but let's say a strong possibility exists she'll attack one of the other chimps. She's small and comparatively weak, isn't she? She'll get her ears flattened. Then what?"

"That's what I don't know," Deena said. "That's what worries me. Duckmore attacked and vanquished his enemy. At least, he's not around any more as far as Duckmore is concerned. He seems completely normal now, except for that persistent drop in the *pa* factor. But what will Fannie do if she is defeated and the enemy is still there?"

"What do you think?"

"Either she'll assault one after another of the adults, or she'll turn on the infant then."

There was silence in the office for several seconds as they considered it. Clark shook his head. "I can't buy it," he said finally. "Why?"

"I don't know why. I only know that when behavior is predictable up to a point, then it's usually predictable past that point. There comes a time when it's safe enough to say because this happened, this will happen."

"On a statistical basis, not an individual basis," Clark said.

"Watch."

"How soon?"

"Within two weeks, probably; perhaps a bit longer, but I doubt it."

Clark stood up, but there was no place in the small office he could pace, and he sat down again. "That's too long."

"I can't help that. Now, Gus, if you don't need me, I'll go home. Clark, can you get home, or go now?"

"I'll get a ride," he muttered, not looking at her.

"Okay. See you in the morning." She left, taking her charts with her.

"That woman drives me up the wall," Clark said. "What makes her so sure of herself all the time?"

"Success helps," Emory said mildly.

"You'd better speak to Virginia before she leaves," Gus said. He went to the dart board and pulled out the darts, took them across the room.

Clark nodded. "She's waiting for me to relieve her at Lola's cage. I'll tell her." He heard the first dart hit as he closed the door.

Virginia was making notes when he approached Lola's cage. The girl looked up at him and smiled. "More good news, Doctor?"

"Yeah." He looked at Lola. She had changed again. Now she sat staring at the lab with her teeth bared, clutching, releasing, clutching again the bars of the cage. Behind her everything breakable had been broken, water had been splashed about, food strewn all over the cage. "How long has she been like that?"

"About an hour now. I think she suspects I'm over here out of sight. She tried to reach around the corner just before she sat down there."

Clark nodded. "Have you ever run a quality deterioration temperature test?"

"Yes, sir. I've done several for Dr. Diedricks."

"Can you set it up, the works?"

"Yes, sir."

"Okay. We're going to need the tests on the *pa* factor. I'll pull you and Phil off this, and bring in whoever worked with you before on it."

"That was Ernest James, but I think he's tied up with Dr. Diedricks right now."

"Okay, let's bring in Brighton. You go work out the schedule. Use my office. I'll look it over before I leave." He glanced at the clock over the far door and swore. "First thing in the morning. It's after hours already."

"I can do it now," Virginia said. "Will you be over here?"

"Here or somewhere." He watched her walk away, pleased she had asked no unnecessary questions, that she had not protested the lateness of the hour, had not made any demands of any sort. A good girl, he thought, and turned to find the transport cage. Time for the chimps' blood tests, then return the infants to mothers, analyze the samples taken, write up the notes . . .

## NINE

HARRY had called at four and asked if he could drop in later, and now at seven he was in the bedroom holding a gray, tiger-striped, half-grown cat.

"I can't keep it," he said, stroking the animal.

"What do you intend to do with it?" Anne asked.

"Give it to you."

"You're out of your mind! We can't have a cat here."

"Yes you can. I called the landlord and asked. He's a very nice cat, Anne, about three months old, I guess. House-broken."

"But where did you get it?"

"An anonymous student left it on my desk, in a box, with a note saying his or her father wouldn't keep it and it was going to the pound."

Anne studied the cat. It was handsome, with almond-shaped green eyes and a bushy tail that seemed to stay erect no matter what.

"I've never seen a tiger-stripe with this much fur," Harry said. "Listen, it's purring."

"Harry, no. We don't want a cat. It would be alone all day, cooped up in an apartment. That's no life for an animal."

"Exactly what they like best," Harry said. "After a few days, I'll install a cat window so he can get in and out, and you'll never know he's on the grounds, except when he wants to play or be petted."

He put the cat in Anne's lap, and the little purring machine stopped momentarily, then resumed as her hands began to stroke it automatically. It was a very soft cat.

"I've brought a cat box and kitty litter, food, a feeding dish, water bowl—everything he'll need."

"You're the cat freak," Anne said, stroking the purring animal. "Why don't you keep it?"

"We've got a cat poisoner in our block."

The cat began to paw at the tie on Anne's blouse. She moved the tie end slightly and the cat pounced on it. "For a few days," she said. "But you'll have to look around for a permanent home for it. What's his name?"

"Doesn't have one, far as I know."

"There's coffee in the pot," Anne said, watching the cat, who was exploring her chair. He reached for the wheel and slid down to the floor, leaped straight up in the air, all four feet and legs rigid, landed, and ran as if he had come down on live wires.

"He's a maniac," Anne said, laughing.

"Crazy kitty time," Harry said. He poured coffee and sat down opposite her. "You like him, don't you?"

"How could anyone not like a kitten?" She looked at him sternly. "But only for a few days."

"Clark tied up at work?"

"Yes. There's an emergency. He'll be late every day this week."

"I've been thinking about your experiment, Anne, and I've come to the conclusion there is no way you can do it and remain ethically pure."

"Harry! For God's sake!"

He peered at her for a moment, confused by the sharpness of her tone. "Oh, not you personally. I was thinking of it as a problem in ethics. A philosophical point."

"I should have kept my mouth shut."

"Don't feel that way about it," Harry said. "I'm very glad you told me. I never really gave this much thought before, but there is a real dilemma here, isn't there? If a person is terminal and everything's been done that can be, then to offer him an experimental drug, serum, or whatever, poses no problem. You throw a drowning man whatever you can, even a rotten rope, hoping it'll hold long enough. No fault can be found. But a relatively well person? One whose suffering is known to be temporary? To carry the analogy perhaps too far, isn't it like offering that same uncertain rope to save one in a boat that is bouncing about on the waves, maybe causing some upchucking and discomfort, but a boat that is all the time drifting toward the shore, with the goal in sight? What really puzzles me is why would that person, in sight of shore, or with the smell of land in his nose, why would he accept a rotten rope, or at best an uncertain rope?"

"If you had any idea of the steps we've gone through," Anne said, "the tests, the debates, the delays waiting for results to become conclusive before we can go on to the next step . . ." She pointed to the table with the notebooks. "I'm still dreaming up new tests. And we're on the primatology tests now. Chimps. Their reactions to something like this are almost human, as human as you can get without going to men and women. And up to now everything's checked, tested out, been okayed. It's been eight years!"

"From a handful of chimps you can generalize to over a hundred, two hundred . . . How many women will you use?"

"A thousand. Five hundred will get the stuff, the others won't. They won't know which ones are which; the doctors who administer it won't know. Only after phase one has been concluded will the records indicate which women got the factor."

"So, from a handful of chimps, to a thousand women, or at least five hundred, you can generalize to over two hundred million people?"

"That's how it has to be. There are laws governing new drugs, serums, everything. After that phase, there is the usage test, where doctors prescribe it to certain patients and keep records of their reactions. Only after that has been successfully reported is the new drug or serum approved for general use. Another two to three years, at least."

Harry shook his head. "What woman would risk her infant's well-being with an experimental drug? I just don't understand."

"The literature has studies on that," Anne said, annoyed with his devil's-advocate role. "Some people really do have altruistic reasons, strange as that may seem."

"I bet less than one tenth of one percent."

"But by then we're so sure of its safety we can assure them the risk is infinitesimal."

"Women in prisons, in welfare clinics, state-run hospitals, the poorest, worst-educated women in society."

Anne shook her head helplessly. "Not my experiment," she said. "It isn't going to be like that."

"Ah, then you do see the ethical point I'm making. You've seen it all along."

"Harry, you know, you drive me crazy? Every week you come here to start an argument with me. Why do you feel you have to engage in some kind of Socratic dialogue with me all the time?"

"Because I want to keep you human, honey." The cat was stalking the shadow of a table leg. They watched. Harry began to rummage about in his pockets and found a ball of yarn. It was red, much frayed at one end. He leaned over Anne's chair and tied the end to the arm. "Next you'll tell me you intend to try the stuff out on yourself before you go on to phase one. Right?"

"Yes," she snapped.

"Thought so." He started to straighten up, leaned forward instead, and kissed her forehead. "Ever tell you how proud of you I am, honey? Leaving you my little house and garden, and my books, everything. Thought you'd like to know."

Anne blinked at sudden tears. "You're as crazy as that cat is," she said. "Just plain crazy."

"Yes, probably."

"I'll call him Tyger," she said. "With a y." She threw the little ball of yarn and she and Harry laughed when Tyger attacked it ferociously.

Harry didn't stay very long. Papers to grade, he said. He promised to come back in a few days to check on the cat, but really to check on her, Anne thought, because he hated for her to be alone so much. She turned the television on, then turned it off again. There never had been time enough to become addicted, and the few things she did want to watch always seemed to be clumped at awkward times. She looked at the table with her papers and notebooks, but didn't approach it. She had been making tentative plans for following up the stress experiments, but she didn't want to get too firmly set on any of them until she had some results. Later.

The kitten had been playing with the fringe of the bedspread, and now it raced to the door and ran out into the hallway in its crazy rocking-horse gait. Anne wheeled herself to the doorway and looked for it. She crossed the hall to the study, now Clark's room, and paused inside. The sofa bed was open; the matching desks on the far side of the room looked naked, hers especially, since the contents had been carried across the hall. The cat wasn't in the room. She returned to the hallway and looked up its length, and then, instead of returning to her room, she began to wheel herself through the hallway.

Anything was better than staying in there all the time, she thought. Even the hall was better, narrow as it was, bare as it was. She longed to be able to run and play, as the cat ran, freely, without any consciousness of self at all. Run like the wind. If she could only get to the kitchen, she thought, rummage in the refrigerator. Perhaps get a glass of milk, or juice. Give the cat some milk in a saucer, watch it lap it up. Just poke about in the cabinets. Anything except stay in that room any longer. The apartment was divided by a hallway from the entrance door, with the two bedrooms on either side of it, to a turn where the living room opened on the right, and a narrower passage went on to the kitchen and dining room. The turn had proven impassable before, not because there wasn't room enough, for Ronnie or Clark could work her chair through it without any real trouble, but because the thick pile carpeting was hard to navigate for Anne, and because she needed to grasp the wheels of her chair on the outside to manage a turn. And grasping them on the outside instead of the top caused her to scrape her knuckles at that particular corner. She wheeled herself to it and paused, considering. There was nothing in the living room that attracted her. They seldom used it even during the best of times. They preferred the study, or their own bedroom with its easy furniture. Besides, the shag carpeting in the living room was an impossible thicket for her.

If she could only stand long enough to get the chair turned, she thought, and slowly, holding to the corner of the wall, she lifted herself and stood unsteadily, keeping her weight on her left leg, but now she couldn't move at all.

She fumbled behind her for the chair. It was caught at the corner. Desperately she tugged it and managed to move it farther from her. She thought of her pelvic bones mashing together from the unaccustomed weight and she thought of the long scar on her thigh, pulling, pulling, reddening, seeping . . . She shut her eyes hard. Not true. She couldn't damage herself now at this late stage. It was a question of strength and confidence, just as that stupid, pretty-faced imbecile had said. Confidence to lift her right leg and put it down again. She couldn't do it.

How rough the wall was against her hands. She had become baby-soft. If she could flow down the wall to the floor, flow back to the chair, haul herself into it again . . . She was crumpling, she thought in wonder. Like a tired paper doll, just folding in on herself, and she couldn't stop. And what, she asked herself sternly, will you do with that stupid leg when it's time for it to bend? She didn't do anything, as it turned out; her leg simply bent itself at the knee and she was sprawled on the hallway floor. She hadn't fallen, she decided. She had melted. In the strangeness of the apartment in the past few days, or maybe weeks—she couldn't be certain now when the strangeness had first appeared, not the night of the ice storm, that was simply the night she had acknowledged it—but since then anything had been possible, including a melting woman. And it really was all right, she was more mobile this way. She could get to one knee and creep quite easily, in fact.

She could move now, but for a time she lay unmoving, her cheek on her arm on the floor. Tyger tried to leap over her in a single bound, and missed, landing on her stomach, digging in in alarm. Anne disengaged the cat and it came up to sniff her face, and then bounded away in pursuit of a prey only it could see. She had to get up, get back to the chair, press on to the kitchen, or back to her bedroom, something. She couldn't stay there, although it felt very comfortable now not to be trying to go anywhere at all. What if Clark came home now?

Tyger ran past her again, the other way this time. She smiled and considered what she should do next. She got herself turned; pointed once more at the wheel-chair and the bedroom at the end of the hall, but when she tried to bring the chair closer to her, she realized she would not be able to reach the brake, and without it she could not climb back into it. Finally she began to inch her way down the hall, dragging her right leg, pushing the chair ahead of her, until she reached the end and the outside door, where the chair stopped and became stable enough for her to pull herself up.

For a time she didn't move, was content to sit in the chair against the front door of the apartment and re-gard the hall. Well, she had had her little adventure, she thought ruefully, and to show for it she had a scraped knee, and a sore leg where she had dragged it on the carpeting, whose softness was illusory.

Finally she sighed and pushed herself back into the bedroom; Tyger was sitting on the bed, his eyes round with alarm. She nodded to him. "Don't tell," she whis-pered. "And don't laugh. I couldn't stand it if you laughed at me for crawling like a baby."

She had tried, she thought, heading for the bathroom to clean herself up. She had been perspiring heavily, her hands felt gritty, and her legs were dirty, she was certain. She had tried. And would again, but not too soon, she added, when she inspected her red knee. Not too soon.

Gus stood in the doorway to Clark's office and watched him for a minute before speaking. Clark was engrossed in a computer-analysis print-out.

"It'll keep until tomorrow, Clark," Gus said.

Clark looked up then. He seemed to have trouble recognizing Gus.

"Go on home," Gus said. "Your eyes are glassy."

"I'm glassy everywhere. I'm afraid I think Deena's right. Fannie's going the way of Duckmore."

"Yeah." Gus lighted a cigarette. "Come on, I'll buy you a drink, or a doughnut and coffee. Christ, I had a lousy turkey sandwich at the cafeteria. Heartburn ever since. Hungry?"

Clark began to stack the papers on his desk. "Had that same kind of sandwich. Think the annex boys have got to the cooks?"

"I'll kill them if that happens." He looked like an old, tired, brown gnome, his suit coat dirty and wrinkled, his trousers a bad match, clashing in color, blue against a dark green coat, his trousers were too short, showing his socks, yellow and brown, scuffed shoes. Clark looked just as disreputable with his frayed slacks and ancient corduroy coat with a button missing. A couple of lab bums, he thought, switching off his light, following Gus through the dimly lighted laboratory that looked like something out of a Grade B horror movie at this time of night.

They met the night watchman as they left the lab. He waved to them and continued his round. He looked better-dressed, neater, than either of them. Clark needed a shave. His beard was always dark by evening, and by this time, ten, it was obviously trying to become whiskers. If a strange night watchman caught them in the building, he'd yell cop, Clark thought, grinning.

"Let's look in on Fannie," he said, almost apologetically.

The animal division at night was strangely peaceful, and although the cats in particular seemed wakeful, they made no sound as the two men strode down the aisle to the rear, where the individual night cages for the chimps were.

Duckmore looked at them as they passed his cage. He should have been sleeping, not waking up for anything as routine as a man strolling by. The watchman made this round periodically; he was instructed to report any undue activity, and undue activity included wakeful chimps. There had been no such report. Fannie, when they paused before her cage, moved from her perch to one higher and watched them. None of the other chimps stirred.

"Stress symptoms," Clark said. "Wakefulness, restlessness at night."

"Right." Gus touched his arm and started for the door again. "Tomorrow," he said once more.

They went to Al's Place for steak sandwiches and beer, and Gus talked of his wife and their two sons. "Funny," he said. "You expect so goddamn much out of them, you know? You see the potential when they're still in diapers and you watch it come along and know you're right about them, what they can do if they want to. And then they just plain don't seem to want to. Funny."

"They'll snap out of it," Clark said. "Lot of kids their age don't know what they want yet."

"Look at Virginia," Gus went on, ignoring him. "Brains, plenty on the ball. She should have gone on to school, be working on her Ph.D. right now instead of locked into a job like she has."

"Maybe it's what she likes to do."

Gus shook his head. "Not that. Too impatient to serve the apprenticeship, that's it. Can't see studying four, six, eight more years. Can't see how open it is after that time."

"It isn't very open, Gus. That's what they see. Look at us, aren't we just as locked in?"

"You're just tired now."

"No. Look at you. Me. They're screwing up what should have been a beautiful piece of work and there's not a damn thing we can do about it. Not a goddamn thing."

Gus sighed and raised his hand for another beer.

"Anne might escape," Clark said. "She senses the need to escape. God, I don't look forward to telling her what we're doing."

"I'll do it," Gus said. He put his hand on Clark's arm when Clark started to protest. "It's my job, remember. I was going to be the one to tell her about Grove and his test subjects anyway. When the time comes, I'll level with her right down the line."

"And break her beautiful dream world into a million

bits," Clark said. "You know she and Deena have worked it out, how to recruit subjects, what they'll tell them, the educational program they've been developing for them. Deena shouldn't have encouraged her. Deena knows it doesn't work like that."

"She really thought Anne could pull it off," Gus said mildly. a hand on Clark's arm. He patted the arm and moved aside for the waitress, who brought two more mugs of beer. "Deena thinks Anne can move mountains, dry up rivers, make the Red Sea part, whatever she sets out to do. If she hadn't got hurt, she would have done it her way. Bob's scared to death of her, and Helverson's afraid she'll take her lovely brain and go somewhere else."

Clark felt himself withdraw and couldn't keep the stiffness from his voice when he said, "I know. And one day she's going to look at me and think to herself, If it hadn't been for you. And that day everything goes down the drain."

"For Christ's sake, Clark! Don't be an idiot. That girl is wild about you."

"Until I get in the way of her dream," Clark said. "Just that long."

They were all afraid of her, Clark thought. The assistants, the management, everyone. Even he, her husband, was a little afraid of her. It was her single-minded pursuit of this one thing, he knew. Everyone recognized a drive like that, even encountering it for the first time. It was as if she had blazoned on her forehead a message: *I'm going here, and don't get in my way!* No one wanted to be the one who got in her way. His fear was both more and less than the others'. He knew he could never be the one to get in her way, but he also knew he was deeply afraid he might somehow lose her. And this fear was more terrible than the other one. That he even considered ever losing her struck him as terrible, as if he intuitively realized he might do or say something wrong, something so horrendous that, once done or said, it could never be undone. He didn't know the source of this insecurity he felt surface now and again; he never had been insecure in any way before, and this proof of a basic need didn't assert itself often, but when it did, he became almost paralyzed with dread.

Now someone would have to tell her there was a flaw, they might have to start over, they might use women prisoners after all . . . He was startled by Gus's voice. He had forgotten him.

". . . sleep. Going to be a hell of a week." Gus had paid the bill already. They left and Gus drove him home.


## TEN


ALL DAY Thursday the test chimp, Lola, sat on her haunches, staring at the laboratory through the cage bars. The other two chimps had accepted their condition, apparently; one sat swinging on a tire, the other groomed herself. When the infants were brought at five, the difference was even more pronounced. Hermione heard the baby's whimpers before it was in sight; she raced about her cage in excitement, caroming off the walls, pausing at the bars, then tearing about again. As soon as the infant was admitted to her cage, she clutched it to her breast and withdrew with it to the highest ledge to let it nurse. Lilith repeated this performance. Lola remained hunched down, watching the large room, apparently unaware her infant was being transferred to her cage, until it actually was inside, the small door secured once more. Then she grabbed it roughly and swung herself to a perch. The infant was trying to reach her teats, but first she examined him minutely, ignoring his cries. When he finally began to suckle, she turned her gaze once more on the laboratory room and continued her vigil.

"She gives me the creeps," Deena said, hugging her

arms about her. "Just like Duckmore and Fannie, only accelerated."

Clark could see no one individual in Lola's line of sight. There were other animal cages, people moving in and out of the aisles between cages; Emory, attendants, came and went, but still the animal stared straight ahead.

"It's going to be something else trying to get those babies away from them," Deena said.

They would use tranquilizers only as a last resort. The cages were equipped with movable sides, and up to now they had been able to maneuver the animals into the corner where the door was, and then offer food to the baby, opening the door only enough to permit it to pass through to the transport cage, not enough for the mother to follow. The stratagem worked once more with Hermione and her infant, who scampered through the small doorway without a backward glance. Hermione reached for it, was distracted by a bunch of grapes, and by the moving bars as they rolled into their original place. She began to pick off grapes and eat them, glanced at the transport cage as it was taken away, and returned to the grapes. Lilith made whimpering noises and watched her baby depart, then she too began to eat.

Lola clung to her infant tightly, too tightly. It cried out with rage and pain and she tried to climb to a higher ledge with it. The wall of bars moved inexorably closer, forcing her from the shelves, toward the door. The baby screamed again. She tried to force it back to the nipple, but it was trying to climb out of her arms, trying to get free. The wall was touching her, forcing her to move inch by inch. She bared her teeth and made a low, growling sound. She grabbed a bar and tried to shake it, all the while moving back inch by inch. Finally she was in position and the transport cage was attached to the front of her cage, the small door slid up partially. She clung even tighter to the infant, and now it fought back until she cuffed it sharply on the side of its head. The baby stopped struggling, but continued to whimper.

Clark held the tranquilizer needle. He went quickly to the side of the cage where Lola's body was pressed tight against the bars. She twisted her head to glare at him, but she couldn't move, confined as she was by the two sets of bars. He injected her in the hip, and within seconds her grasp of the infant loosened and it scampered to the safety of the transport cage and cowered in the rear, watching its mother fearfully as her head lolled and only the bars supported her.

"I'll take the blood sample now," Clark said, and at that moment Virginia appeared with the tray of equipment. The movable wall was rolled back, so Clark could enter through the large door. He extracted the blood and withdrew. Already Lola was twitching, and before the door was locked again, she was shaking with long heaving tremors as she fought back to wakefulness. An assistant wheeled the infant away, and now Lola was pulling herself up from the floor. Dazedly she looked about for a moment, and then she straightened and leaped at the door. When it didn't give, she howled with rage. Screaming maniacally, she streaked back and forth in her cage, crashing into the walls, leaping into the air to race along the ledge, then flung herself back into the bars again. As abruptly as her rampage had begun, it ended. She sat on her haunches, edged her way to the front of the cage, her breath heaving her entire body. There was froth on her mouth, her eyes were wild. Clark had remained in front of the cage, and now her gaze fastened on him, her eyes sought his and she stared at him, baring her teeth widely, the aggressive, straightforward challenge that usually only the males exhibited, and only to each other.

For a moment Clark shared a full measure of her impotent fury, her despair, her madness, her hatred. Beside him he heard Virginia take a deep, quick breath. "You should get out of here," she said.

He turned and left. Deena caught up with him before he was out of the animal division. "I've never seen anything like that," she said.

Clark stopped and looked at her. "Will you decide I'm crazy if I tell you something?"

She shook her head.

"That damn chimp was telling me she's going to kill me the first chance she gets. I could feel it coming from her."

"I believe," Deena said. "My God, I could feel it!"

Virginia joined them, carrying the tray. "Are you going to run this through, Dr. Symons? Shall I find someone to do it?"

"You're still on the temperature test, aren't you?"

"Yes. I was between runs and had a minute. I wanted to see Lola for myself." She shivered. Clark took the tray from her. "If I were you," she said, "I wouldn't let myself be caught in a room with her for a single second."

"Yeah, I know. Thanks, for thinking of the tray. I intend to put it through myself."

At eight Virginia tapped on his door, and when he answered groggily, she looked in and said, "Have you eaten yet? I'm going to the cafeteria now. I could bring you something."

Clark stood up and stretched. "Jesus Christ!" he moaned. "I'm as stiff as a corpse." He looked at his watch in disbelief. "I'll come with you."

On the way they talked about the temperature tests. Nothing unpredictable there anyway, Clark decided. They had assumed the *pa* factor would be unstable at temperatures over eighty degrees. The tests would continue until they could predict exactly how long it could be stored at eighty, at seventy, sixty, and so on, and then they would narrow it even further. So many hours at seventy-three, or sixty-two. It would take time. Everything took time. And suddenly their time had been eradicated. Just like that, no more time. Ladies and gentlemen, we have an announcement. Henceforth there shall be no more time . . .

They met Deena leaving the cafeteria. She turned and went back in with them. "I wouldn't advise the ham or the turkey tonight," she said, and made a face. "My God, if they're experimenting on us, I'll blow up that goddamn annex!"

Not many people were in the cafeteria, a few people from the skeleton crew working a second shift to fill a government order, and a handful of people from the PR department, who were readying a campaign to introduce a new line of hypoallergenic cosmetics. There were three of them lingering over pie and coffee, their table littered with sketches and photographs. One of the watchmen was taking his break. The cafeteria echoed dismally with so few people in the cavernous space.

"I sent Marcie off to stay with my mother," Deena said when Clark and Virginia joined her with their trays. She was having more coffee.

"Anything new?" Clark asked, not even trying to conceal his fatigue.

"I'm not sure yet. Let you know later. How did that last blood analysis turn out?"

"Down, not sharply, but down. I called Anne and told her what happened, told her I'd stick around and run one more blood test at ten."

Deena nodded and sipped her coffee. Anne wouldn't have been surprised, she suspected. Anne must have figured this out on paper; putting it to the test was simply to verify what she already had decided. She realized she had been wrong about Anne, they had all been wrong. She looked up from her cup to see Virginia gazing at Clark. At her look, Virginia blushed a deep red that extended down her throat. She stood up. "I'd better be getting back," she said, and left very fast.

Clark looked startled, glanced at her departing back, then shrugged and pushed his food around on his plate.

Deena watched the girl walk away, and the fiercely maintained neutrality with which she regarded Clark flared with the pale painful fire of hatred. He knew and relished the anguish Virginia suffered. You always know if you hurt someone like that. For him it was a roller-coaster ego trip: for Virginia, a long slow slide into the shadows of despair. Deena stirred her coffee until there was a whirlpool and watched it until the motion ceased and the surface was calm again. Only then did she look at Clark, and by then her face was masked, the fire again banked.

"Saturday night we're having dinner with my parents," Clark said, "and I'll be damned if I'll give it up for more of this junk. No matter what happens around here between now and then."

"Atta boy!" Deena murmured. She lighted a cigarette and said deliberately, "We should tell Anne everything."

Clark sighed. "I keep coming back to that," he said. "If there was anything she could do about this mess, I would. But there isn't. Helverson, Grove, the human tests . . . It would drive her nuts."

"She should know," Deena repeated. "Let her intuition get to work on it, see what happens then. This stress experiment seems proof enough to me. She is working. Let her work on the real problems now."

"Look, Deena, she has therapy of some sort every day. She is out for several hours for that. She comes home exhausted. After she rests she works out on the exerciser, then she's supposed to soak and get massaged. It's an all-day job, just trying to get her strength back, learn to walk again. What part of it should she give up?"

Deena didn't have an answer then. Only much later, at home, after working until two, lying awake in bed, too tense and tired to go to sleep, did the elusive answer come to her mind. Anne could be thinking while she worked her body, she realized. She could think and tell Clark what had to be done even if she couldn't do a bit of it herself. She would tell Clark tomorrow, today, Friday, she thought sleepily. But on

Friday too many things erupted all at once and she forgot.

And at two Anne was sitting in her chair looking at the dieffenbachia that had turned its back on her, on the room. She didn't blame it, she thought. If she could, she would turn her back and never see that room again.

Her bed was mussed, the sheet twisted into a hopeless tangle, the ashtray by the bed was full, magazines were on the floor by the bed. Her notebook was also on the floor. She had looked at it a long time, wondering if she could retrieve it some way, had decided not, and had gone to the window instead.

How dark the park was every night. She thought of the small hill on the other side of the park, lovers' lane, where she had done a certain amount of necking and petting as a teenager. How innocent it had been, she thought, and remembered her fear of being caught by the patrolling police, of having the bright light turned on in her face, hearing the scornful, hateful voice telling them to get the fuck somewhere else.

But all she had done was neck and pet a little. Not even enough to arouse her still-sleeping libido. That had come later, in college.

She should thank Clark, she thought soberly, for giving her this opportunity to discover she was hollow. Take away her work and what was left? "Nothing," she said. Hollow casing stuffed with work. She was tempted to pinch her arm, to see if her fingers would meet since there was nothing between to stop them.

The rubber treads of her wheels left faint marks on the hardwood floor of her bedroom. The marks didn't persist very long, and this was the first time she had seen them. It must be the lighting, she thought. Only a night light was on, low on the wall next to her bed; it cast a pale glow over the floor. She studied the tracks. How they crisscrossed. She tried to find a pattern. To the door, turn, to the window, turn, to the bed, to the bathroom door, turn, to the window . . . In the center of the room the lines converged, like the center of a spider web.

Like a spider, unseen, unheard, she could roll about the apartment, into the hall, which looked dark and unfamiliar, with only a suggestion of light coming from her room. It was like a cave passage, she thought, and tried to see if the marks were visible. It was too dark. She went into Clark's room. Her eyes had adapted to the dim light and she could see his form on the bed, no more than that. A shape that her mind instantly identified as Clark. She watched him sleep.

"It's inconclusive, of course," she said at breakfast with Clark. He looked very tired. "It would take a full-scale test, but it's indicative of a trouble spot."

"It's trouble, all right," Clark said. "I wish you had seen that chimp last night when she realized I was coming toward her. If she'd had a gun, she would have shot me."

Anne nodded. "Do chimps have high blood pressure naturally?"

"I don't know."

"Will you ask Emory? We know we can't induce high blood pressure clinically without trouble, but what about animals with hypertension? Is there an adaptation process over a long period? We have to know."

"I'll see if Emory can help. Anything else?"

"I don't know. Something is nagging, but I haven't been able to put my finger on it. You're sure Lilith is fine?"

"Yeah."

"Are there other drugs that are used to elevate blood pressure? Some might produce different effects. We should try them all, same conditions otherwise. Drug, induce a state of stress, and wait. Clark," she said, her gaze inward, "it could mean a delay, couldn't it? We have to know." She shook her head. "After all this time."

"Don't worry about it, honey. Okay? Just don't get

in a sweat over it. If you think of anything else, give me a ring. I'll be late again."

Anne swam again that day, and this time was less exhausted afterward. She could even turn off the smiling idiot, she realized on her way home. Miss Westchester had hardly bugged her at all. The sun was shining, and on the way home Ronnie drove through the park, stopping at the edge of the lake so they could watch a flock of eider ducks for a few minutes. Anne liked the way they upended and vanished under the water. The surface of the water was opaque; the ducks looked like toys being moved by magnets from underneath. When they finally returned to the apartment, she felt as if she might scream. She sat at the window, and could believe the end wall was moving closer, closer, pinning her in place, keeping her immobile while the experimenter prepared yet another test . . .

## ELEVEN

THE HOLDING CAGES were not very large, they could house two or even three adult chimps, but not comfortably, and not for long. One chimp had enough room to swing up and down from the shelf, take four steps to the front of the cage, four from one side to the other, back to the ledge. The bars were too close together to permit a chimp to get his hand through them.

In the rear of her cage that Friday morning, Fannie sat as the watchman made his check. Her lips were pulled back tightly, her eyes unblinking, unwavering, as she watched. He vanished. She continued to stare at the laboratory before her. Clinging tightly to her belly, her infant shifted position, awakened, hungry. He tried to get to a teat. Fannie growled. For a moment the infant hesitated, then began to mouth her again, groping. Fannie pulled him away, put him on the ledge beside her, not looking at him. The infant crept back to

her, nearly slipped off the shelf, whimpered, and re-
gained his balance. He had to crawl over her leg to get
to her belly. Fannie continued to watch the laboratory.
Again she growled, and again she pulled the infant
away, and this time he fell to the floor.

He lay quietly for a minute, then began to whimper
louder, and now he crept about, looking for a way back
up to the shelf. A dog barked, and as if encouraged by
this sound of activity, the infant chimp wailed and
looked up at his mother. Fannie stared ahead, but as
her baby crept back and forth crying, her gaze was
drawn to its dark form and she transferred her stare to
it. Her teeth remained bared, and she growled. The
baby cried, tried to climb the bars of the side of the
cage.

Suddenly Fannie leaped from the shelf and grabbed
the infant by a leg and soundlessly began to tear about
the cage, dragging it behind her. She raced up the bars,
leaped to the shelf, back to the floor, to the side bars ...
Around and around, leaping, climbing, dashing first
one way, then another, she ran. Now the infant's head
struck the shelf, now his back slammed into the bars,
now he was thrown against the floor. He screamed and
struggled briefly, then became limp, like a rag being
swished over surfaces, leaving behind a trail of excre-
ment and blood.

Other animals were excited by the frenzy; a cat
howled, a dog barked and another growled continuous-
ly, another cat screamed. The chimps were all chattering in fear and excitement. The din rose and became
tumultuous.

The watchman punched out at seven without returning to the animal division. The day man hung up his
coat and lighted a cigarette, coughed long and hard,
and started his first check. Outside the animal division
he paused. He ground out his cigarette underfoot,
something he had never done before in his fourteen
years there, and ran into the room. Moments later he
called Emory Durand.

*        *        *

"Okay," Clark said. "They go crazy. Now we have two psychotic animals. The only question I can see right now is, which one do we sacrifice?"

"Three," Deena said. "Lola's less than a step behind Fannie in her deterioration."

"Not Lola," Clark said quickly.

Emory nodded. "I'd say Fannie," he said. "She's still showing symptoms, while Duckmore seems completely normal again."

"Fannie," Clark agreed. "Immediately." He looked at Emory, who kept averting his gaze. "Will you help?"

Emory shrugged helplessly. "Sure."

"I want that brain sliced from one end to the other," Clark said.

"Are you going to return Lola's baby this morning?" Deena asked.

"Yes. Right now. Someone else can extract the blood. I'll run it later."

A tap on the door was followed by Gus entering the room. "Can I come in?" He was already in. "You fixed with enough people, Clark?"

"Hell no!"

"We'll get them," Gus said, then added, "This is first priority, remember?"

For ten minutes they talked about procedural matters, then they all went to observe Lola's behavior when her baby was brought to her. It was a repeat of the previous day. Clark breathed a sigh of relief when the baby was taken away again.

"We're ready for Fannie any time," Emory said after consulting with one of the staff veterinarians.

Clark smoked a cigarette first, then he went to the operating room to cut up the brain of the newly killed chimp.

Sunlight coming from the stained glass cast pink and blue shadows in the little world of the terrarium. Anne looked at the broad leaves of an ivy that climbed up a twig, to cover it completely. The ivy was blue, green, and rose-colored.

They had played a game, she and Clark. A getting-acquainted game, they had called it. It had evolved from something one of them had said. Something like, I hate prunes. Gradually the rules had emerged and they had settled back warily to test it. The rules were simple—Clark had seen to that. He hated complexity when simplicity would do.

"We'll take turns," he had said, "naming things we hate. Personally hate, I mean. Not abstracts like war, or suffering. Okay?"

"Okay. But no Aha! reaction allowed."

"Right. And after we've got ten each, we select one of the other's things and try to explain why. I try to tell you why you hate roses, you tell me why I hate canned vegetables."

"And you have to confess if I hit it," she had said. "And if I miss, you have to explain it yourself."

"If we can," he had added.

"I'll start," Anne said. "I hate baseball."

Clark nodded. "Artichokes."

Anne considered it, nodded reluctantly. "We could use up all ten things by naming various foods." She thought, then said, "Dirty dishes left from the night before."

"Musical comedies."

"Being wrong."

Clark looked startled, then said, "Perfume."

Anne looked at him quickly, decided he was serious, and said, "Hairy soap."

"Sweaty or dirty feet."

Anne had gone on to name, in this order: Sharing a comb, hair brush, or most especially a toothbrush. Family reunions. Menstruation. Sentimental movies. Men over six feet tall. Hamburger in any form.

Clark's list had been: Gelatinous food. Writing compositions or papers of any sort. Situation comedies. Homosexuals. Mean drunks. Cheaters.

It had started in a light mood, with each of them

intent on being honest, on keeping the other honest. By the time they finished, they were both subdued and serious.

"You want to drop it?" Clark asked.

"No! Why should I? Do you?"

He shook his head.

"You go first this time," Anne said. "Explain one of my things to me."

"Men over six feet tall," Clark said. "You are tall for a girl. You feel superior until you get beside a man over six feet tall, and then you feel small again. Okay?"

"Wrong. Men over six feet tall have been conditioned to believe tallness is manliness, that to be big outside is somehow to be big inside, and it's been my experience that they are very little inside. Little and curled up like timid worms, always afraid someone will guess, so they develop big loud voices and their feet always trip anyone who gets near them. If they think you suspect the truth about them, they become bullies."

Clark took a deep breath and said, "Whew! A live wire there, isn't it?"

"Yes. My turn." She closed her eyes, trying to remember what he had said. "Perfume. Your first girlfriend wore perfume and she threw you over for a jock."

Clark laughed. "Wrong. I drank my mother's perfume when I was a kid. Made me sicker than a dog."

"You drank your mother's perfume! Aha!" Anne cried, and clapped her hand over her mouth. They had struggled and he had kissed her and she had kissed back and later they both agreed it was that minute that they knew this was it.

She thought of her brothers and her father, all over six feet tall, all bullies. Come on and play with us, they'd yell at her, you're big enough and strong enough. She had been both, but they had hurt her anyway. They loved picnics and grilling hamburgers

outside and going to ball games and friendly wrestling
that always got something broken. They didn't hurt her
sister, who had somehow missed the tall genes, and was
small and dainty. They were always very careful with
her, protective.

Clark's family was so different. He was the only
child, dearly loved by mother and father, loving them
in return. No hostility there, no remembrances of ugly
things past, only good will and mutual respect. They
had let him go without a struggle and he reciprocated
by never really leaving them. Knowing you can re-
moves the need to break away, she thought. They had
accepted her with kindness, some reserve naturally, but
nothing overtly unfriendly. They weren't sure how to
treat her, she had realized early. She obviously was the
equal of their son, whom they adored. They responded
to her with uneasy kindness. His mother would have
liked her better, she thought suddenly, if she had been
a black militant. Then she could show her off to her
friends. Anne would have become a cause for her.

Maggie Symons was a liberal who collected causes
and antiques, and tried to sell both. Anne dreaded the
day her parents, conservative Republicans, got into
politics with Maggie Symons. Maggie would annihilate
them. Mr. Symons was a mild man who was president
of a bank, chairman of a hospital board, member of
several other boards, and a founder of a youth camp.
Anne supposed they were very rich. She supposed one
day Clark would be very rich. If they had a child, it,
he or she, would be very rich. That always seemed
unimportant.

When they were not visiting them or not intending a
visit in the near future, the Symonses seemed quite
unreal to Anne. They were the sort of people who
inhabited a world whose reality touched only briefly,
sporadically, on the reality of the world Anne knew.

It was a wonder they hadn't spoiled Clark inordi-
nately, she mused, and then realized she didn't know if
Clark was spoiled or not. You only find out when you
cross the person, she thought. And she never had

crossed him. Their goals had been identical from the start. Neither of them had ever wanted anything the other hadn't wanted equally, or else had not cared enough about to oppose. And if I said no when he said yes, and if I made it stick, she wondered, what would he do? She didn't know.

When things went wrong, everyone in the department was affected, Gus thought. Francis Kirkpatrick and Ronald Medgars were feuding over sharing one lab assistant. Personnel was being funneled steadily away from everyone else to work under Clark now. Steve Ryman and Bert Cheezem had asked for an interview, and Gus had stalled them. More computer time for their soybean runs. He knew what they wanted, demanded. Damn Bob Klugman's eyes, he thought, but without heat. Bob on the job would be more trouble than Bob sick at home, or drunk at home. Here, he would tell everyone yes, take what you need, schedule time for the analyzer, or computer, or whatever, and he would let them fight it out at the site when three of them showed up at the same time. And the hell of it was, Gus knew, each one was involved in work that was vital, that had immediacy. All lab freaks are born equal, he thought, signaling his secretary to admit Walter Orne; only some are more equal because what they're doing will make zillions of dollars for the company.

"What's up, Walt?" he asked the stooped man who slouched into his office and looked at him with an oblique gaze that never seemed to center on his face, but held at his ear, or at the top of his head, or his Adam's apple.

"It's my capsule," Walter Orne said. His gaze roamed the room, as if searching for something. "I think I have the twenty-four-hour capsule ready for testing now."

Anyone else would be celebrating, Gus thought, and at any other time he would have joined in the celebration. A twenty-four-hour capsule for aspirin, for decongestants, for whatever the hell they decided to put in them. And here Walter Orne was practically apologizing for bothering him with it. He pumped enthusiasm into his voice. "Walt, that's swell! Good Lord, we're the first! Work out the test procedures and we'll start as soon as it's set up!"

Walter's eyes paused on his shirt collar, then resumed their scrutiny of the small office. He hadn't sat down. Now he turned and walked his shambling walk back to the door. "Everything's ready."

Gus sighed. "Sit down, Walt. You have your notes with you?" In his mind he could visualize Clark slicing, slicing, preparing slides. They would photograph them with the electron microscope, feed them into the computer for analysis. Clark, of course, would ruin his eyes studying them personally. The problem was, he decided, taking the detailed notes from Walter Orne, he didn't give a damn if the world had to take a cold tablet every hour or once a day, or never. He was interested in that autopsy and its results. Gradually he began to make out the words, and the meaning of the words, and gradually Clark faded from his mind and he gave his full attention to Walter Orne and his twenty-four-hour capsule.

"What we think happens," Clark muttered to Emory Durand, "is that clumping occurs at the nerve endings. That's what I want most now." Fannie had been dissected, her organs preserved for future study. Her frozen brain, exposed to the electric scalpel, was now being sliced neatly, spread out like so many leaves of a book to be read by the computer.

"Too bad you can't get a piece or two to study before the introduction of the *pa* factor," Emory said. "You know, a before-and-after examination."

The dissection room was as modern as a hospital operating room, with shining stainless steel, pale green gowns for the attendants, and a look-through panel in the door for observers. Now Gus's face appeared in the

opening. He was not gowned, did not enter the room.
It was three-thirty.

"Enough," Clark finally said, nearly an hour later.
His legs ached, his back ached, his head ached. He
knew his eyes would be bloodshot, and now that he
had decided to stop, he was suddenly racked with pains
in his stomach. "Buy you some lunch," he said to
Emory as they stripped from the surgery gear and
scrubbed.

"You're on."

When they left for a restaurant, Emory was as im-
maculate as a camera-ready male model; Clark felt
grimy beside him. "What you said before, about a
before-and-after comparison," he said. "Look, are you
familiar with the divided hemispheres technique?"

"Not really. Read about it. Used in major epileptic
cases, or massive brain-damage cases, isn't it?"

"Usually. But the relevant part to us is that a person
can and does survive massive brain surgery. We could
do a before-and-after examination. Take out a section
of the left hemisphere; after recovery, inject the *pa*
factor, and later do a study of the right hemisphere."

They arrived at a small French restaurant, and over
lunch made plans for the experiment. Their waitress
viewed them from behind the serving screen and shuddered, wondering how they could eat and talk about
the things they talked about.

"It's just like all the other variations in the body,"
Clark said. "Those born with high *pa* levels adapt to it
at an early age. There's clumping in the brain, but they
adapt. If the levels are too high, most often they don't
survive childhood. When we artificially raise the level
of *pa,* the same kind of clumping takes place in the
brain, preventing the pain stimulus from registering.
After six to eight hours the level has dropped back to
normal, no more clumping, and pain is felt normally
again. What Anne's been working on is the effect of the
*pa* factor in conjunction with increases in chemical
lactate in the blood, associated with anxiety, high blood

pressure, hypertension, and so on. I don't know if there's any connection with the other effects we've been observing, but it's a lead. And we by God can use any leads we can get right now. I'll talk to Gus about a before-and-after examination as soon as we get back. Thanks, Emory. Great idea."

Gus turned it down flat, however. "Clark, who could do it? Do you realize we've got seventeen people tied up more or less full time on this now? Half of them acting as if we'll go ahead next week with human testing, the other half trying to find out what's gone wrong. I can't pull anyone else off other work for this."

"I'll do it."

"When? You're working double shifts as it is. It's a fine idea, and you'll do it, but not right now."

"We need it now!"

"Clark, sit down." Gus went to the dart board and pulled out the darts. He returned to his desk with them. "This is your first setback, isn't it? Everything's been going great right along until now." He threw the first dart, wide, almost off the target altogether. "Damnation. Well, it isn't mine. I've seen dozens of experiments go sour after longer years than this of checking out right down the line. Relax. Go with it." Another dart thudded into the board, this time a bull's-eye. "There's nothing we can do now except what we're doing. If Helverson agrees to a postponement, we'll have more time available, but not until then."

"What do you mean, if? There's no way we can go into human experiments now! Not with this new development."

"Relax, Clark. Take it easy." He threw again and again cursed. "Lost it," he said. "It comes and goes. One day, all dead in the middle; next day, nothing." He sighted the dart, looked at Clark, and said, "I might succeed in making Helverson understand that, and I might not." He sighted the dart again and this time threw it, but didn't watch where it landed. "If I fail, Clark, I'm counting on you to make it as foolproof as you can with what we know now. No hypertension cases, things like that. Can do?"

Clark shook his head. "I won't be a party to it, Gus. I can't."

Gus leaned on his elbows and studied Clark. "You can," he said. "So can I. We make it as safe as we know how, and go on that basis. It's all we can do, or get out of the game when it comes to the crunch. And it might come to the crunch next week. Either you'll do it, or someone else will. I prefer you."

"An ultimatum, Gus?"

"I guess so. Whatever you choose to call it, Clark, there never will be a time when you'll know it's one hundred percent okay. Never. You do the best you can."

"Even if you know it isn't safe?"

"Even so. There are categories of people who will have to be excluded. You exclude them for now. The testing goes on, you keep trying to improve it, find the reasons that necessitate the exclusions. Maybe you find them, maybe not. Meanwhile, you go ahead."

"Or get out," Clark added bitterly.

"Or get out," Gus agreed. "Sooner or later every new drug, every new serum, everything comes down to this, and you get scared, and should get scared, but you go ahead. I'm going to try like hell to get more time, but if I can't . . ."

"And if those women go the way of Fannie and Duckmore, what do we tell them, Gus?"

"Not a damn thing," Gus said. He threw another dart, bull's-eye. "Can't understand why it comes and goes like that," he said, examining a dart.

Clark stood up, stared at him for a moment, then turned and left. Gus looked at the door for a long time, ignoring the darts now. He pulled the phone to him and placed a call to his wife, the third for the day, and while he waited for it to go through, he continued to stare at the closed door until his eyes hurt.

# TWELVE

ANNE watched Ronnie playing with the small cat and smiled. Ronnie loved animals, and children, and was very good with them. She was pulling a string tied to a strip of heavy plastic now. The cat's claws could not grasp the plastic, and time and again it watched in frustration as the captured strip moved out from under its paws. It crouched, its tail flicking out of control, and pounced again, and once more the plastic got away. Ronnie laughed heartily at it.

"He's a beauty, isn't he?" she said. "Harry is a good sort to bring him over. Keep you a lot of company, he will."

Tyger lost interest in the elusive plastic and began to clean his tail. It was a handsome tail, tall, full, white underneath, gray above. Ronnie laughed at him and tugged the string. Tyger pounced instantly.

"You can't fool an old cat hand like me," Ronnie said. "I know your tricks." She tied the string to the arm of the chaise where Anne could watch the cat play with it. "I'll just finish up your dinner and feed the crazy cat," she said. "Be back in a minute."

At six, Ronnie was ready to leave. "Honey. are you sure you don't want me to stay until Clark gets home? I wouldn't mind a bit. Really I wouldn't."

"It's all right," Anne said. "He won't be very late. And I'll need you in the morning for swimming again. Is that a problem?"

"Nah! I've been wondering if they give swimming lessons at that place. I should take lessons. Scared to death of water. I've heard if you take lessons you get over being afraid. But I've always been afraid to take the lessons. That's how it goes, isn't it?" She pulled on her coat and tied a scarf over her hair. "Going to rain cats and dogs again," she said. "Smell it in the air.

114

God, I'm tired of this weather." She glanced about the room, nodded, and waved. "See you in the morning. Good God, Tyger! You're going to get stepped on and mashed flatter'n a pancake if you don't learn feet are dangerous."

Anne could hear her good-natured scolding as she went down the hallway to the back door. Presently Ronnie was back again.

"Honey, that damn cat ran out when I opened the door. I'll try to find him and bring him back, but he was running like a fire was on his tail last I saw him."

"He's probably up in the top of one of those maples by now," Anne said. "Don't worry about him. If he can't find his way back, that's his tough luck. Just leave the dining room window open a little for him."

"Damn cat. He ran out like greased lightning. His first big adventure. Just like a kid. Zip, gone!"

Anne waved her away. "Don't forget the window."

"Right. Can't get over how fast . . ." Her voice faded out as she left once more.

Anne turned on the television, turned it off again after several minutes, and looked at the little world instead. She smiled dreamily. At the pool she had successfully eliminated everyone else, and had swum alone, just as she did in the little world, where the water was in distinct bands of color that didn't mix, didn't become diluted, but remained emerald, jade, pale blue, brilliant royal blue . . . If she stretched out full length in the water, her fingertips were pale blue, her toes emerald, and her body a deep, almost black blue. Passing from one zone to another, she could feel the changes in the water. The emerald was best; it made her tingle with cool ripples of erotic pleasure. She could turn and follow the emerald, staying wholly inside that band, but she couldn't remain there long; it was too sensual, too arousing, and the pleasure became painful as eroticism grew and became a need. Then she dove into the midnight blue and all feeling left her and she was aware only of the satiny water on her skin.

Suddenly she jerked. She must have dozed, staring at the terrarium. It was eight o'clock. She heard again the noise that had roused her. A cat's scream. Tyger!

Somehow she got her chair down the hall to the corner which she could not turn. "Tyger! Come here, Tyger!"

He was crying pitiably now. She called him again and again. She backed up her chair and tried to get around the corner, chipped plaster and paint off the corner, and got stuck. Working the chair loose, she scraped both hands, and hardly even aware of them, she gave one final tug on the wheels and got around the corner, heading toward the kitchen and dining room.

Tyger was on the floor, breathing in hard, racking gasps that sounded hollow. He was not crying now. His eyes were closed. She got closer to him and he pulled himself to his feet and staggered away from her chair.

"Tyger! Come here. Tyger!"

Blindly the little cat tried to run from her. He started to bleed. Anne eased herself from the chair to the floor and crept after him and finally caught him. He struggled to free himself and clawed her arm and she dropped him. He ran a few steps, stopped, fell down in a convulsion, and died.

Anne stared at the small cat in horror and disbelief, then she vomited and it seemed the room was spinning, faster and faster, and she felt she was falling a great distance.

It seemed a long time later that she began to pull herself back up to her chair and got down the hall to the corner again and stopped, knowing she could not turn from this side. This passage was narrower than the main hall. There was no way she could turn the chair from here. She sat still for several minutes and then left her chair and crept down the hall, dragging her right leg, to her room, to the bathroom. She didn't try to stand up, but washed her hands and face and rinsed her mouth at the bathtub. She was shivering uncontrollably and she felt hot as if she had a fever.

She had blood on her clothes. She undressed, leaving the things where they fell. The smell of vomit was heavy in the air. She felt the bathroom start to tilt, and she put her head down until everything was stable again. In her panties and bra she dragged herself to the side of the bed and pulled the telephone to the floor, not caring if it broke or not. She dialed the number for Clark's office. There was no answer. She was shivering too much to dial again and she pulled her robe from the foot of the bed and got it around her shoulders. She could hear a hard, pounding rain beating against the windows. It would break the windows, she thought. She should close the drapes so it couldn't get in all the way.

Her fingers trembled as she dialed again, this time the lab number. A woman's voice answered after half a dozen rings. Virginia Sudsbury.

"Dr. Symons isn't here right now," she said. "I think he's gone out for dinner. Probably to the cafeteria. I can find out for you."

"Please do," Anne said, fighting hysteria, fighting to keep her voice as calm as the girl's. "Right away. Please."

"I'll call back in a couple of minutes," Virginia said. "Are you all right?"

"Find him!" Anne cried, and bit her lip. "Please just find him."

Ten minutes later Virginia called back. "I'm sorry, Dr. Clewiston. I can't find him. I think he went out to dinner with Dr. Wells and a couple of the others. As soon as they get back, I'll have him call you. Is there anything I can do?"

Tears were standing in Anne's eyes. She shook her head. "No. NO! Just tell him!" Fumbling, she hung up the phone and the tears now ran down her cheeks.

This was the reality, she thought. The floor was cold and hard and she was too weak to climb up into the

bed, too dizzy and sick to try to get to the chaise. She
could only sit there on the cold hard floor and wait for
her husband to come do something about it. Thunder
rumbled distantly and the rain pounded as if frenzied.
In a minute, she thought, she would try to get herself
up to the bed, get under the covers, get warm. In a
minute.

She thought of the wicked or cruel things she had
done in the past. But she hadn't been evil, not really,
not as evil is measured in the courts. She never had
harmed anyone, not deliberately. She had lied a little,
but not maliciously. She had not abandoned God.
There never had been a God to abandon. She didn't
deserve this, she thought, weeping. The agony of the
accident, the operations, the months in this prison
room, and now this solitary confinement and the de-
struction of the one thing that might have eased it for
her.

The weeping stopped finally and she wiped her face
on the sheet. "Ah, well," she said to herself, "crying
doesn't make the fire burn." Her grandmother had said
that, she remembered. Her grandmother had died
when Anne was only six, how strange to remember her
now. Very old and brown, with silver hair and merry
blue eyes, and a quick tongue, that had been her
grandmother. Even after she had become too frail to
leave her bed, her mind had been sharp, her tongue
sharper. "Fretting doesn't make the train run faster,"
she would say if the children fidgeted, in a hurry to do
something or get something. Anne thought of her
grandmother as she worked to get into the bed with the
telephone beside her.

It was after nine when Clark called, and by then she
was calm. She kept having to banish the image of the
small gray heap of fur; over and over she was successful at banishing it.

"Clark, I need you," she said, and was amazed at
the steadiness of her voice.

"Are you all right?" His voice in contrast was almost
shrill with apprehension.

"Yes. Please come home. I can't talk about it, not on the phone." No more, she thought, no more talk now or I'll break and that will frighten him too much. No more.

"I'll leave now," he said.

She closed her eyes, tried to recapture the lovely water, and saw instead the tiny animal blindly trying to escape its hurt. It would take him twenty minutes, maybe more in the rainstorm. Half an hour. The thunder was drawing closer, breaking with the sharp, close explosions of a summer storm. Probably there were tornado warnings out. May weather. Someone must have hit it in the parking lot, and it dragged itself back to the apartment, through the window, and died. Deena would drive Clark home, might come in with him. If there was nothing going on with Clark and Deena she would come in, they would have to pretend nothing was changed, all of them pretending, pretending. Deena looking at her from the corners of her eyes, wondering if she suspected. Clark uneasy with her, staying at the lab longer and longer hours . . .

He arrived twenty-two minutes after her call. She told him what had happened. Under the covers her hands were clenched so tight that when she tried to open her fingers they felt paralyzed. Clark's face became set in the way it did when he received bad news. A stranger might think he was not reacting at all, but she knew he was shocked, more than just shocked, he was filled with the same horror she had felt.

"Oh, my God," he said in a low voice. He left her, came back very quickly, and sat on the side of the bed and held her. "It must have been awful for you. Are you all right? Do you need anything? Can I get you coffee, a drink?"

"Coffee," she said.

He brought it and then left again to clean up the dining room. He was very pale when he returned the second time. He had her chair with him.

"I'll draw a bath for you," he said. He went out and came back with a tall drink that appeared to be straight bourbon with a single ice cube floating in it. He drank deeply, then started her bath while she got into the chair.

Clark lifted her into the tub and washed her back. He examined the long scratches on her arm and when she was dry put Merthiolate on them, and a Band-Aid on her knuckles where she had scraped them on the corner wall. Neither spoke until he lifted her hand and kissed her fingers.

"Oh, Clark, don't or I'll cry again."

He held her close for a minute, and then took her back to the bedroom, to the table by the bay window. He closed the drapes, and the storm became distant, not threatening, the room became the haven it should have been and she felt dry, warm, and safe once more. Clark's presence was too strong for the strangeness, she thought. When he was there, everything was normal.

He had almost finished his drink, and he showed its effects in a sleepiness that came over his face, softening his expression, slurring his words a bit when he spoke. "Anne, this won't do," he said, in his different, more Southern, voice. He had lost his accent, but it came back when he was very tired, or a little drunk, and he was both then.

"I don't know what you mean," she said.

"You can't stay here alone again. I don't know how in hell you got back to this room from the hall, but what if you hadn't been able to? What if you got stuck somewhere and had to stay for hours and hours? Where the hell is Ronnie? I thought she could stay until I get home?"

"She needs some time off, too," Anne said. "She has to be here tomorrow, maybe Sunday. You can't expect her to stay day and night."

Clark closed his eyes. "We'll get someone else to relieve her," he said. His accent was more pronounced. It was nearly twelve and he would fall asleep where he sat if he didn't get to bed soon, he knew. He shook himself and stood up. "Tomorrow. Do you want to call the agency, or shall I?"

"Let's talk about it in the morning," Anne said. "You're so tired. Go on to bed. Should I call your parents and tell them we can't make it tomorrow night?"

He shook his head. "I already told Gus I won't be staying late tomorrow." He leaned over her to kiss her and for a moment rested his cheek against hers. He needed a shave. Then he sighed and pushed himself away. "Can I help you get to bed?"

"Not yet. I'll go soon." She watched to see if the strangeness returned with his absence. It didn't. Afraid he'll come back, she thought. He would be taking a shower, maybe getting another drink, fooling around. At one she knew he would be in bed, probably already sound asleep, and she could feel the other reality seeping in from the corners of her room where it lived now. The room became plastic that flowed into new shapes. Now it was a ship's prow, she the captain staring out at the storm that threatened to capsize them all. "A female captain! By Thunder, no wonder we're sinking!" And she, the captain, fought the wheel and sensed the power of the waves and was one with the ship beneath her. She smiled and the room flowed again, back to her bedroom, with its elephant adorned with rare and costly jewels, and now she swayed with the rhythm of the elephant's measured tread, and on either side she could hear the excited murmuring of the boys as they neared the killer tiger. Only she, with her innate sense of danger, could be certain the tiger was near now, ready to spring, murder in its evil heart. She could feel it nearer, nearer. The elephant knew. He snorted. (Do elephants snort? she wondered.) He snorted and tossed his trunk. (Scattering her clothes in every direction.) She sighed and willed the scene away, but the feeling persisted. The tiger at her back, ready to spring . . . Springing. Leaping through the air . . . She twisted in her chair and shot, and knew she had missed. She screamed and tried to smother the sound with both hands.

Trembling, she waited for Clark to appear, to demand to know what had happened. She could hear the scream bouncing off the walls, up from the floor, down from the ceiling, beating at her as the rain beat the windows, fading so slowly it seemed it would persist for hours, days even. Minutes passed and Clark didn't appear and gradually she relaxed again. He hadn't heard. She would be murdered here in her room and he wouldn't hear her screams for help.

She had been hallucinating, she thought in wonder, getting into bed. Really hallucinating. The feeling of a tiger had been real, the fear had been real. She almost laughed. In spite of herself, she had been able to reach a state of transcendental meditation. It was the isolation and the quiet, she thought. Sensory deprivation. Your mind will create its own diversions if none is provided by the outside world. And her mind was functioning perfectly in that regard.

She slept and dreamed that Tyger played on her bed, and every time she tried to pet him, he scratched her.

## THIRTEEN

MAGGIE SYMONS stood in the doorway of her living room and looked back into the hall, then into the room. The entrance hall was a rather large room in itself, but it didn't seem so. Sixteen feet wide, twenty feet long, the room looked like a furniture storeroom, with narrow passages, one to the hall, another to the stairs, and this one that led to the living room. There was enough room for Anne's wheelchair, she hoped, but probably none at all to spare. She spread her arms and walked through the hall, stopped at a carved coat rack and frowned at it, drew in her hands an inch, then walked on to the door. She nodded.

Maggie Symons was only five feet two and over the years she had gained weight, one pound a year. She often thought with wonder at how they had accumu-

lated. She had been petite for so long she still thought
of herself as petite, until she looked in a mirror and saw
a short, stout woman with a pretty face, naturally curly
brown hair, who really should lose at least twenty
pounds, and twenty-five would be even better. But she
had kept her face and her hair, and her teeth. At that
point she would always smile at herself, and she knew
it didn't matter so very much about the weight. There
were clever clothes, and she was fifty plus, after all.
The smile would broaden and she would add, Joseph
liked her plump.

There had been two bad times in their marriage.
The first had been when Clark was a baby and she had
come to realize her life was the house and the child,
and a husband who was absent more frequently than
necessary, who worked longer hours than he needed to,
and who put in weekends on the golf course, or in
traveling to meet with other businessmen, or something. The other young wives had the same complaints,
but it hadn't mattered about them. She had suffered,
and she had found relief. For three years the marriage
had teetered. Then, with no explanation then or ever,
he had started to court her again. He had sent her
presents—flowers, candy, a mink stole, a trip for two to
New York for a weekend. Neither of them ever mentioned those lost three years. And it had been good
then until Clark went away to school.

Maggie knew who the girl had been, how long it
lasted, where they went, what he bought her. This time
she waited, and when the time was right, she sent him
a present—an antique pocket watch, ornately carved
gold, with a dent in the cover, said to have been made
by a gambler in Summit, California, who had claimed
it when a loser tried to welch.

She could remember, with some pain, and some
amusement now, the look on his face when he had
come home carrying the watch in his hand. He had
stopped in the doorway of their bedroom and said
something quite inane that she hadn't heard. Since
then, everything had been fine, lovely in fact. And she

believed him when he said she was prettier now than when they married. She knew he believed it.

Clark was like her, she thought. Clark was passionate, sensuous. She shied away from visualizing him with Anne, who always seemed very cool, too controlled, too cerebral. She shook herself and studied the cluttered entrance hall again.

"What do you think?" Maggie asked, reentering the living room. She sat on a rose velvet love seat, 1848, and addressed her husband, who was seated in a sturdier leather chair of Spanish origin.

"About what?" he asked, glancing at her. He was trying to read the paper, and he knew he would not be allowed to.

"Can Clark get her chair through the hall? I had Edgar clear it out a lot, but you know how he is. He means well, but you have to stand over him and point and explain in one-syllable words, over and over."

"They'll get through."

"But did you really notice when you came in?"

"I would have noticed if I hadn't been able to get through," he said, turning again to the paper.

"Just go look, will you, dear? Just to make sure. It would be so embarrassing for Anne if we had to start moving anything after they got here. She's so sensitive."

He didn't even sigh as he got up and walked to the front door, just as she had done. He was under six feet, but always felt and appeared much taller. His hair was white, fairly long. He looked like a successful banker. He sat down again. "It's fine. Don't get in a stew."

"I'm not in a stew. I don't think she thinks we like her much, that's all. I don't want to hurt her feelings. Clark would be annoyed. They might not come back for months and months. I really can't understand that girl. Can you?"

He shook his head. "Nothing to understand. She's just like Clark. If you can understand him, you can understand her. Just alike."

"That's the problem," Maggie said with a soft sigh.

"I don't understand him a bit, and somehow it doesn't seem right for her to be so like him. I really think he would have been better off with someone altogether different. Like us. I don't have an inkling of your business and I don't want to. What would it be like if we got up and had breakfast and went to work together, had lunch with the same people every day, came home together? What would we have to talk about?" She paused and tried to imagine such a relationship. She said, "She doesn't know a thing about art or music or anything except their work, I guess."

"Neither does he," her husband said, turning to the comics.

"That's the point. She should know something, be ready to coach him, or fill in for him, or, you know. The way I do for you if someone brings up opera."

"Maggie, everybody doesn't have to be an opera fan."

"Do you suppose they just talk about bugs and microscopes all the time?" He didn't answer, and presently she said, "I bet they talk about sex a lot. They probably spend a lot of time in bed. They have sex books in the apartment. I saw them."

Behind his newspaper Joseph Symons took in a deep, inaudible breath. Now she would say, I wonder if she intends to have a child . . .

". . . With a woman like her, you never know. I wonder if she can have children. I think they turn to things like science when they know, even if only intuitively, that they won't have babies. Clark would be such a good father. I can just see him helping his son fly a kite. Like you did with him."

Joseph Symons chuckled at *B.C.* He turned the newspaper to the local news section.

"Should I give her her present first, I wonder," Maggie said after a pause. "If I take Clark upstairs to show him the Chinese chest first, she might feel left out and be hurt. I should have told Edgar to bring her case in here. Then I could give it to her, and then take Clark . . . Joseph, are you listening to me at all?"

"No, dear," he murmured.

Maggie frowned in his direction, but not at him. She wasn't even seeing him. "I think I'll have Estelle help me get them both in here now," she said. She stood up, then sat down again. "But then he couldn't get her chair in," she sighed.

Joseph Symons liked the long-legged girl his son had married. He liked the way they looked at each other, and thought they probably did spend a lot of time in bed. He liked her reserve, the way her eyes twinkled just before she ducked her head when Maggie said anything especially ridiculous, like her method of attaining instant culture.

"You see," Maggie said, "it's so simple. Everyone is expected to know something about everything these days. And there's always someone to put you to the test. So you just have several things ready. Like you should know four different composers and specific compositions, and if music comes up, you can say your favorite is . . . oh, something like Glière's *Red Poppy*. Or the Bernstein Mass. You see, not the usual things. Not Beethoven's Fifth Symphony, for instance." She beamed at Clark, but she was directing her little lecture at Anne, who had ducked her head in order to concentrate on her salad.

Joseph grinned and said, "I always tell 'em my favorite music is country fiddling."

"And you lie about it," Maggie said calmly. "His favorite really is bawdy sea chanteys. No music to it, just dirty words."

Joseph chuckled.

Clark said, "And you should have a favorite moviemaker. Not Cecil B. De Mille. Someone obscure that only three other people in the room ever heard of."

"And a favorite dish," Joseph Symons said. "Nothing as common as chili con carne—which really is, by the way—but exotic, like escargots stuffed with shallots and truffles, served in a champagne sauce, as made by

Chef Jobert in some fancy hotel down in New Orleans." He smacked his lips.

"And a favorite little ocean cruise," Clark said laughing. "Nothing like the Atlantic or even the Caribbean. A little out-of-the-way ocean, like the Caspian Sea, on this delightful little steamer that leaves promptly at ten every Tuesday."

For a moment Maggie's lips tightened, but then she laughed, and after she caught her breath she said to Anne, "My God, think how dishonest I would be without them!"

Going home, Anne said, "I'm so glad we went. That was fun. I really am jealous of you for your parents, you know that."

"I know. And it's so dumb. You're taken in like everyone else. Didn't you see how they treated me? As soon as I go in that door, I'm seventeen again. Mother lectures me, gently, and never directly, but she's still trying to turn out a proper son. Dad . . . well, Dad is himself. I never did know what he was like, really."

"But they love you so much. It's so obvious."

"Not this me that I've become. They don't even see me. They see that awkward kid home from school, and they see a messy room with a microscope and an insect collection, and chemicals that scare them to death. They quit looking after I grew out of that phase."

Anne was silent. He just didn't understand. It was easy at his parents' home. They wanted to please him. His mother and the presents she couldn't resist buying for Clark and Anne. It gave her pleasure to buy them, to give them.

"I go because every now and then it's nice to be that kid again," Clark said softly. "It's nice to feel even for a couple of hours someone else is being responsible. I don't have to do anything, be anything, except there, ready to kid them along, or be kidded."

Anne laughed. "And when you said you'd keep your opium and LSD and coke in that chest, I thought I would crack up. Did you see her face?"

Clark laughed. "I know I shouldn't do it to them, but I can't seem to help it. What in God's name will I do with a fancy Chinese chest that cost five hundred dollars and is too fragile to hold booze?"

"Keep your fossils in it. You can't keep them in my jewelry case!" Anne laughed until she felt weak. "That was an awful thing to tell her, by the way. She thinks we're barbarians as it is, and you tell her things like that."

Watching Anne that night, being away from the gloom of the lab, laughing with her and his parents, Clark had felt a surge of confidence. He could tell her about the approval of the IND, he realized. It would never occur to her that anyone was considering going ahead, not in light of the trouble her own stress experiments had caused. She would think they were investigating that, being as cautious now as they had been from the beginning. He remembered their past successes and felt his heart lurch. It would be like old times, he thought, just like before. He had driven to the front of the apartment building without thinking. He turned off the motor and reached for her.

"Honey, I've been bursting with this all night. I couldn't tell you before them. We got the IND approval!"

She didn't move. She seemed to be holding her breath. Then she said, "You're serious? It really came? This soon?"

"It came."

"Clark! They approved? An approval?"

She laughed and wept and asked questions and didn't wait for answers before she asked other questions. And it seemed all the wine she had drunk at dinner, the brandy after dinner, all went to her head together and she was dizzy and floating and incoherent. Clark carried her chair to the apartment door, then returned for her. He kissed her when he picked her up, and again when he placed her in the chair.

"And my news," she said. "I thought you were so tired all week, working so late, it just didn't seem like the time to mention it. I've been swimming every day this week!"

"Good God!" Clark cried, swinging her chair around. He kissed her again. "You just didn't mention it! You idiot!"

"My. Symons, is everything all right?" a voice asked from the stairwell. Anne, looking over Clark's shoulder, saw spidery little Mrs. Ochs peering down at them.

"Everything's beautiful!" Clark called back. He opened the apartment door and pushed Anne's chair inside. The apartment was dark; they had forgotten to leave a light on in the hall. Laughing, Clark pushed her chair through the bedroom doorway and groped for the switch.

She was drunk, Anne thought. Alcohol mixed with the adrenaline of excitement, release of tension, everything combined, and she was quite drunk. The room was unquiet. The space capsule tilted in a banked curve. "Don't turn on the light," she whispered, her eyes adjusting now. He was with her this time, they could share the strange room.

"I don't have much choice," Clark said, still laughing. "I can't find the bugger."

Gradually the darkness gave way to a dimness, light through the wisteria tree softened the bedroom, made the walls recede into distance, made the bed appear very large. Clark carried Anne to the bed and she floated serenely. Free fall, she thought. Although the bed might waft gently from side to side, might even turn over all the way, she was safe there. No top, no up, no down. She felt the bed bobbing as Clark leaned over to kiss her. Now, she thought. Now she should tell him the other piece of good news. *The doctor said have fun, screw*.

She opened her eyes and saw him then. An intent look had come over him, and he was strangely exposed, as if a mask had vanished leaving his face almost twisted in pain and need. No hiding now, no pretense, only pain and need. And when he saw her, what would he see? Broken body, scarred, disfigured, crippled. She had a momentary vision of herself tied down by restraints, immobile while he fucked her, and when his lips touched hers, she jerked and tried to twist away from him.

Clark kissed her hard. He knew when the moment passed, when she withdrew in fear, and he could feel the tension in her body as his hands moved down her, taking off her skirt, unbuttoning her blouse. She was rigid with fear. He kissed her throat and whispered, "It's all right, Anne. It's all right. Your doctor said it's all right. I won't hurt you. I'll be gentle." He kissed her collarbone and then her breast and his hand moved down her stomach, rested a moment on the sharp hipbone and moved on to her thigh. She tried to hold his hand, tried to pull it away, and he kissed her palm, her fingertips, and then put her hand in his left hand and held it. He kept whispering to her, kissing her, and she was trembling now. "You're so beautiful! I love you so much!"

"No!" she moaned. "Clark, don't . . . !"

"I won't hurt you," he whispered at her ear, and then his mouth went to her nipple again, and his hand was at her pubis. "Don't be afraid," he whispered. "It's all right."

"No!" she cried, shaking her head. "No! Don't!"

She pulled her hand out from under him and tried to push him away, and he whispered and kissed her and his hand found her clitoris and no words made contact.

She didn't know what he was saying, what she was saying, nor did he.

He knew she wanted him as much as he wanted her, her need was as great as his. He had felt it flowing from her, stronger every day. It was a palpable thing in the apartment. He knew he wouldn't hurt her, cause her pain now, and she would realize that, too, and they would be together again. "Not just for me," he said hoarsely. "We have to. For you too." And, over and over, "I love you so much!" And, "I'll be so careful.

I'll be gentle. Please, don't be afraid. I won't hurt you. I promise I won't hurt you."

She knew he would do it, and she struggled harder, then stopped. She couldn't move. A long shudder passed through her and she could hardly even feel him any longer. Tears of rage and self-pity and helplessness burned her eyes.

A new rhythm was beating in Clark's ears. *Now! Now! Now!* As carefully, as gently as he could, he rolled her to her side and lay down beside her.

She was dry, his penetration painful, and suddenly she began to weep convulsively, and he ejaculated. For several minutes neither spoke or moved, then he withdrew and left her.

She groped for Kleenex and wiped herself, then worked the bedspread down under her and got herself under the covers. She couldn't stop weeping.

When Clark returned, he had on his robe and slippers, carried a tray with coffee and cups. With his back to her, standing at the small table before the bay window, he said softly, "Anne, forgive me. If I hurt you . . ."

"You didn't hurt me."

He came to the bedside and started to sit down. She turned her head away and he returned to the chair by the table.

"It's been driving me crazy," he said after a moment. "Seeing you in bed day after day, looking prettier all the time, wanting you so goddamn much. I dream about us, about sex. At the lab, it comes over me like a shock, the illusion of being with you. And tonight . . . I've never seen you so beautiful as you were tonight. Anne, I swear to God I thought you wanted me! I thought you were afraid, that afterward you'd see it isn't going to hurt you now."

"Once," Anne said, looking straight ahead, "we were making love and it was one of the good nights at the beginning, and then something happened, and later you said we never had been so out of rhythm. Do you remember?" Her voice was toneless, dead. She didn't wait for his reply. "I know what happened. It was a year or so ago. I had my legs almost flat, and you were on me and it was building, building, to a slow beautiful climax. And you suddenly decided I would perform better with my legs up, and I resisted, not long, not hard, but I rebelled, and everything went away. It had to be your way. You always know what will be best for me, don't you, and I have to do it that way. If my legs ache, or I get a cramp in my thigh, or whatever, it has to be your way. For my sake, of course."

Clark cleared his throat. "All you ever had to do was give me a sign, say something . . . Good God, Anne, if there's any one thing we have had together it's been sexual freedom."

"No," she said. "I took it for granted we were equals in all ways. At work, here around the apartment. All ways. But I was kidding myself. All I have to do is say something. Tonight I said something and you went on anyway. Always your way. You know best. If there's something we do that you don't like, don't enjoy, it's simple, you just don't initiate that again, and if I start to, you ignore me. It has to be your way. If there's something I don't like, all I have to do is tell you, plead with you not to do it again, try to explain why, how I feel, explain I'm not rejecting you, but only a small act. And you'll stop, won't you? Just like you stopped tonight!"

"What don't you like that we do? Just tell me, for God's sake!"

"Don't you understand what I'm saying to you?" she cried. "I won't be a supplicant! I won't plead with you, try to explain myself to you, beg you."

"Jesus! I don't expect you to plead or beg. Just tell me." Clark started to pace. He went to the bed, and when she continued to stare, dry-eyed now, past him at nothing at all, he reached down and turned her face, hurting her cheeks, knowing he was hurting her cheeks. "Anne, you know tonight's the first time I've ever forced myself on you in any way, and I was wrong. I thought that was the way it had to be, to show you it was all right now. I was wrong. We should have talked first. Anne, I swear to you I thought you wanted it too."

Now she looked at him, and a tremor passed through her. He yanked his hand away as if it had been burned. He looked frightened.

"Anne, I've really upset you. I didn't realize it would do this to you. Anne, Christ, I'm sorry!"

She stared at him. "It doesn't matter any more," she said. "It just doesn't matter."

"Anne! Don't look like that. Don't talk like that. What's wrong with you?"

"I don't know," she said, in that same lifeless voice she had used earlier. "It doesn't matter."

Clark dropped to the bed and tried to put his arms about her. She didn't protest, didn't resist, and after he had held her for a moment, she said once more, "It doesn't matter at all. Please bring my chair over here."

"Anne, I can't leave you like this. Something's terribly wrong. You're in shock or something. Lie down, try to relax. I'll get you a drink."

"I don't want anything. Just my chair. And then go on to bed and leave me alone."

Clark grabbed her by the shoulders and shook her. "Stop it! Snap out of it!"

"Get your hands off me!" she cried in a low voice that was almost a sob. "Don't touch me again! I want to go to the bathroom and clean myself. I feel filthy, used! I feel like a whore who let the slimiest prick in the world smear her up. I can feel it on my legs, on the sheet under me, and it makes me want to throw up! All at once here I am, a cunt for you to empty yourself into. Why didn't you go out and buy yourself a cunt? Why didn't you jerk off? You've killed it! Can't you see, it's dead, gone, and all I feel is dirty. If I thought you were coming at me again, I'd vomit. Now get out of here! Get out!"

## FOURTEEN

CLARK drove until almost three. He had gone out to put the car away, and instead had driven through the park, out the other side, and had kept going. He had stopped at red lights, at stop signs, and then, when he stopped in the middle of the street and a driver behind him had pressed his horn angrily, he had come to, as if out of a deep sleep, and had turned and gone back to the apartment. He couldn't recall what he had been thinking during the two and a half hours he had been out. He was cold and tired, the damp February night was in his clothes, his hair; he felt clammy all over.

Her light was still on. Her door was closed. It was the first time since they had been married that the door had been closed with one on the inside, one on the outside. Before he went to her, he had a hot bath, made two drinks, and entered her room.

"Are you all right?" he asked. She was sitting at the window, the drapes open now. The room was thick with smoke. She didn't look at him, didn't answer.

"Look, Anne, I said I'm sorry. I truly am. Will you talk to me?"

Still she didn't respond. He put her drink on the table where she could reach it, emptied the ashtray, and sat down opposite her. "Anne, please don't do this. Try to see it as I saw it. We were happy, celebrating two pieces of incredibly good news. You said don't turn on the light. You lay there smiling, the way you do when you're inviting me, and my God, I wanted you." She didn't move. He leaned toward her and said, "Anne, I've known for a month you were ready to have sex again. I talked to your doctor and he told me. He said you were afraid but there was nothing to keep us from resuming our sex life. He said you'd regain your strength and lose your fear naturally. Nothing to

134

worry about. I thought you were telling me you were ready."

She looked at him then, and her eyes were very dark, almost black. She looked stricken, ill. "You've been checking up on me behind my back?"

"No! It isn't like that," he said. "I've talked to Dr. Radimer a lot since the accident. In the beginning I called him every few days. Now maybe once a month. My God, Anne, I've been out of my mind, seeing you like this, hurt, helpless. If I'd been able to do something myself it wouldn't have been so bad, but knowing I could do nothing . . . I had to know how you were. I had to talk to him."

She continued to look at him, and her gaze was that of a stranger who didn't like what she saw.

"Anne, he said you were ready! I wouldn't have touched you if I hadn't known that!"

"It wasn't his decision to make," she said distantly. "It wasn't yours, either." She looked at the window again. "You raped me. No amount of talk will change that. Go on to bed. Leave me alone."

She felt only a great impatience with him for coming back, interrupting her thoughts, forcing her to pay attention now. She had managed to get a great distance away from the room, from everything, and he had brought her back; she wanted only to be alone again. She was hardly aware when he left her.

It always came to this, she thought. She was a woman, she belonged to him to be used or not, and all the rest of it was a sham. Just so long as their desires coincided she had been allowed to believe she was free, and she had believed wholly, harboring no doubt whatever. This is what happened. This is why women suddenly began to break up the crockery, smash up the house, this realization hit each and every one of them eventually, and while they might now articulate it, or think it through as she had been doing, the knowledge lay like a lump in their hearts. Or their wombs.

They can't talk about this, she thought, so they talk about everything else—jobs, being tied down to children, no money of their own. But at bottom it was this: if he wanted to do something, he did it; if he didn't want to, he didn't do it. If she wanted it, she had to ask, or explain; if she didn't, she had to struggle, beg, reject the act without rejecting the person, or he might lose his erection, or ejaculate prematurely.

All the little things she had overlooked, excused, because her sex drive had been satisfied. The times she had felt ridiculous with her long legs waving in the air, the times he had changed her position when she had been enjoying the act and hadn't wanted to change. Just tell him, she thought bitterly. When? When she was riding the crest of a coming orgasm? Afterward, when she was floating serenely? The next day? When she had tried to have her way, one time only, everything had gone, it had become awkward and unlovely and frustrating to both of them. What made him think he knew with a god-like certainty what she would enjoy most? What made that doctor think, with godlike certainty, she was ready to resume a sex life?

"There, there, now didn't that feel good?" That was their attitude after the fact. And after the fact she had felt good; unvoiced complaints became childish, selfish cries of a sated spoiled brat who would continue to eat even though he might become sick, or who would deny himself a goodie simply to hurt his parent.

She had gone inside her own brain to register a complaint, she thought, and she had found this tiny, almost invisible door to the right department. When she had opened the door she had discovered, to her amazement, the room stretched out in all directions; it was boundless, and there, waiting for her to recognize them, were all the minor complaints she had filed over the years. Each one had been belittled, its sharpness rubbed off by her easy acceptance of results, and her belief, unproven, untried, in her own freedom.

Now that belief was shattered and she felt strange, as if she had become someone else. A person she had to explore, that she needed time to accept. She didn't think she liked the person she had discovered. It seemed urgent for her to maintain as much distance as possible from that person until she understood her better, and she had succeeded in separating herself earlier while Clark had been out. He had forced her back, and the confusion had started again.

She realized she knew as little about Clark as she had known about herself, and this seemed a revelation as staggering as the first. She wheeled herself to the hall, across it to his room. She rolled close to the bed where he slept, and for a long time she sat motionless studying him in the dim light from the hallway. She shook her head. She didn't know him at all.

On Sunday, Clark went to the lab to observe the chimps on the stress experiment. Hermione and Lilith had accepted the new routine. They greeted their infants with delirious joy, nursed and groomed them, and when the babies were removed, resumed feeding themselves with no outward show of concern. Lola's baby was brought only after the others had been returned to the infant cage. Lola sat clutching the bars of her cage, staring at the laboratory. She transferred her unblinking gaze to Clark when he approached. A low moan seemed to issue involuntarily from her and she bared her teeth but otherwise didn't move. Clark felt the same prickles he had felt before under her stare. He motioned the attendant to bring the baby and stepped out of the way, around the side where he could get at Lola with his tranquilizer gun if he had to.

He glanced at the two assistants on duty, John Lincoln and Frank Egleston, both good enough, but not of the caliber of Virginia Sudsbury or Bob Brighton. Neither of them had been working with the chimps during the week. His tension mounted when Lola now fixed her gaze on the transport cage that was being maneuvered into position to release the infant. Something . . . Something . . . He didn't know what, but something was wrong, badly wrong, dangerously wrong. Then the cage door was being raised, and he knew what was wrong. Frank hadn't locked the transport cage into place. He raised his tranquilizer gun and at the same time Lola snatched her baby and threw it over her head and lunged at the opening; her long arm snaked out, shoved the wheeled cage away. Her hand fastened on Frank's lab coat and yanked. Clark's first shot only grazed the moving chimp. He fired again as she tore at the air to get at Frank. She slumped, half out of the cage, her arm dangling over the side. Frank was on his knees, his arm bleeding, his eyes large with shock and fright.

Moving very swiftly, Clark unlatched and pulled open the full-sized door and hurried inside the cage to retrieve the injured baby. He handed it to John Lincoln and tugged at Lola to get her fully inside so they could close the small door. She stirred and rolled over and lashed viciously at Clark. Her hand hit his thigh and he fell to his hands and knees. Lola tried to rise, was overcome with convulsive shaking, and before she could recover, Clark pushed himself to the door and rolled out. For a moment he thought she had broken his leg. John Lincoln slammed the door shut and locked it. He already had the small door closed and locked. Lola was shaking her head from side to side now. She stood up unsteadily, the effects of the tranquilizer fading, and she began to scream.

"You all right, sir?" John asked, helping Clark stand up.

"Yes. What about him?" He motioned toward Frank.

"He's okay. Pretty deep scratch down his arm, that's all."

"Good. Get him to the infirmary, will you? Does he drive to work?"

John Lincoln shook his head. "Bus."

"Tell the infirmary to send him home in a cab, fill out an accident form for him. They'll know."

"Sure," John said. He led Frank from the animal division.

"You bitch," Clark muttered, looking at the chimp, who had stopped howling and was again merely staring at him. "You dirty bitch. You wanted to kill me, didn't you?"

He looked at the baby chimp in the transport cage and sighed. It was breathing. He started to push the cage toward the animal surgery room and winced. His leg would be good and sore for a while. He paused and glanced back at Lola once. She was still staring at him.

He had to get the blood samples, he thought, wheeling the injured baby to the veterinarian. Had to check out the temperature quality test. Had to check on the progress of the autopsy sections that were being photographed through the electron microscope. His head ached and his leg throbbed with each step.

Dr. Jerry Levy was on duty that day. He examined the baby chimp and shook his head. "Broken neck, I think," he said.

"Save it if you can," Clark said, and left him. Another dead baby. Another crazy chimp.

He did the blood samples as quickly as he could, looked in on the other people working on this job, and then went home. He'd be back for the six o'clock feeding, he promised John Lincoln.

Anne still wasn't talking to him and he was too tired and preoccupied to care. He had stopped in a delicatessen for sandwiches, and when she didn't even look at hers, he shrugged and left it on the table where she could reach it later.

"I have to go back around six," he said. "I'll make us a steak after I get back. Is there plenty of coffee in the pot?"

She nodded.

"I'm going to see if I can sleep an hour."

He dreamed they were flying kites in the park and it was fun with the sun hot on his face, the wind hard and fresh. Then his kite nose-dived and broke. He had another one, this time a yellow and red dragon that rippled sinuously. Anne's kite rose higher and higher, pure white, like a giant bird flying to the moon. His gaudy dragon began to climb, then it, too, nose-dived and fell. He looked at the ruins and sobbed like a child, and woke up, covered with sweat, as if he had been having a nightmare. He couldn't remember for a time where he was, or that it was Sunday afternoon, anything. He sat up and switched on the lamp and the light hurt his eyes. He had slept an hour and a half. For several moments he sat on the side of the bed, feeling the soreness in his leg, his aching head, stiffness in his back. Then he saw the lines on the rug. Parallel lines from the door to the bed. They stood out only because he was on the same side of them as the light; he could see the faint shadows cast in the depressions made by the wheels.

Images flashed before his eyes: the mangled kitten; the dead chimp infant; Fannie's stare that had become more and more malevolent; Lola's injured baby; the way Anne had looked at him with her stranger's eyes; the withdrawal of the chimps from normal contacts; Anne's withdrawal, her silences, and most of all the many times recently he had turned to her only to find her averting her gaze, as if she had been staring . . .

He shook his head and the dull ache flared. She had rolled in, stopped, backed up, making an arc with the wheels, turned and left again, silently, not touching him, not making a sound to disturb his sleep. How long had she sat there staring at him? Why had she sat there staring at him?

She had wanted to talk, had found him sleeping and had left. He nodded. She wanted to make up. That stupid quarrel had upset them both and she wanted to make up. He stood up and grimaced at the soreness of his leg. He could no longer see the marks from her wheelchair. He stopped on his way to the bathroom and looked back. Not a sign of them. How many times had she done it? Did she come in every night and look at him as he slept?

Hurriedly he washed his face and brushed his hair. He needed a shave, but not yet. First they would talk, clear the air of the tension that was as poisonous as gas in the apartment.

Anne was on the chaise, a book in her lap. She didn't look up when he entered the bedroom. The sandwich was untouched. Clark poured coffee and sat down.

"Are you all right?"

"Yes."

The coffee was thick and bitter. He put his cup down. He unplugged the pot, gathered the cups and sugar, cream, the sandwich. The table needed wiping. He'd remember to bring a dishcloth back and do that. When he looked again at Anne, he found her staring at him with an unreadable look on her face. She looked down at her book. Clark felt a chill.

## FIFTEEN

CLARK found himself on the ramp leading to the back door of the apartment. He had had the ramp installed the day before Anne's release from the hospital. The ramp led to a walk to the parking lot, covered for the occupants, open spaces for visitors.

The rain had washed it all clean. That goddamn, pounding, driving, relentless, scouring rain. He examined the windowsill again. Nothing. Nothing on the ramp. Nothing on the walk. Nothing in the parking shed. Nothing in the open lot. Nothing.

He leaned against the rail of the small porch. It could have been hit down there, dragged itself up the ramp, to the low window left open. It could have.

There had been blood under the window, on the carpet. None on the windowsill. It hadn't started to bleed yet. It coughed, cried out, then bled.

He went inside and searched every inch of the windowsill, the wall below it. Nothing. He sat at the dining-room table and stared at the wall.

He could ask the other people in the building if any of them hit a small cat or saw an injured cat. And skinny Mrs. Ochs would say, "Oh, yes, come to think of it, I did." He rubbed his eyes. The cat would have been invisible in the rain against the black pavement of the parking lot.

Images: Anne lying absolutely still, pale as death, her vital signs too low. The pain relievers they used, one after another, all depressed her too much, all were dangerous for her. Low blood pressure, respiration bad. Dr. Radimer: "I think she will suffer less after you take her home. The psychological effects of being hospitalized, on top of her inability to tolerate the drugs, is impeding her progress. Take her home, Clark. See if that helps. We can put her back in if we have to."

Home, around-the-clock nursing, and a nearly miraculous relief from pain, or from the expression of pain. After returning home she had never complained.

But how? One of the nurses? He'd check. If she had had the stuff in the apartment, she could have administered it herself, if she had a syringe.

The ifs were too big. He pushed himself away from the table and returned to her room. Anne was as he had left her, a book on her lap that she picked up when he appeared.

"You should eat something," he said. "I'll scramble eggs. Will you eat them?"

She shook her head.

"I'll call Harry, then. He can fix you something. I'll get a bite at the cafeteria."

She made no response and he turned and left.

When Harry came in, Anne looked at him in surprise. She had forgotten Clark had said he would call him. "The cat was killed," she said.

Harry nodded. "Clark told me. He said you weren't feeling well."

"I'm all right. I don't want you to stay. Please." She stopped and realized she was near tears. It was strange. Suddenly there was the constriction in her throat and her eyes were hot. She picked up the book.

"I won't stay. I'll just make you some dinner. Don't talk if you don't want to. I won't, either."

She watched him leave, a nearly grotesque figure, with his too tight and too loose pants, straining the seams at his hips, flapping about his ankles. Scarecrow figure, she thought, and when he was out of sight, she forgot him.

They kept bringing her back, and it was so hard to get away again each time. She looked at the little world with longing. She had been unable to escape into it. The glass walls were infinitely high now, and unbreakable. She had circled it, had tried to rise over the glass walls, and each time she had failed. Her one refuge gone. She felt herself withdrawing again from that motionless figure in the wheelchair until she was distant enough to see that other person completely, and only then could she think.

She thought about freedom, not as abstraction, but her own freedom. Hollow word. That was how they fooled you. Pretending you were free to choose anything, everything, and you weren't. Everything fell into place and you walked among the pieces and believed you had put them there because you wanted them. Her thoughts changed and she was with Clark on his motorcycle, her arms tight about him as they roared down a glaring white concrete road, as straight as a rope stretched between two posts. The air had been so hot her skin had peeled later. Windburn, sunburn.

How casually his hand would find her breast, feel it, squeeze it. How casually her hand would pat his crotch. Sometimes he would gently remove her hand, as if to say not now. She never had removed his hand from her breast, or her buttocks. "It's different," he had said once. And she had accepted that. He could be aroused at her touch. She, because she didn't run a flag up the pole, obviously couldn't be, wasn't.

She was jolted once more when Harry appeared

carrying a tray. She shook herself. "I must have dozed," she said faintly.

He nodded and prepared the table. "Spanish omelette, salad. Okay?"

"Yes. Thank you."

"Anne . . . Nothing. Come on and eat."

The omelette was good and she was hungry. Harry looked on approvingly as she finished it off. "I'm thawing some raspberries, they'll be ready in a minute or so. Anything else?"

She shook her head. "Harry, I keep thinking of Grandma, your mother. I was so small when she died. I keep wanting to cry for her."

"You loved her very much. And she loved you. You were her favorite. When she died, everyone thought you were heartless because you pretended not to believe she was dead. I didn't understand either then."

Anne looked at the small table top that was cluttered with dishes. She wanted to sweep them all off to the floor, to throw something through the window. "My mother spanked me because I played the day of the funeral. I played hopscotch all afternoon and I sang."

"You were about six," Harry said, remembering. "Six. A baby. Children don't know how to express grief of bereavement. They're not physiologically able to express it, there's no understanding possible to them. They think the person has gone away, that he'll return, or she will. Or they think they're being punished for something they did or said. It's abandonment they suffer from. Purely egotistical and purely normal. It's the nature of the little beast. Few people understand that, and the child carries it like a nickel sack of jelly beans all his life, guilt wrapped in layers of shame, ready to come undone at the most unexpected time. Anne, the only danger is in letting yourself substitute that ancient death and its feelings for whatever is going on in the present. If you're feeling the agonies of bereavement, it isn't for your grandmother, honey. You have to face that." He stood up, an awkward, ungainly figure, too long in the arms and legs, and he said, "I'll go get the raspberries, get rid of this stuff."

He cleared the table and left. But she did want to cry for her grandmother, she thought. She hadn't cried then, now she wanted to.

They ate raspberries with thick cream and had coffee, and Harry said, "The Sunday-night concert has already started. Mind if I turn it on?" She shook her head. He turned on the radio and sat down again with his eyes closed. "Gluck," he murmured. "I've been looking forward to this."

Anne felt herself drawn to the music and she found she could lose herself much easier with it on. She closed her eyes and there was only the music that filled the apartment.

Anne sent Harry home shortly after ten when the concert was over. "You've helped," she said. "You're a good man, aren't you? I never thought about it before much, but there aren't many really good men. Thanks."

"Now you're being maudlin," Harry said, laughing. "Are you sure you don't want me to stay awhile?"

"I have to think," she said. "It goes better alone."

He nodded. "See you in a day or two."

She didn't blame Clark, she thought. It wasn't his fault. It was hers. It was everyone's fault, or no one's. She had accepted an attitude without question, and he had accepted her role also without thinking about it. Now they could think about it, talk about it. Maybe. Not just yet. But that it loomed as a possibility was hopeful. That she had thought of it was hopeful. It was like a bereavement; she wondered at Harry for knowing that. Like a painful bereavement, it could not be spoken of just yet. She was too near tears; she would weep and spoil everything by becoming incoherent when she needed to be reasonable, by becoming too emotional when she needed to make him understand, not with his reflexes that would want to love her into quietude again, but with his mind. He had to understand what she was discovering, had to look at her with different eyes, just as she was examining him with new eyes. If, through rediscovery of each other, they lost what they had once had, that too would have to be faced. If they could not build something else, then they would have to deal with it. But later. Not until she could finish thinking through her own attitudes, her acceptance, the reasons for her acceptance. Not until she could talk without crying.

When Clark came home at twelve, he was haggard. He needed a shave badly, and his clothes were rumpled and dirty-looking. Standing near the doorway, he stared at her intently, and asked, "Anne, did you bring home some of the *pa* before the accident?"

"What's wrong?"

"Just tell me!" His voice was harsh. He was trembling.

"Yes. What's wrong?"

"Where is it?"

"I threw it out."

Clark rubbed his eyes and came into the room in a lurching walk, as if he were drunk, not from liquor but fatigue. "Anne, for God's sake don't lie about this. How could you have thrown it out? Where was it?"

Anne shook her head. "No more. You tell me what this is all about first."

Clark sat down and put his face in his hands. For a moment she thought he was weeping and during that moment, if she had been able to, she would have gone to him, would have taken him in her arms to comfort him. She started to move her chair, and he raised his face and stared at her. His eyes were bloodshot.

"There's something wrong with it. Three chimps have become psychotic. Two infants have been killed. Three out of twenty-three! And tonight Lilith began showing symptoms exactly like the others. It isn't just chimps on the stress experiment. Others too."

"No!" she cried. "No!" She moved without being aware of turning the wheels. "You're lying to me! You want to pay me back! You're just tormenting me!"

"Anne, stop it! For God's sake, you know I wouldn't lie about it."

"I don't believe you! What have you been doing down there? Who's been messing it up?"

"It just began happening Monday," he said. "Duckmore attacked a lab assistant, put him in the hospital. Then Fannie killed her baby. Lola injured her baby today, probably it will die before morning. It was just barely hanging on. It won't live."

The wheel of her chair touched his foot and he jerked back. She stared at his foot, then raised her eyes to look at his face. "And you think I . . . Because I objected to being raped, you think I'm going crazy!" It ended high, too high. She wanted to scream. She turned her chair away from him. He caught it and swung it back. "Let go! Don't you dare touch me!"

"You can't dismiss it like that," Clark said desperately. "Anne, if you took it, tell me!"

"I told you and you chose not to believe me!"

"Tell me how you got rid of it. Who helped you?"

"One of the night nurses. The first one. Ruth Gorman. I told her to bring me the package from the refrigerator. I looked at the stuff and wrapped it up and threw it in the waste can by the bed. I was afraid it wouldn't keep until I could test it on myself."

Clark groaned and shook his head. "As soon as you came home from the hospital, you stopped complaining of pain. In the hospital you were in constant pain."

"I was in constant pain here," she said furiously. "How could I have complained! You would have taken me back!"

"Anne, that's not true! I didn't want you in the hospital!"

"You didn't want to see me suffer. It was easier on you if I did it somewhere else. I know you protested over bringing me home too soon. They told me."

"Because I was afraid."

*No! Because you didn't want to know!* You put me in the hospital and you didn't want to see any of the rest of it." He was still holding the wheel of her chair, preventing her from moving away. Brutally, she said, "You knew it was your fault, all of it. You smashed us up, crippled me. You knew how I suffered, and now if you can ease your conscience by thinking I took the *poena albumin* to relieve that pain, you'll jump at the chance, won't you?"

Clark stood up and knocked over his chair. He took a step backward. When he let go, the wheelchair rolled slightly. "You've thought all this time it was my fault?" He shook his head; his face was the color of putty. "It was an accident! There was nothing I could do to prevent it."

"If you had kept your head, it wouldn't have happened! You lost control of yourself and the car. You overbraked, overaccelerated, oversteered. You put us in a spin and let that other maniac hit us broadside. On my side. You know it. I know it. And I guess that poor slob we're suing knows it. And we'll all know it forever!"

Clark was shaking his head hard. "It was an accident. The investigating police said there was nothing I could have done."

Anne turned in disgust. "It's late. Go to bed." She was trembling and couldn't stop. She clenched her hands on the rims of the wheels and pressed her knees together to try to control her spasms.

"Anne, we have to talk about this tonight. I know you planned to try the stuff out first. I meant to do it too, when you did. I remember the day you ran our blood analyses to get our *pa* levels. Yours was about as low as it can get, remember? Is there a chance you could have used it and have forgotten doing it? You were on various things back then. One of them might have affected your memory."

"Ask Dr. Radimer."

"Is there a chance that happened?"

"No! I told you. I threw it out." She didn't look at him again.

"Christ!" he muttered after a moment. "Oh, Jesus Christ!"

She thought of the little cat, and jerked the chair around to stare at him with disbelief and fury. "Get out of here!" she cried. "For the love of God, just get out of here!"

Neither of them moved. Clark stared at her and she at him, and each was a stranger to the other. After a moment, Clark righted his chair again and sat down, his hands dangling between his knees.

"Anne, just let me tell you what's been going on since Monday." He didn't wait for her response, but started with the announcement of the acceptance of the IND, and Helverson's orders for human testing. He didn't look at her as he spoke. His voice was almost singsong, he elaborated nothing and left out nothing.

He was doing it, too, she realized. He had put that part that could be hurt, that had been hurt, far back where it was safe, where it would not be trampled underfoot. The part that was left, that was detailing the long terrible week, was emotionless, toneless, a machine. And she, watching, listening, she was a machine. They could kill each other now, but neither of them would bleed, and if they touched, neither would be warmed by the touch of the other. Metal on metal. Her gaze slid past him to rest on the little world. Cool, misty world without pain, without torment, without accusations and guilt . . .

"Anne, are you even listening to me?"

"Of course. Are you through?"

"I asked you why you thought of that stress experiment? What led you to suspect the results?"

"I don't know. A daydream. An article in a magazine."

"Try to remember."

"Why?"

"Anne, put yourself in my place. If I were the one here in this room acting as you've been acting, and you knew I'd had access to the *pa*, that I had desperately needed it, wouldn't you want to follow it through? Wouldn't you have to find out?"

"But I already told you." She almost smiled at the

reasonable tone they both used now. The return of sweet reason, she thought, how calming, how soothing, how phony.

Clark's face darkened and he looked away from her. Anne felt almost smug. He couldn't maintain the separation as long as she could.

"I'm very tired," she said. "I have a busy day tomorrow. If you don't mind . . ."

When he walked to the door, his legs had lost their spring, his feet seemed almost to drag. He turned and regarded her with puzzled and unhappy eyes at the doorway; he didn't say anything else.

His thoughts were circling in tighter and tighter as he showered. Anne naked in his arms, laughing up at him. Anne in the hospital, her face gray with pain, tears standing in her eyes that were red-rimmed and sunken. Anne cool and distant, somehow superior, in her chair, staring past him with her lips not quite curled up in a smile. Anne at his bedside, staring down at him as he slept. The dead kitten. The dead chimp baby. Anne looking at him with an unreadable expression, a stranger's expression. Over and over, around and around they went, each forming and being chased by the next before the edges firmed. He sat on the side of the bed and knew he couldn't sleep. He went back to the bathroom and found sleeping capsules, for emergency, Anne had said, years ago, and now the emergency was there. He took two of them and went to the bed again, but again he paused, and then he went to the door and locked it. For a long time he stood with his forehead pressed hard against the frame, and his eyes were hot.

## SIXTEEN

"How's Anne?" Deena asked when Clark got into her yellow VW.

"She's fi . . . Deena, I have to talk to you and Gus as soon after I get those blood samples as possible. In his office."

"Sure. About the *pa?*"

"About this whole fuckin' mess." He looked out the window, seeing nothing, and Deena didn't ask anything else.

They sat in Gus's office with the door closed and locked. "I think Anne used the stuff on herself before Christmas," Clark said harshly. "She denies it."

Gus exhaled softly and picked up his darts. He didn't throw them, just held them, turning them over and over from one hand to the other.

"She knows better than that," Deena said, frowning. "I can't believe she'd do it under those circumstances."

"I don't want to believe it, either," Clark said, still too rough, too abrupt. He felt old and tired, and knew he looked old and tired. The sleeping pills had made his head ache even more than the day before, and he had a bad, fuzzy mouth. He glanced at Deena and said more quietly, "I'm edgy. Sorry. I checked the records last night. She took enough out to last her two weeks. She had it all figured out long ago. For both of us," he added.

"Bloody Christ!" Gus sighed. "Start earlier, Clark. Why did you check the records?"

"Right. She's been acting strangely for weeks. Withdrawn, avoiding any personal talk, sending Ronnie home too early, staying alone too much. I don't know. Just not like her, not like she's been. Then Harry, her uncle, brought her a kitten, nearly full-grown. Friday

151

night she called me home. Virginia said she was nearly hysterical on the phone. When I got there she was absolutely normal, very quiet, watchful. She said the cat was dead, out in the dining room. Her wheelchair was in the hall near the kitchen. She hadn't been able to get it around the corner again to get back to the bedroom. I didn't even know she had been leaving the bedroom." He swallowed hard, then continued, speaking fast. "I went in and found the cat. It was mangled, bleeding from the nose and mouth. She had vomited in the dining room near it. She said it must have been hit by a car in the parking lot, dragged itself through an open window to die in the apartment. I believed her." He could hear the raspy quality in his voice without being able to do anything about it. He cleared his throat and lighted a cigarette. "Saturday night we went to my parents' home for dinner and afterward she told me she's been taking swimming therapy for a week. I told her the IND had been approved. We were happy, laughing, both a little smashed. Then she went all to pieces, became hysterical, made accusations. She lost control completely. And since then she's been alternately wholly withdrawn or else in a fury. She sits and watches me. Just like Fannie. Just like Lola. I found the marks of her wheels on the bedroom carpet when I woke up. She had been sitting there watching me."

Gus was shaking his head when Clark finished. "For God's sake, she sounds normal to me," he said. "I can imagine myself cooped up like that for months. I'd really be in a rage most of the time."

"Listen, Gus, don't you think I know how it sounds? Her pain-threshold index on the scale she worked out herself is two point four, on a scale of ten. Mine is six point three, a little higher than normal. Gus, she suffers if she bumps her arm on a doorway. Her *pa* count is one half mil per liter, mine is fourteen. Point ten is the lowest we've ever found. And when she came home from the hospital she was in agony. You remember she couldn't tolerate anything they gave her. And within days she stopped complaining. She began to get interested in her notebooks again. She acted as if she had no pain."

"Hold it right there, goddamn it!" Deena said. "I was around her then, remember. She was scared out of her mind that she'd have to go back to the hospital, and she hated it with a passion. More than that, she has what amounts to a phobia about hospitals. She's afraid a stupid, or malicious, nurse will stick the wrong thing in her or something. She associates hospitals with people dying, not with people getting well. She told me if she continued to have so much pain they would put her back in. Under those conditions, she would have had to go into shock from pain before she would have admitted it."

"Her index is two point four!" Clark said, nearly shouting. "Two point four, Deena! How could she have concealed it?"

"Maybe you just didn't want to see it!"

Clark stared at her. *Déjà vu*, he thought. Again. He said, "I could be wrong. God knows, I hope I'm wrong. But what if I'm not?"

"You've told her what's been going on, I take it?" Gus said.

Clark nodded. "She thinks we're screwing up her work."

Gus nodded. "Can't blame her for that. You told her the symptoms the chimps showed before they went bananas?"

"I told her everything," Clark said impatiently. "Gus, what should I do?"

"Damned if I know," Gus said, playing with the darts, examining the feathers. "Is there anything else?"

"I keep seeing her hands and arms, scratched up, bleeding. One knee was bleeding. There was blood on her chair, on her robe . . . Gus, she's alone every day with Ronnie for hours and hours. What if . . . ?"

"Who's Ronnie?"

"She's the practical nurse–companion we hired. She's supposed to stay until I get there, but Anne's been sending her home no later than five, but even so, from nine until five they're alone in that apartment."

Deena stood up, her face very pink, her eyes glittering. "I think this is a lot of bullshit. I'm going over to see Anne."

"She's at the doctor's office getting crutches this morning," Clark said. "She'll be back around eleven. Wait until after lunch."

Gus, looking at Clark, stood up then and motioned Deena to go away. She glanced at Clark, shrugged, and left.

"What am I going to do?" Clark said again, and this time his voice broke and he cradled his head in his arms and his body shook.

Gus took aim and threw the first dart. Ten, almost off the target. He threw again, and again, and presently gathered the darts and started over. His score was four hundred ten when the phone rang. "No calls yet," he said, then listened. "Tell him you can't find me. I'll call back when I have the chance." He threw another dart and said, not looking at Clark, who had grown quiet now, "Helverson. He's got his wind up over possible trouble. Third time this morning he's wanted to talk to me. Poor bastard. Had his tongue out to lick the chocolate and they took the spoon away."

Clark got up and went to the window and stood there with his back to Gus. "I'm scared," he said. "Really scared. And I don't know what to do."

"Either she did or she didn't," Gus said. "I can buy her actions as normal, the result of the accident, her inactivity, all the rest of it. It gets harder when you can see the end ahead somehow. That way with kids. Good as gold while they're really sick, but when they start to recuperate, then whammo, all hell breaks loose."

Clark shook his head. "And if she did use the stuff?"

"That's a tougher one. But you're right, we have to know. Think she'd tell Deena anything?"

"I don't know. She won't talk to me."

"What set her off, Clark? Something must have started it all?"

"I made love to her. She's okay, the doctor told me. But she's calling it rape. Maybe it was. I don't know."

Gus sighed and aimed another dart. He didn't throw it. He put it on his desk and asked, "She's always liked me all right, hasn't she?"

"Yes, you know it.".

"I'll go see her."

"Not Deena," Clark said. "She'd agree it was rape."

Neither of them added to that.

"I'll go now. She should be home by the time I get there. If not, I'll wait." He stopped at the door. "You've got a hell of a lot of work to do, Clark. If anyone asks for me, just say I'm wandering about somewhere. Be back soon."

Clark looked out the window at the back parking lot until his vision cleared and he was able to pick out individual cars, and then he went to the door, but he didn't leave just yet. He returned to the chair and sat down. Gus was right about the work, on both levels. It was there to be done, and Gus knew once Clark got caught up in it, he would be okay. But he wasn't ready yet. What no one, not even Anne, understood was how much he loved her. It was true he hadn't been able to bear her suffering. He had wept uncontrollably over it. He had haunted the doctor, urging him to do something, anything, to relieve her. And he had objected to having her sent home too soon, because he had recognized his own helplessness.

He loved her long smooth body, her sexuality. She was the most sexual woman he had known; before her, he hadn't realized a woman could be so responsive. He liked to contemplate how, even if their sex life diminished in time, they would still have everything else together. Their work, all their interests, their friends. He, never a romantic before, had come to believe that for each person there was one ideal mate, one other who was the perfect extension, the perfect complement. She was impatient with details, an innovator; he had infinite patience for details. It was as if she viewed the world through a wrap-around picture window that allowed her to see broad vistas at a glance, and he looked through a peephole that magnified one very small section at a time, so that when they combined their knowledge, and they always did, they saw the world in a way no one person ever could. The reality they shared had a breadth and depth few others could imagine. Once they had talked of their likenesses and their differences, and she had summed it all up: "Where I go in, you go out." And it had not been a facetious remark at all. It included everything.

They had become like two vines that intertwined to climb up into the sunlight, so that if you pulled off a leaf it would be impossible to say from which vine it came. And she had called it rape. He knew he could never forget that, never forgive her that. Nothing else she had said really mattered, he couldn't even remember what else she had said, but that had been too deliberately hurtful. That one word had ripped them apart, mutilating both of them, until now they stood with that barrier word between them, two separate beings, neither whole now, neither able to undo the damage one word had done.

But if she had used the *pa* factor, he thought, then she wasn't responsible, any more than Fannie was, or Lola. He saw again the look of shock and hatred on her face, heard her voice, "If I thought you were coming at me again, I'd vomit." And he knew she had used the *pa* factor. There was no doubt.

Gus was stunned by Anne's appearance. She was in bed, very pale, with deep dark lines under her eyes outlining them owlishly.

"My doctor is a brute," she said with a faint smile before he could conceal his reaction to her condition. "And we haven't had much sleep around here for several nights. Clark sent you, didn't he?"

Gus sat down on the side of the bed and held her hand for a moment. "No one sent me. I came. Okay?" He got up and dragged a chair near enough to touch the bed. "I'd fire a quack who sent me home looking like that."

"We worked hard this morning. See?" She pointed to the new crutches. They were aluminum, with tripod ends capped with black rubber. "More for balance than support, the doctor said. I believe. Who ever saw such hideous things?"

Her voice was strained. It must have been a bad session, Gus thought. "And did you walk with them?"

"He wouldn't let me leave until I mastered them." Her voice became more animated. "You wouldn't believe how goddamn tired I am of being treated like a thing. Do this, don't do that, try again, you can't sit down, raise your foot, watch how you put it down . . . Programming a computer or something, that's what it's like."

"*Alles was nicht Pflicht ist, ist verboten,*" Gus said, grinning at her. She nodded and there was a hint of a smile. "Can a guy get coffee around here?"

"You met Ronnie, didn't you? She's out making lunch. Tell her. I'd like some too."

He nodded and went to the kitchen.

"You know who I am, Ronnie?"

"Sure. You're the boss, aren't you? She's talked about you from time to time." Ronnie looked him over and then nodded. "Okay, what can I do for you?"

"We'd both like coffee, if it isn't too much trouble." Again she nodded. "Ronnie, there may be a problem with Anne's medicine. Stuff she took months ago. It might begin to have an effect on her behavior. We're not sure, but there's a possibility. Have you noticed anything? Anything at all out of the ordinary?"

Ronnie's cheerful, open face closed, and she became very professional, very distant. "Sorry, Dr. Weinbacher, but since when are you her doctor?"

"I'm a scientist, Ronnie, and a friend of them both.

Did her physician recommend you?" She nodded. "If you notice anything about her behavior, it's your duty to report it to him. You know that. I don't mean her physical condition, Ronnie. A change in her attitude, in her disposition, her appetite, anything. It could be dangerous to her."

"I know my job." Ronnie turned her back on him to stir something in a pan. "I'll bring you some coffee in a minute."

Gus hesitated, then shrugged and left. Whips wouldn't open her mouth, but he believed she would be alert to any change now, would report any change to Anne's doctor. They would have to get in touch with him right away, get a list of the medications she had taken.

"In a minute," he announced to Anne, entering the room. Anne's eyes were closed. She opened them and motioned him to sit down again. "You want to talk?" Gus asked.

"No. Not really. He thinks I'm crazy. Did he say I strangled the little cat, or ran over it with my wheelchair? I began to wonder how he thought I had done it."

"He didn't say."

"How will you resolve it, Gus? I say I didn't, he says I did. How do you resolve it?"

"Wish to Christ I knew."

"A sanity test? I wouldn't submit to one. I believe I may be a little bit insane right now and I wouldn't like it officially confirmed. Bad news for an employment record."

Gus grinned at her. "You're a smart cookie, Anne. What else have you thought of?"

"Separation. I won't live with him now. He's afraid of me. Last night he locked his door." She smiled, a chill, bitter smile. "I checked just to see. I didn't believe it until then, what he was saying, I mean. Then I believed."

"It's tearing him up, Anne," Gus said. "The scientist

in him knows what he has to do, the man in love with you is unwilling to do it. Right down the middle."

"It's the man who thinks I'm crazy," Anne murmured. She raised herself on her elbow, and her face became tauter, harder. "From now on, everything I do will have a double meaning. I've been thinking about it. If you don't want to find insanity, avoid all mirrors, Gus. You'll see it there first every time." She reached for a cigarette. Gus held a match. Then she said, "I want to go over all the records, everything that's happened since last week, since before then. Something like this doesn't just pop up overnight. There must have been clues, indications. No one was paying attention."

"I'll send over everything this afternoon," Gus said. "Are you up to it?"

"Better that than lying here thinking about how not to appear crazy to someone who's looking for symptoms." A slight change came over her, she looked at him with an expression at once sly and bashful. "Do you believe, in the abstract, a man can rape his wife?"

Gus shifted in his chair. "He told me. In the abstract, I'd say only under certain conditions. If they were separated. If she was trying to sell something he thought should be free. If it had become a weapon. All those things happen."

Anne nodded and lay back down. She looked at the little world and yearned for the solitude there.

"Anne, that man worships you. You know that." He had lost her, Gus knew. She was withdrawn, paying little attention to him. Her fingers were working with the fluff of her cover, rolling it up into small tight balls.

"Anne, look at me. I have to ask. You know I have to ask. Did you use it on yourself?"

She glanced at him, then away. "No. Poor Gus. You should have listened to Bob Klugman. He didn't want to hire a man-and-wife team, did he? He predicted trouble from the start. You should have paid attention to him."

Gus stood up and went to the window. He turned the dieffenbachia around. How beautiful its leaves had become, she thought, all streaked with white, pale greens, dark greens. Poor thing, it had worked so hard to escape, and with one careless motion it was captive again.

"Bob was wrong," Gus said. "You and Clark are the best people I have. As a team you're unbeatable, and you know it damn well." He looked at her and said distinctly, "I want a blood sample from you. I want to send in someone to talk to you, observe you, if you choose. You can take that with a damn female put-upon reaction, or you can accept it rationally and know it's necessary."

She shook her head. "You want too much. You send me the records, and we'll go on from there."

"You won't cooperate?"

"You won't take my word?"

They stared at one another for what seemed a long time, until Gus shrugged. "For the time being," he said, and Ronnie appeared with a tray. Gus sat down again and patted Anne's hand. "We'll work it out," he said.

"You still pooped?" Ronnie asked. She winked at Gus. "I thought she was going to hit the doctor the last time he said, 'Just once more and then you're through.' "

She was mocking him, Gus thought. Make something of that, she was saying. He grinned back at her. "Aluminum's too light. She should carry a monkey wrench for things like that."

Ronnie arranged the coffee things on the night stand. "Lunch in twenty minutes. You staying, Doc?" She was already at the door.

"Can't," he said.

"Dirty shame," she called over her shoulder.

Anne laughed. "You must have pinched her bottom or something out there in the kitchen. She likes you."

"Just my irresistible charm. They fall down in droves before me."

Anne refused to let the talk come back to her. She asked about his wife, their plans for another vacation, and he promised to send stuff over that afternoon, and presently he left, dissatisfied. She looked awful, not only tired, haunted almost. There had been a look about her, something different, remote, watchful, knowing. A look he was sure never had been there before. He had always thought of Anne as terribly young, so young, he had complained to his wife, he felt he had to watch his language around her. She had that look of innocence. And today he hadn't felt that at all.

## SEVENTEEN

"I could ask her mother to come," Clark said. He and Gus were having lunch in the cafeteria. "They don't get along, though."

Gus shook his head. "I talked to her doctor. The list of medications is being sent over by a delivery boy. The nurse will call back as soon as she's off duty, around three. We've done all we can right now, Clark. Try to relax. If it's any help, I believe her. I don't think she used it."

"She really said she wants a separation?" Clark's voice was dull. He had eaten nothing, was drinking his third cup of coffee.

"She said it," Gus admitted. "But you're both pretty upset right now. God, why is it no one can hurt you like the one you love, who loves you? Elaine can ice-pick me without even half trying, just off the cuff. She knows where to stick it in, how deep to stick it with a precision that's admirable."

Clark grinned. "You're a son of a bitch, Gus. Okay, it's our first real quarrel and we're both making a big deal of it. I could buy that, if this other thing wasn't hanging fire. And it scares me. This morning Duckmore is starting to withdraw again. He's moody, irritable, watchful. Is he working up to another outburst? And this time I know damn well there was nothing to stir him up. We've been handling him with kid gloves."

Gus glanced at his watch. "Got to see Helverson," he said. "I'll be in touch later."

Gus had intended to return to his office for his coat and tie, but he forgot and didn't think of them again until he was inside Helverson's office. Bob Klugman was there already, in coat and tie, looking nervous and ill at ease. Helverson, as always, was elegantly dressed.

Helverson came around his desk to shake hands and propel Gus gently toward the small leather couch against the wall. He took one of the matching chairs, Bob Klugman the other.

"Gus, this problem, how's it coming?"

"It's a little soon to say." Gus waited. Bob Klugman was twitching more than usual, and he avoided Gus's gaze.

Helverson nodded. "Bob tells me it's confined to those chimps with high-blood-pressure symptoms, or those on a regimen to induce an increase in blood pressure. Seems a simple thing to list those conditions as contraindications."

"We're getting the computer data now," Gus said. "The albumin tends to agglutinate at various nerve endings in the brain, and this in turn could be responsible for the psychoses, but we can't be certain yet. We don't know why it affected those chimps, not the others, or if it will affect the others also. None of the chimps had high blood pressure at the start."

Helverson frowned and tapped his long slender fingers on the arm of his chair. "Gus," he said, "I wonder if you realize the magnitude of this discovery. An end of needless pain, the dream of mankind since the beginning of time. It's our duty, Gus, to make this available to humanity just as quickly as we possibly can. I'm not a scientist, but I think I understand some of the caution a scientist feels. I've been around scientists for a good many years, and I respect that caution. But, Gus, there are times when the view from outside the lab just isn't the same as that from within. As I see this, there is really only one chimp whose case is in doubt, the male. Do you wonder at the females, with infants, in captivity, under conditions of induced stress? Of course they act strangely. It's such a normal, even human reaction, if I may say so. And the male. Can you say with no doubt in your mind that the lab assistant did not provoke an attack? Of course not. It's well known how animals in captivity harbor grudges against keepers. It's been documented time and again."

He paused, his voice fading out to nothing, but his fingers kept tapping, tapping. Gus thought again of Anne's fingers balling up the fluff of her cover. Don't look in the mirror, he thought. Mr. Helverson, don't look into the mirror. He said, "It isn't merely overcaution. If this had come up before we turned in the application for human testing, approval would have been denied until further work was carried out. We all know that."

"But they didn't turn it down, Gus. That's the point. The work is brilliant, irrefutable. An end to pain, Gus! It's worth the risk of needing psychological counseling afterward! I've already spoken with Dr. Wells, who will be in charge of that department. Those woman will receive the best medical care, physical and psychological, that any group of people has had since the first witch doctor shook a stick at a patient. We'll see to that."

"Does Dr. Grove understand the complication that has arisen?" Gus asked.

"I've kept him informed," Helverson said, and now his voice was cool and the interview was to be terminated. He glanced at his watch, discreetly, but not hiding the fact that he had other, equally pressing matters to attend to.

"Why did you want to tell me this now?" Gus asked.

"I understand there's been a good deal of discussion in the laboratories about this," Helverson said, honey-smooth now. "I rely on you, Gus, and Bob, of course, to keep in mind that once administrative decisions have been made, we're all united, like an army with a common battle to prepare for, a common enemy. Dissension after decisions have been made can ruin an army, a company, a family. When it's time to close ranks, Gus, I want every man and every woman to stand shoulder to shoulder, with no holdouts, no dissidents to cause confusion and delay the day we can make our glorious announcement to a suffering world. Think of the cancer patients, Gus . . . the agonies of inoperable tumors . . ."

Horse apples, Gus thought, and glanced at Bob Klugman, who was watching Helverson as if hypnotized.

Helverson stood up. "I want you to make certain that every bit of new information is given to Bob immediately. And, Bob, you see it gets put into English I can understand and get it to me, day or night. When Dr. Grove gets here Wednesday afternoon for our meeting, I want to have a positive report ready for him. A positive report." He escorted them to the door and held it for them. "Do you need anything, more manpower? More money? Anything? Now's not the time to skimp, you understand. There are times for economy and times to expand and make use of all the resources of a great company. This is that time, gentlemen. Expand! Work! We're on the brink of a day that will revolutionize all humanity!"

Gus shuffled away, cursing under his breath, his head bowed, seeing nothing on either side. He knew Bob was trotting along, but he paid no attention to him.

Deena met him at his office door. "He's going ahead with it," she said. "He told you?"

"In so many words. You're to be in charge of the psychological testing."

She nodded. Bob Klugman joined them and they fell silent. Bob said, "After all, we knew the albumin agglutinated at the brain nerve endings. That was the whole point." His voice was a near whine.

Gus shrugged and opened his door. "Not nine or ten months later," he said. "Did you want to see me, Deena?"

"Gus, wait a minute, damn it!" Bob said. "Helverson had a point. Everything's been fine up to now. That damn experiment Anne wanted done just wasn't proper at this time. You can't include those reactions with the bulk of the experimental material. I could think of any number of experiments to distort the findings. So could you." His voice was rising and he was breathing very fast, as if he had been running. "Look, what Helverson didn't say, something we discussed before you got there. No more experiments that aren't cleared with me first. Not at this time. I'm the head of this department, damn it, and I must be consulted! We're at a crucial point here! All results, every experiment, must pass through my office from now on." Neither Gus nor Deena replied, and he said, almost falsetto, "Helverson's right! You can get results with humans! Results that aren't possible from animals. They can tell you if they're losing their grip. Or if they have headaches. We'll have them under close observation twenty-four hours a day for the next two to five years. They can't avoid telling us if anything's going wrong!"

Deena examined her fingernails and Gus looked at a point somewhere over Bob's head. Neither spoke. After a moment Bob Klugman said, "Where's Clark? I want him to understand, no new experiments that aren't okayed first."

"I'll tell him," Gus said.

"I'll tell him myself! I don't want any more foul-ups

now!" Bob's face was red and he was sweating heavily.

"Leave him alone, Bob," Gus said pleasantly. His ugly face looked uglier than ever as he smiled at his boss. "He's been working twenty hours a day practically all week, and he's tired. You go in there yelling at him and he just might rip out your tongue and stuff it up your ass." He looked at Deena. "You wanted something? Come on in."

They turned together and left Bob Klugman in the narrow hallway. The color drained from his face and he shook with rage, but he didn't go down the hall to Clark's office, didn't go back through the laboratory, but went out instead to the main hall and from there to his office.

"He won't fire you, or turn in a bad report, nothing like that," Deena said, inside Gus's office. "But he will begin a slow poison campaign. That's his style."

"Been underway for months," Gus said. "He's running scared for his own ass. You're going along with Helverson?"

She shrugged. "No choice. They're moving. We go with them or get out and let someone else go with them. I figure I know more about what to look for than an outsider would. I'll keep it cleaner than an outsider."

"Sure. Sit down. I went to see Anne."

"I meant to, but Helverson kept me tied up."

Gus nodded. "She wants to leave Clark. I'm worried she might have taken the stuff. If she did and recognizes the danger, that would explain her wanting a separation. Also, she wants everything we've got about the series of incidents last week, all the charts from the preceding weeks. She wants to make a general review of everything." He sighed. "Got a truck handy?"

"If you can get the material from your department, I'll get it from ours and take it all over myself," Deena said. She looked at Gus, then averted her gaze. "I can stay with her for a while. Marcie can stay with my mother for a while. She can go to school from there."

"Clark thought he might ask her mother to come," Gus said. He didn't like the way Deena avoided looking directly at him. He didn't like the idea of putting Deena in charge of Anne. She's not a lesbian, he thought, but close enough. And she admired Anne perhaps too much.

"When I met Anne's mother," Deena said bitterly, "she said to me"—her voice became falsetto—" 'Isn't it too bad Anne didn't study just a little harder, get a better recommendation so that she could have gone to one of the really big companies?' " Her face was hard and set in an expression of disgust. "Bitch. She's been giving Anne that crap from the day she was born. If Anne killed her, it would be justifiable. I don't think she should be given the opportunity."

"I had the same impression," Gus said. "Go get your stuff together and I'll talk to Clark about it. He may dig in his heels and stay in spite of what she said. We'll see."

Clark was in the projection room. It was a tiny room, hardly big enough for two people, where the images could be projected manually or through a computer system. Clark had the slides on a table at his elbow.

"I need a brain man," he said in greeting as Gus entered. "Look at this. A massive clumping here, and here. Clumping, but not so much here." He changed slides too rapidly for Gus to follow. "And we'll need to sacrifice two more of the chimps, a control and a test animal. I'll do it this afternoon. I need comparative data."

"You can use a man when? Wednesday, Thursday?"

"Better make it Friday," Clark said. He had two slides side by side now and was going from one to the other, muttering under his breath. He cursed and put in a new set of two, and Gus withdrew.

Wilmar Diedricks was waiting for Gus at the end of the office hallway. "We're going ahead, is that the word?"

"Looks like we might. What kind of shape are you in?"

"We'll be ready in ten days to two weeks. Is Grove going to furnish us with blood samples from his subjects? Do we have to collect them ourselves? It'll make a difference. And someone has to post a notice we'll have the super-centrifuge and the refrigerator room tied up until this is over."

They talked as they went toward the office clerical pool, where Gus stopped and motioned his secretary. "We'll need space and setups for two more autopsies this afternoon," he said. "Tell surgery to see to it. And don't take any arguments. I want it ready in an hour."

Mary Johnston nodded and returned to her desk, picked up her phone.

"As soon as we get the subjects' samples, we'll be ready to move," Wilmar Diedricks said. "The program is set, the analyzer, everything. If I'm not allowed at the committee meeting, Gus, I want you to voice my protest though. I'll give it to you in writing. And I'll have to coordinate our matching symbols with Grove, make sure his people understand the system we'll have to use." He paused near the door to his section. "If you can put the brakes on it, Gus, for God's sake do it. I don't think we're ready yet. I can't document it, just a feeling, but I don't like the feeling."

Gus nodded and went on to Virginia Sudsbury, who was monitoring the temperature quality test. "Can you give me a copy of all your preliminary findings right away?" He smiled at her when she looked flustered. She relaxed and he patted her shoulder and turned. He paused and came back to her. "How's it holding up at room temperature?"

"So far it's completely stable at 23 C."

He nodded and left again. A brain man, he thought. Hutchinson, at Harvard. He probably couldn't come himself, although he might. But he could recommend someone else. He started toward the clerical pool again, swerved instead and went to his office, closed and locked the door, and got an outside line. He wasn't ready yet to tell Bob Klugman, or to have anyone else tell him, that he was bringing in an outsider.

An hour later Deena had gathered all the material ready to be taken to Anne. She stopped by Gus's office. "I'll give you a call later, if I don't get back before you leave," she said.

"Right. And, Deena, here's the list of medications Anne had while she was in the hospital, and afterward. Look at them carefully, Deena. Three of those damn things are to stimulate respiration, stimulate heart action."

The crutches didn't fit under her arms at all. There was a strap that went around her wrist, and a leather-covered handgrip that was comfortable to hold, and the tripod at the bottom. They weren't designed to support her weight. Anne stood unsteadily and positioned them. A centipede, she thought, all those feet and she was still afraid she would fall. Left crutch forward. Left foot. Right crutch. Right foot . . . It dragged. She swayed. Lift the foot! Damn it! Right foot, dummy! She had all the feet lined up again. Left crutch. Left foot. Right crutch. Right foot . . . dragging. She made an effort and lifted her foot, too high. The tripods held her and she caught her breath.

"Honey, you're really dragging that foot," Ronnie said.

"Don't you think I know that!" She got her feet aligned again, and only then looked up at Ronnie in the doorway. "Don't watch me. You make me nervous."

"Okay. But you don't have to do it all day, you know."

"Leave me alone, can't you!"

Ronnie withdrew. Anne looked at her feet again. Left crutch forward. Left foot. Right crutch. Right . . . Dragging. You goddamn stupid thing! she breathed at it. Get the fuck up off that goddamn floor!

She was in the middle of the room when Ronnie

came back. "Dr. Wells is here," she said. "She has a lot of stuff with her."

"Not now! Tell her to wait a minute. I'll call you," Anne said breathlessly. There were sweat beads on her upper lip. She didn't move until Ronnie was out of sight.

When Deena brought in the notebooks and record books, Anne was sitting on one of the straight chairs at the table by the bay windows. The table was cleared.

"Hi, honey," Deena said. "Santa with presents. There's more in the car."

"Looks like plenty to start with," Anne said. "Tell me about it all first, will you?"

"Sure. I don't know how much Clark told you. I'll pretend nothing. First there was Duckmore . . ."

At five, Ronnie looked in and backed out again without speaking. They were engrossed in the notebooks, Anne making notes as Deena talked. She went back to the kitchen. At six she looked in again and said, "Anne, I've got dinner ready for you and Dr. Wells. Should I put it in the dining room?"

Anne looked up blankly. Ronnie repeated it.

"No!" Anne said.

"I thought this one was pretty well out of the question," Ronnie said, motioning toward the cluttered table.

"Not in the dining room!" Anne said, and her voice was too high, too tight. "In the living room. Where Harry set the table last week. We'll have a fire."

Ronnie grinned. "Okay. I'll get it ready. Five minutes."

"And then you go on home," Anne said. "I didn't realize how late it was getting."

"I don't mind . . ."

"I know, and thank you. But we'll be working. You might as well go." It was an order, not a request. Her voice was still hard and tight, her face closed.

"I'll clear up the stuff," Deena said. "Don't worry about it, Ronnie. I'll be with her for hours yet."

Ronnie shrugged and went out to set the table in the living room.

"I'm sorry," Anne said. "She gets on my nerves sometimes."

"I bet she does. Somehow the perpetually cheerful ones are the hardest ones to take. You want to go wash up or anything before we go in?"

Deena wheeled Anne to the living room. Ronnie had lighted a fire, but it was small and hissing, at the stage where it was as likely to go out as to burn. Deena blew on it and poked it, and then gave up. "You're on your own, brother," she said, gazing at the smoking flames. "Don't burn, see if I care."

Ronnie had made shrimp creole. There were biscuits and salad and string beans. Anne ate very little. She watched the fire become feebler. They were nearly finished when she said softly, "He thinks I killed the little cat in the dining room."

Deena poured coffee for them both and lighted a cigarette.

"He thinks I'm psychotic. I might be."

"If you are, I'm Joan of Arc, and nobody's ever made that kind of accusation about me."

Anne was sitting on the couch, Deena on a straight chair she had pulled up to the table. Now she moved to the couch to sit by Anne.

"What happened with you and Clark? Want to talk about it?"

"I don't guess so. He did something that made me realize I had to think everything through again. Us. Our relationship. Everything. And he thinks I'm crazy. That simple."

Deena got up and started to pace. She moved out of Anne's line of sight. "Is it true you're leaving him?" she asked from behind Anne.

Anne twisted to see her; Deena touched things as she moved. First her hand lingered on the carved Indian table, then went on to touch a Tiffany lamp, past that to the frame of a painting done by a school friend of Anne's. Anne turned to study the dead fire. With its unprotesting end, gone without even a sputter of sparks, the room had become chilled and unlovely. It needed more light, the furniture was wrong, the painting was wrong, all cool blues and whites and grays, not at all right.

"Is it true?" Deena repeated, and now she came back to the table and sat down in her chair once more.

Anne shrugged and didn't look at her. "True."

"Where will you go?"

"I haven't given it any thought yet."

"Anne, come to my place. With Marcie and me. There's plenty of room. You can have your own room, and it's big enough for a study."

"Thanks," Anne said.

"But will you?"

"I don't know. I haven't given it any thought yet."

"You'll remember? I mean, you won't go rent an apartment where you'll be alone or anything?"

Impatiently, Anne said, "I'll remember. Let's go back to work. Okay?"

"Sure. I'll just move this table, bring your chair over." Deena got the chair and took Anne to the hallway.

"You want to get the coffee? I can manage from here," Anne said. She didn't wait for a reply, but pushed herself down the hall, and when Deena came to the bedroom several minutes later, she was frowning in concentration over the computer print-outs of the $pa$ levels of the chimps.

"Let's find everything that relates in any way to this fluctuation," she said, without looking up. "Test chimps and controls."

Hours later she pushed papers away from her side of the table and threw down her pencil. "Damn, damn, damn. Has anyone made a real effort to explain this situation to Helverson?"

"Sure. He's convinced we're at the point where human reactions are necessary. I saw him this afternoon. He's adamant about going ahead. He thinks human subjects will report any changes as soon as they happen, changes in perception, headaches, anything."

"He can't. It's this damn fluctuation. That's the key. I knew it was trouble! I knew it in my bones from the start, when it first showed up. We should have followed through on it back two years ago, last year. We have to stop Helverson."

"We can't," Deena said. "Why didn't you follow through if you were bothered by it?"

"We finally decided it was normal. It shows up in every animal, everyone we've tested. We decided it was the norm."

"We! You mean Clark, don't you?"

"Clark. Me. It was our decision."

"Look, Anne, isn't it a fact that it was an intuitive urge that made you want to follow through on that? Just as it was an intuitive jump that led you to suspect something like the *poena albumin* existed in the first place? That's what it's all about. And someone like Clark, all rationality, all tests and proofs, hasn't he hung back when your intuition said go? I've seen it with you two a dozen times over!"

"That's not so. We always talked over every step and agreed before we did anything. It was mutual consent from the start."

"Nuts! I know what I've seen happen again and again!"

"You don't know at all if that's what you think."

"Don't defend him, for Christ's sake! Everyone knows this is your work, he's riding your coattails. And he's been a drag! You should have followed up on the fluctuation if you had even an iota of a suspicion something was wrong there! And you would have, if he hadn't urged you on. Wouldn't you?"

"I don't know. What have they been saying at the lab?"

Deena groped in her purse for a cigarette. "You do the work, he gets the credit. He has half the girls watching him with bedroom eyes! And he knows it. He already has his name on this and he'll take it through the human tests, and when it's time for the bonus, and the glory, you know who'll be right there. You think it's yours, but it isn't. Who do you think will be invited to speak at seminars and conferences? Who'll get the promotion when Gus moves up? You? That's a laugh! They'll think of a million ways to keep you tied up, too busy to leave your hot little microscope, and let Mr. Big represent the firm! I've seen it happen before! Listen to me, Anne. Please believe me. I know." Deena kneeled at the side of Anne's chair and took her hand. "If you're serious about leaving him, do it now, before anything's announced, before there's a success with this stuff. It's your work, and yours alone. Get his name off it! You know he won't stay around if you simply tell them it's all yours. There'll be no reason for him to stay around, and then there won't be any doubt about whose work this is!"

Anne pulled away. "You don't know what you're talking about. Of course it's his, too. He made it possible."

"Any well-trained lab assistant could have done what he's done! You've told him every step of the way what had to be done next, and when you didn't force him to do it your way, it got off the tracks! You admitted that yourself!"

"Deena, you're talking crazy! You haven't an idea at all what went into this work before you even knew it existed! This phase, the phase you've been working on, is the result of seven years of hard work that we've done side by side!"

"It isn't crazy! It isn't crazy! You know what I am in that company? An assistant to Emory Durand! That's all I can ever hope to be! An assistant! And if he's promoted, and he will be, then I'll be Benny Bobson's assistant! And he'll be promoted and I'll be someone else's assistant! And you! You think you'll ever be anything more than what you are right now? Clark will take Gus's place one day, and eventually he'll be offered Klugman's job and he'll take that, and you know where you'll be? Exactly where you are right now! That's the way they play the game, baby! That's how it is and has been and will be!"

"And if you and I freeze Clark out and maybe put your name on the work, at least in this phase, we'll change that system?"

"You're damn right we'll change it!"

Anne felt her knees shaking, and her hands were sweaty. She wiped them on her pants legs. Deena was still kneeling at the side of her chair. Anne didn't look at her now. "Why do you hate him so? What has he done to you?"

"I don't hate him! Not just Clark. Can't you understand what I'm telling you? I can see how they're working to take this away from you and me. It won't be ours at all! It will be his, and Klugman's and Helverson's, the company's!"

"And what makes you think it's yours now? Your work with the human experiments. Every idea we've worked on has been mine! *I* said we have to educate the women! *I* said we had to have personal interviews! *I* said no prisoners!"

Deena got up and went around the table. "I didn't mean that the way it sounded. I know that. I misspoke myself. I just mean ours in that we've worked together to make it as good as we can."

Watching her, Anne said, "You said what you think. Ours. Freeze out Clark and add your name, isn't that it? Why do you hate him?"

"For the same reasons you do!" Deena cried. "It's taken you longer to discover them, that's all!"

"Why did you become a psychologist? Why are you working with animals instead of people?"

"What are you driving at?"

"I don't know. But don't you see what you're doing? You're urging me to do the very thing you're accusing them of. You want me to take from Clark what is legitimately his, and you pretend it's what they are doing. Don't you see that?"

"That's not true!"

"Why aren't you urging me to make up with my husband? That's what a psychologist should do, isn't it? Try to reconcile differences? You're trying to drive a wedge even deeper. Take his name off, put yours on. Come to your place to live. Why?"

Deena paled and for a moment she seemed to sway, then color flared in her cheeks, and clutching the edge of the table, she leaned forward and whispered, "That's a lie! That's what they say about me, isn't it? It's a lie! It's a damn lie!"

Anne watched her without speaking and Deena came around the table; her chin quivered and a twitch distorted her mouth, went away, and returned. She put her hand to her mouth, her finger shook. "It's a lie!" she said hoarsely. "You have no right to say something like that to me. I've been your friend! I've stood up for you over there all week! I've had faith in you and your work from the start. I've risked my professional life on this work. You have no right!"

"I didn't accuse you of anything," Anne said. "I think you'd better go home now. We're both tired."

"It's what you think, isn't it?"

"I don't think anything."

"You'd rather think that than face the truth about him, that's it. It's easier for you this way. And you don't have to think about how he betrays you . . ."

"Deena, for God's sake, don't try to psychoanalyze me! I don't need you to explain me to me!"

"But I do need psychoanalyzing, is that it? You think I need help?"

"I don't think anything! Deena, go home. I'm exhausted. I can't play this game with you! Just forget everything I've said. Everything you've said. We're both tired!" She heard the rising note in her voice and bit her lip.

"I'll go," Deena said after a moment. "But I won't forget. I'll never forget!"

# EIGHTEEN

LOLA's black leathery fingers plucked hairs from her flanks, first the left side, then the right. She pulled a few hairs, extended her hand, let them fall, then she pulled some more. Bald spots, larger than half dollars already, oozed blood, a spot here, another. She stared ahead fixedly.

"When did she start that?" Clark asked Bob Brighton.

"I don't know. I got here at ten-thirty, a little too early to relieve Virginia, and wandered over to have a quick look at the chimps before I started on the temperature quality work."

"Christ!" Clark felt a rising nausea, and despair. "I'll have to find someone to come in to keep her under observation. Will you stay put until someone comes? I'll tell Virginia you'll be a little late."

Bob Brighton nodded, keeping his eyes on the chimp. He had a notebook, already one page was filled with notes. He sat down again, the notebook on his lap.

Clark's mind refused to supply a name and finally he called Emory Durand at home. Durand said he would take care of it and Clark went back to watch the chimp again. Lola stared ahead and her fingers plucked out hairs and dropped them. The bald spots were becoming elongated. Clark stood helplessly before the cage for another minute or two. Then, shoulders drooping, he returned to his own department.

In the pharmaceutical division half a dozen people were working; others were in the computer room, a technician was at the electron microscope. Diedricks's night staff was processing blood, extracing the *pa*. It was eleven-thirty.

"Dr. Symons?"

He turned to see Virginia Sudsbury approaching. "I know Dr. Wells isn't here tonight," she said. "When Bob's relief comes . . . I thought, if you wanted a ride . . . I think we go the same way. I have my car." She began to blush as she spoke, and looked about almost desperately, as if searching a way out of what she had started.

Clark nodded absently. "It'll be twenty minutes or so."

"I'll be by the back door," she said.

Clark longed to go back to the electron microscope and try to speed up the man working there. He clenched his hands and went instead to his office. It was all going as fast as it could.

At twelve, Gus entered his office. Clark looked up bleary-eyed. "What are you doing here?"

"What the hell are you doing here still is more like it," Gus snapped. "And did you know Virginia's waiting to take you home?" He had a paper bag, which he opened now, and flashed a bottle at Clark. "Therapeutic dosage, one good jigger—and then off with you." He produced two paper cups and poured. "You must be seeing everything twice by now."

Clark gulped his drink. "What are you doing back?"

"Can't sleep with Elaine away," Gus grumbled. "What damn difference it makes I don't know, but there it is. I start itching. My legs actually start to itch. So I thought, what the hell, be better off down here than there scratching." He sipped his bourbon and sighed. "Good stuff. You know, I watch my hands start to scratch before I can stop them. Make sores, and I know damn well nothing's there. Not a bite, not a rash, nothing. But I scratch until I make sores. Thought Bierley would probably have some slides ready in another hour or two. Sneak preview."

Clark finished his drink. "You say Virginia's waiting? Christ, I forgot about her."

"Yeah. I thought so. Go on home, get some rest."

Clark looked about vaguely, remembered his corduroy coat and pulled it on, and left. Virginia met him at the door. Her hair was loose on her back, lustrous, heavy, beautiful.

"My car's almost at the end of the lot," she said. "That's the worst part about coming in at three, no place to park closer than that. You want to wait while I go get it?"

"No. I'll come. The air feels good." It was cold and still, the sky overcast. By the time they got to her car, he was shivering hard.

"My heater isn't too great," Virginia said. "But it'll help in a couple of minutes. You live on Cherokee Drive, don't you?"

He nodded, and it didn't occur to him to wonder how she knew. He didn't ask where she lived. He slumped down in the seat, huddled in his coat, and closed his eyes as she backed up from the parking space, drove slowly through the lot, and picked up speed on the highway, nearly deserted now.

From time to time Virginia looked at him, but she didn't speak; it made her glad that he slept in her car, that she was able to do this much for him. She knew where the apartment building was; she had looked up his address and had driven past a few times. She liked to think about him living in an elegant apartment overlooking the park. When they arrived, she slowed the car gently and came to an almost imperceptible stop. She shifted to neutral and twisted to look at him. He was sound asleep. She reached out to touch him, to awaken him, then moved her hand back and clutched both hands together. Not yet. In a minute. She watched him sleep.

Deena's little yellow car jerked away from the parking space, stalled, died, and jerked again as she drove through the alley, turned and entered the street without stopping. Halfway down the block she saw Virginia's car parked before the building, and without volition, she stopped at the curb. Her heater hadn't had time to warm the car and she shivered, but didn't start the engine again. She hugged herself and watched the old Ford. Its lights were off. Minutes passed and she was chilled through and through. Her fingers dug into her arms through the coat, released, dug in again. Finally the door opened and Clark got out. He swayed, leaned against the car, spoke to Virginia, then mounted the stairs, holding the rail, walking like an old man. Deena didn't start her VW until Virginia's car was gone, out of sight.

She'd tell Anne, she thought, tell her about Clark and that fat slut, open her eyes about him. She shook her head. Anne wouldn't believe her. She could never tell her anything ever again. Not after the vile, vicious things Anne has said to her.

She drove too fast, screeching to stops at red lights, behind slow-moving cars; she killed her engine several times, and by the time she reached her apartment she was furious with the automobile. She'd take it in for a checkup, make them fix whatever made it stop like that. And the brakes. Brakes shouldn't scream in agony. She made herself a Scotch and soda and sat down in her own living room and thought about Anne.

She was sick. If Deena had not reacted personally, had treated her more professionally, she would have seen that at once. It was hard to separate her professional self from the personal. That's why we don't treat friends and family, she thought. Of course, Anne needed professional help. Projecting like crazy. Like crazy, she repeated, and sipped her drink slowly. Sexual maladjustment of some sort, projecting to Deena what she was suffering. Anne felt a tug there, that was clear. Refused it, refused to acknowledge it even, and instead projected it. That much was clear.

Feelings of persecution there. *They* were ruining her work. *They* were trying to take it away from her. *They,* even Deena, probably the only real friend she had, were conspiring against her.

She probably had killed the cat, repressed it thoroughly. It fit the pattern. Deena had noticed the scratches. It was impossible not to notice them, and

Anne had acted as if they didn't exist. Maybe she blanked them out, hysterical blindness.

It was almost a classic case, Deena thought. Interpreting a simple invitation as a homosexual threat. Classic. Anne was the type. Long legs, slender hips, boyish figure altogether. Hormones out of balance, obviously. Confused by her conflicting desires, repressing her urges . . . Deena finished her drink and started to undress. Now she could pity Anne; with understanding came pity, not the fury she had felt earlier.

They had to know, of course. Anne had to have treatment. She had used the *pa* and it was having an effect on her. They had to know.

Clark hesitated outside Anne's door, his hand on the knob, but he didn't enter; he turned and went into his own room. The brief nap he had had in Virginia's car had cleared some of the fuzz from his brain, and he realized he had to get Anne's diary, and also that he could not ask her for it. She was too fine a scientist not to have kept scrupulous notes from the start. It would be there, dosage, times, reactions if any.

Across the hall Anne listened for him, and when it was apparent he was not coming in to her, she relaxed. After a time she became aware of the soreness in her arms and shoulders and she knew she wouldn't sleep soon. She thought longingly of a hot bath and wondered if she couldn't manage it alone; she was afraid to try. Getting out of the tub was hard. She turned off the light and sat in the dark room looking out the window and thought about the work being done at the lab, thought about Lola and Fannie and Duckmore. This long after being administered the serum. Why? A process of facilitation, obviously. The *pa* tended to migrate to the brain, and in normal subjects, accustomed to it from birth, it did no harm there. In subjects with high, artificially induced *pa* levels, the adaptation wasn't made. Why? There had to be another factor, she thought. Something they had overlooked, hadn't taken into account. The fluctuating *pa* level had to be the key.

They had to work with a brain specialist, after all. They had discussed it early and had decided not to bring in yet another person, but they needed that specialized knowledge. Gus would know someone. She remembered the early days after the accident, when Dr. Radimer had told her they would have to operate on her leg again. He had said, "There's so damn much we don't understand, can't anticipate. Why the tibia is so hard to heal is a mystery." Why the *pa* factor was agglutinating in the brain now was another mystery.

What would Clark say if she admitted she couldn't remember long stretches of her convalescence? The early days in the hospital were a blank, explainable because they had kept her doped all the time. Then there was a clear piece, hours of torment, days of torture. The trip home was a solid memory. Being brought into the house on a gurney, the transfer to bed. All that was clear. More days of torture, then another blank until the day she fell.

There were snatches, a piece here, another there. A visit by her mother, and her accusations, phrased as questions: Were you two drinking? Was he speeding? Were you arguing? Are you going to collect a lot of money? She remembered that visit perfectly.

She was evading what she had started to think through, she knew, and drew her thoughts back to the blanks. Traumas often brought their own amnesia, a simple protective mechanism, easily understood, usually easily overcome if the blank could be outlined. This period, starting with event A, lasting until event B. The fall was event B. Event A? She didn't know.

The fall. Sitting on the side of the bed, the chair within reach, knowing she could stand and draw the chair close enough to seat herself in it. A surprise for Clark, who was in the bathroom. He would return to find her in the chair, pouring coffee at the table by the bay window. She closed her eyes, visualizing what had happened. She had swung her legs over the bed, steadied herself with both hands on the edge. Then, still confident, she had stood up, unsteady to be sure, but she had stood and had reached out, and now the image she got became distorted. She could see her own hand reaching for the chair, her hand groping as the chair seemed to move away. She had lost balance and with a twisting motion of desperation had tried to grab the bed again, and she had fallen, dragging the blanket off with her. She might have screamed. She couldn't remember if she had screamed. Clark had come running; she must have screamed. And then she had felt pain and terror.

That had been months ago. Why had she been so certain she could do it? What had given her that false confidence? Most of all, why did she have those blanks?

If she had used the *pa* factor, she would remember, she knew she would remember. She saw again Ruth Gorman, a pleasant, middle-aged woman of medium height, tending to overweight. Ruth had knitted all night, night after night. Making an afghan with lovely orange and brown and gold yarns.

"There's a white plastic bag in the refrigerator," Anne had said late one night. She had slept very little those nights. "Will you bring it in here, please?"

Ruth asked no questions. Anne had been accumulating notebooks, magazines, boxes of slides, practically everything from her desk in the study that had become Clark's bedroom.

And later Anne had looked at the contents of the bag. There was a box with two dozen stoppered, one-dram sample bottles. Two dozen disposable syringes. Her passport to freedom, she had thought, looking at the bottle filled to the top with the colorless liquid.

The next day the doctor had come and they had done something new with the traction and the agonies had started over again. She had been in a hospital bed then, she remembered. She had forgotten that.

And, sometime, she had asked for the bedside table instead of the hospital stand on the right side of the bed. The table had a door that automatically locked when it closed. She had the key. She remembered opening it, putting the plastic-wrapped box inside the storage space, along with her original notes on the *pa* factor.

She had unlocked the door and put the package inside. It had hurt her to move that way, stretching down to reach. And sometime she had opened that door again, removed the package and wrapped it in newspaper and dropped it all into the waste can. She knew she had done that. She could remember wrapping it in newspaper.

Why had she wrapped it up? Why not just throw it away as it was?

She had wrapped it in newspaper. She had wrapped it carefully, as if it were something she wanted to preserve, not something to be discarded. She had tucked the ends in. So it wouldn't come open again. She had overwrapped it, tucking in opposite sides. She dropped it into the waste can, and then she folded newspapers and dropped them in. She dumped her ashtray out on top of them. She put a magazine in the waste can. And sheets of notebook paper, crumpled loosely. She had buried the package completely.

"I was afraid it wouldn't keep," she whispered. "There were so many strangers in and out of the apartment. I was afraid someone would take it, might even use it." She heard the whispers and clamped her mouth shut. That wasn't the reason.

She had wrapped it in newspapers. Back, before that. She had opened it first, looked inside . . . She unlocked the door and took the white plastic-wrapped package out. No one was in the room then. She always had to choose her moments carefully. They never left her alone. She wore the key on a charm bracelet on her wrist. She unlocked the door and opened it, leaning far down over the side of the bed. She groped for the plastic, it always felt cool, a little bit sticky. She put it on her stomach and lay back against the pillows. The plastic bag was ripped almost all the way down one side. She had the newspapers beside her on the bed. She opened the box . . . She wrapped it in . . .

Back, before that. She had opened it, had taken out one of the tiny bottles, held it up . . . Why? She remembered holding it up, looking at the clear fluid. "I discovered it! It has my name on it!"

Anne felt her heart thumping hard, and she closed her eyes and finally remembered that day. Her mother had been there. Weak with pain, dizzy from sleeplessness, she had tried to follow her mother's monologue, and had given up. Then her mother had said, "He probably has a new girl to help him now. Have you seen her? Is she pretty?" Malicious bitch, Anne thought. How can you do this to me now? Her mother looked like Harry, tall, long arms and legs, thick through the middle. She looked unhappy also, but she had always looked unhappy.

"I am not his assistant," Anne said, working to keep her voice firm.

"They'll let you back, won't they? But there must be lots of jobs for good laboratory people, even women."

"I still am on full pay," Anne said. "I told you that."

Her mother raised her eyebrows.

And Anne had twisted to reach the door of the cabinet, unlocked it with her key worn on her bracelet, and had taken out the white plastic-wrapped box, with the plastic ripped almost all the way down one side. The plastic had felt cold, clammy. Her hands shook when she lay down again, the box on her stomach. She opened it and withdrew one of the small, stoppered bottles.

"Look at it, Mother! I discovered it! It has my name on it! Mine! Anne Clewiston! Not Mrs. Clark Symons!"

"What is it for?"

"It will stop pain. Completely stop it."

"Well, if it works, the way you look, you should be

using it, I'd say. Why do you have it here if you don't intend to use it?"

Anne put the small bottle back carefully and kept her eyes on the box, not willing to see her mother, not willing to let her mother see her. She would use it, she realized. She had to. She couldn't bear it any longer. Her mother's voice went on and on, droning about how Anne had always complained so about the least little thing. A scratch would send her crying to her room. Desperately, Anne wrapped the box in newspapers, overwrapped it. A fall, you'd think she had broken every bone in her body. Tres had had a baby with natural childbirth, not a whimper had passed her lips. Anne stuffed the rest of the newspaper in the can on top of the box. And Hal! The day he broke his wrist playing football, he had finished the game! On and on and on and on.

The waste can was full, overflowing. She lay back against her pillow, shaking.

"Why are you throwing it away if it's any good?" Her mother reached for the waste can, and Anne rang the bell for the nurse. "You can't just throw it away. Won't they need it at work? Won't Clark miss it and wonder what happened to it?"

Ruth Gorman entered and frowned at Anne's condition. "Can I get you something?" she asked.

"Please, just empty the can."

Ruth picked it up and carried it out. Anne's mother watched her and then turned to Anne. "That's a sin, just throwing it away like that! Clark might have been able to do something with it! You always did do things like that. I remember when you threw away Hal's handmade fishing flies. Remember? You were mad at him or something . . ."

"I didn't. Tres did it."

"Now don't try to blame it on Tres. She and Hal were very close then, not like you and your brother at all . . ."

"Mother, please go now. I have to rest. I'm tired. Please. Go! Don't come back!" Her voice was rising out of control. "Don't come see me again. When I'm well, we'll visit you."

"If you had something you could use and just threw it away, well, it's your decision. Stubborn, too stubborn for your own good . . ."

Ruth Gorman had returned with the empty waste can and quite firmly had ushered Anne's mother from the room with no more delays.

Anne hadn't seen her mother since. There had been one very hurt letter, which she hadn't read all the way through. Someday, she thought, she would try to get to know her, to see the woman Harry talked about, a woman she never had seen. Someday. She left the window and got ready for bed.

She could tell Clark now, end it. And Helverson would go ahead with the human tests and her work would lie in ruins about her.

Her life. Her work. Everything. She thought how eagerly Clark had seized on this belief, that she had used the *pa*. How important it was for him to believe that. He had to believe it. Even if she told him now, right now, he would have to doubt until he called her mother, talked to the nurse. He might even think she coached her mother in what to say. No, Clark would never believe that. He knew her mother, knew their relationship. Others might believe it, but he never would. But he would call and confirm her story. And then what? He would have to face the same questions she was facing: Why did he have the need to believe she was psychotic?

She was too tired to think any longer. She lay still and tried not to think of the next day. Learning to walk again, swimming perhaps, more arguments . . . Who next? She was alienating everyone she knew. Poor Deena. She never had seen Deena so furious. Again she thought, poor Deena. And poor Marcie, Deena's daughter.

Her door opened and she stiffened but made no sound. She woke up completely. A shaft of light stretched into the bedroom from the hallway. The room had changed from dark to dim. It was possible to see Clark's outline when he came into the room. His face was a pale blur, his hands giant moths that made aimless movements. He stood over the bed a moment, and she closed her eyes at his approach. He didn't touch her. He moved away a step, stopped at her wheelchair, and the moths fluttered about it. He was searching the pockets of the wheelchair. He was looking for her diary. Presently he found it and he left and closed the door without a sound. He would be back to replace it, she knew. He would not find what he was looking for, and he would sneak back in and return it to the pocket, as puzzled as before, as certain as before. And he would reason that she, a fine scientist, would have kept notes, would have recorded dosage, times, dates, results, everything. He would come back to search again and again, certain of finding the notes sooner or later. He was so certain. So certain.

## NINETEEN

CLARK woke stiffly and made coffee, showered, and dressed before he went into Anne's room. She was already up, at the table by the windows. Clark's eyes rested a moment on the locked door of the bedside table. He resisted the temptation to try the door, see if it was locked.

"Breakfast?" he asked.

She shook her head. "No, thanks. Just coffee."

"Be right back."

It was so normal, he thought, preparing the coffee for them both. Just like always, except he was no more than a servant now. Anne was studying the tree outside the window when he returned. Without turning to look at him, she asked, "Can you make Helverson reconsider? Can you stop him?"

Clark put the tray down and poured the coffee,

handed hers to her and sat down before he answered. "I don't think so. Gus doesn't think so."

"He won't believe the risks, is that it?"

"Partly. And he knows it will all be kept secret. Deena's working on it, you know. Prisoners. They'll be under observation for as long as it takes. Grove will see to that. All very hush-hush."

Anne's hand was steady when she lifted her cup. She was facing Clark now, but was not seeing him. Her gaze was on a distant point, something not even in that room.

"There was a new development with Lola last night," he said. He told her about it and she nodded.

"Is her *pa* increasing?"

"Yes. Not much, but steadily. I'll call and give you the exact figures if you want." She nodded. "You think she's manufacturing *pa* now. Is that it?"

"Looks like it, doesn't it?"

"And it's accumulating in her blood," Clark said, narrowing his eyes. "It could be the break, Anne."

"And it could be disaster. If it continues to build to the level of her dosage, and then drops, especially if it drops very fast, she'll probably have a seizure. You should have close observation constantly from now on, for the next few days anyway."

"We're doing that. What do you think?"

"I think we've taught them how to manufacture *pa* without at the same time knowing anything about the control of it. If Lola responds like I suspect she will, the stuff will begin to agglutinate at an accelerating rate, and since it seems non-selective, with this new assault on her brain, vital functions can as easily be affected as simple pain receptors. She's likely to die this time."

Clark stared at her in horror. "What can we do?" He wasn't asking about the chimps.

"Nothing, except wait." Anne poured more coffee. "You'd better call for a cab."

She couldn't look at him now. She heard the horror in his voice and knew what he was thinking and couldn't look at him. You chose to believe, she thought, stirring her coffee. You chose this as the lesser of the evils, and now you have to accept all of it. And this is one of the parts. There are others, will be others. But she couldn't look at him. He had spoken.

"I'm sorry," she said. "I was thinking, I guess."

"I asked why I need a cab. Did Deena say she wouldn't be here this morning?"

"She didn't say. We had a quarrel last night. She was pretty pissed off at me, and through me, you. I doubt she'll come by."

"What did you fight about?"

"It doesn't matter. We were both tired, I think. It'll pass."

Clark felt that things were happening he couldn't comprehend. Anne was different, cool, remote, abstracted, so deep in thought she hardly seemed aware of him until he spoke. Withdrawn, he thought, like Lola, and Fannie, and Duckmore. Gone into a world of her own where no one could follow her.

"Anne," he said. "Please don't turn me off, just listen to me." She came back from wherever it was she went, and she looked at him, and for a moment he thought he saw pity on her face, something about the expression, something in her eyes. It was gone too quickly to be certain, and she was merely alert, listening, waiting. "Anne," he said, and now he was pleading, "I want to call a doctor to come see you today."

"A psychiatrist?"

"Yes. I can ask Dr. Radimer to recommend someone. We would confide in him, explain everything, what the stuff is, how the chimps have been reacting, how you . . ."

"How I've been reacting? Is that the rest of it?"

"Anne, please. Just try to understand it from my side. Please."

"And what if he found nothing? Then what? Another one? And another? Until you find someone who will say what you want to hear?"

"For God's sake, Anne, stop it! I don't want to hear

anyone say you've taken the stuff and it's hurting you!
But if you have used it, we have to know, someone has
to be on hand to help you."

"I told you I didn't."

Clark shut his eyes and took a deep breath. "You
told me," he said. "It's late. I guess you're right about
Deena. I'd better get a cab."

At the door he stopped and said, "Anne, at least
think about it. I'll try to leave earlier today. We can
talk about it tonight. Think about what I've said."

"I think of little else these days," she said. "What
else is there?"

Gus arrived late that morning. Before work he had
gone to see Dr. Radimer, who didn't believe Anne had
taken anything to relieve her pain. "I would have
known," he had repeated several times, stiffly, as if
being accused. "Not necessarily," Gus had explained.
"The stuff has no lasting effects. Within eight hours, the
level of pain would be exactly what it had been before.
If she knew she had an appointment with you, she
might not have taken it that morning. How could you
be sure?"

"I would have known," Dr. Radimer insisted.

A washout, Gus thought. The nurse had been another washout. She didn't know if Anne had thrown away
the package from the refrigerator. She didn't even
remember getting it for Anne. There was the cleaning
woman, and after that no one else they could ask. Only
Anne, and Clark. Gus had no hopes the cleaning
woman would remember that particular package, that
one day in the middle of winter. Why should she? He
scowled and, still scowling, entered the laboratory,
where his secretary Mary Johnston was waiting for
him.

"Mr. Helverson wants you right away," she said.
"He came down personally to get you."

"Shit," Gus said, and his scowl deepened.

"He wants Dr. Symons at the same time," Mary

added. She glanced over her shoulder. "He's been with Dr. Wells for almost an hour, and Dr. Klugman is with them now."

"Is Clark here?"

"In the animal division."

"Get him for me. Don't tell anyone I've come in yet. I'll wait for Clark in my office. Scat!"

He went inside his own office, to scowl even deeper at the dartboard.

Clark knocked and entered without waiting for an answer. Mary Johnson had alerted him, too, then. "Do you know what's up?" Gus asked.

"Deena? And Bob? Why, unless Deena blew the whistle on Anne. What else?"

"Right. What happened?"

"Christ, I don't know. Anne said they had an argument. Anne wouldn't talk about it."

Gus cursed fluently for several seconds, and then said, "Okay, Deena's blown it. And she must have some ammunition. The question is, what will we do about it?"

Clark didn't answer.

"Goddamn it, Clark, snap out of it! Get on the outside for a quick look! You want a human subject and you find out someone took the stuff three months ago. You've got the subject! Then what?"

"Observation. Tests. Anne won't let them!"

"Can she stop them?"

Clark's eyes narrowed and he lighted a cigarette, thinking furiously. "Is anyone else in on it?"

Gus snatched up the phone and told Mary Johnston to find out who else was in Helverson's office, and waited for her to call back with his hand on the receiver. The phone rang seconds later. He listened, grunted, and hung up. "Grove," he said. "He got here ten minutes ago."

"I won't let them touch her!" Clark said savagely.

"Not even for her own good?" Gus asked, and his voice was almost as savage as Clark's. "You think she took the stuff. Deena must agree. Is she going psychotic? Will she become a psychopath tonight, tomorrow? Next week? Can you say she won't? Clark, she might not even know if she used it. I talked to a brain man, Hutchinson, described generally what we have, and he suggested the possibility that it might act as an amnesic, if it prevents certain synapses firing. She could have used it and have no memory at all about doing it."

"They can't have her!" Clark stood up threateningly, his fists clenched. A muscle worked in his jaw, there was a pallor on his face that made him look ill, old.

"Can you say she'll be all right tonight? Tomorrow?" Gus stood up too and they faced each other across his desk, the little ugly man, as tight and hard now as Clark.

"I don't give a shit if she's all right tonight, or any time. They can't have her. I'm going home!"

Gus got to the door first. "No, you're not! You're going up to Helverson's office with me and you're going to keep quiet and listen to them. You hear me! You're going to listen and keep your big mouth shut."

Clark sagged. "For now," he said.

"Right. Now let's go."


Dr. Lawrence Grove was almost bald, with a few pale hairs across the top of his skull, and a fringe that ran from ear to ear in such a way that a head-on view of him made it appear he had tufts of hair poking from behind his ears. His dome was very red, redder than his face, redder than he was anywhere else. His face was long and full, rectangular, with large features, a bony nose, full lips, large myopic eyes. Recently he had switched to glasses that darkened according to the available light, and now the glasses were violet-tinted, a hideous contrast to the redness of his scalp.

He tapped his fingertips together and shifted his feet, crossed his legs, automatically moving in such a way that the crease was not distorted. His shoes were highly polished. "Dr. Wells," he said, and his voice was surprisingly vibrant, alive. He would have been very good on radio. "If this young woman is mentally ill, from whatever reason, it is our duty to care for her."

"You don't listen to me," Deena snapped. "I admit that. What I am saying is that I'll have no part in trying to get her committed to any kind of institution. There are plenty of private hospitals. Even an experienced nurse in her apartment. Anything except one of the institutions."

"I understand," Dr. Grove said. "And I heartily endorse what you say, but, my dear, this is an extraordinary case, and we must be absolutely certain that the doctor we select to handle her case is in sympathy with our cause. I can assure that in any of the hospitals under my jurisdiction, you see. However, if we go to a privately run hospital, a privately engaged physician, then . . ." He turned to Helverson, who was nodding. "Yes. Now, naturally we will not take any precipitate action. This is understood. Nothing hasty, nothing to regret. Right?"

Edward Helverson listened to them without adding to any of it; he was planning the next move, the next few hours. That son of a bitch Symons might be a stumbling block. The fool took the stuff, that was certain, and she either was going mad or wasn't, and in either case they had to know. Perfect. Perfect. There was an estrangement, that too was clear from what Dr. Wells had said. Symons's name was on the project; he'd want to protect it at any cost, wouldn't he? He could handle Gus, had always been able to handle Gus. Klugman was nothing. Gus and Symons, then. Gus would play. He'd protest, but he'd come around. Symons had to play. He made a mental note to sic Jack on Symons and that idiot wife of his. Jack Newell would dig out anything there was. Good. There was always something. He realized he was staring at Deena Wells and he put her in the unknown column. He didn't know what was bugging her. A queer probably, that might be useful. Another note to Jack Newell. Trying to break up the Symonses' marriage? Why? No hint of perversion in Anne Clewiston. He underlined Deena

Wells's name in the unknown column. Something about the way her eyes glittered, the way she kept moistening her lips. Jack would find out anything there was about her, too. He began to listen again to Grove.

". . . her physician. A steady dosage of tranquilizers probably is all she'll need. You say the level of the *pa* fluctuates daily?" He was speaking to Bob Klugman.

Klugman could feel sweat trickling down his back, and he kept wiping his hands on his trousers. "He, Gus, knows about the details more than I do," he said. "I was ill last week, you know."

"What exactly do we need to commit her?" Helverson asked.

"No problem there," Grove said. "I'm qualified as a physician to sign the papers. Dr. Wells can be the second consultant. We'll need her husband's permission, also." His voice rose in a near question.

Helverson nodded. "No court order?"

"Not if we have her husband's permission. Or even hers. She can commit herself, you understand."

Deena moistened her lips again. She was cold. "What hospital?" she asked.

"State hospital down in Shepherdsville. Good man there. Avery Meindl. Know him?"

She shook her head.

"He'll understand. I'll brief him myself. We've worked together on other projects in the past. Good man."

A state hospital, Deena thought, and visualized its grayness. Prison. Uniforms. Gatehouse and high fence and guards. She tried to moisten her lips, but now her tongue was also dry. "I won't sign for that," she said in a hoarse voice. "Not a state hospital."

Helverson looked at her and his eyes were very cold, very bright, as ice is bright under the sun. You will do exactly what we tell you, you stupid cunt, he thought. He said, "This is merely a preliminary discussion, Dr. Wells. We must examine every aspect of this extraordinary situation, and keep in mind always that Anne Clewiston's well-being is our primary concern.

We must protect her at all costs. Everything else is secondary."

Deena's hands clenched and loosened, but she still couldn't moisten her dry lips.

Edward Helverson believed people were born to serve in different spheres. There were the natural military men, out of place anywhere else. There were the natural artists, who would produce art no matter what. There were the people like Gus, and Clark Symons, born to play with test tubes and microscopes. And there were the men born to move through the world of business. He knew his place had been ordained from the beginning. There had been no doubt in his mind at any time in his life about where he belonged. And even this mini-crisis was welcome to him, a new test of his skill; this victory would be another in a line of victories that would leave his mark on the world.

He had come to the company while old man Prather had been at the helm, his hand firm, his vision clear about where he was going and how to get there. It had been his goal to make the company the finest in the world, not in size, but in quality. Helverson had moved up the ranks as surely as a salmon moves upstream, incapable of resisting the inevitable, incapable of imagining such resistance. And now, with young Prather as president, suddenly there was no place to go. The boundaries had become visible, and as he approached them under steady acceleration, he knew he could not be contained within them. That was stasis, and stasis was death.

Six years ago the old man had died, and four years ago Helverson had understood what had to happen next. The company was good, but it could never be more than it was—a peanut concession at the World's Fair. Prather hadn't been interested when he first brought up the subject of a merger. There was some pride there, also laziness, and worst of all, lack of vision. Or perhaps he merely felt safe here and was afraid to compete in the real world. Helverson didn't know what held young Prather back, and he didn't care. When the ante became high enough, pride, and fear, and whatever else it was would fade from the scene, and the merger would go through. Prather might retire prematurely to spend his windfall, or invest it in a new peanut stand; Helverson didn't know what he would do, didn't care; he knew what he would do then.

He never entertained a worry that the *pa* factor was possibly dangerous. They would have found that out long ago. It was just the confounding pickiness of the scientific mind that insisted on one more test, one more run, one more delay. They acted as if they had all the time in the world, while he knew time was the everlasting enemy.

With Clewiston's find, the ante had shot up suddenly, and he knew that within a year he would deal himself a fistful of aces, and he wasn't going to let any sudden failure of nerve take that away from him. The IND made it legal; Grove would keep it clean professionally, add some prestige even, and they all knew anyone who stuck his pinkie in this would draw it out dripping honey. A bigger find than penicillin, bigger than the Salk vaccine, bigger than anything on the books. The story would be on the front pages of newspapers throughout the world—Clewiston's name, Symons's, Prather's, they all would be there—but the story that really mattered would be hidden away on the financial pages. In that story it would be his name that the people would read, the people who mattered.

Helverson had seen the power of the corporation when the IND approval had been rushed through. Nothing illegal, but they hadn't dragged their feet the way they would have done had it been only Prather Pharmaceuticals trying to get a decision. It wasn't merely another move up a ladder, he knew; it was a quantum leap, and he was going to make that jump. There was nothing shady, absolutely nothing illegal, in moving forward. If there were, he would not consider such a move. His record was unblemished, and would remain virgin-pure; that was important, he would guard it jealously.

He continued to listen to Grove and Deena Wells arguing about state institutions, and he knew Wells wouldn't be a problem. She was afraid, and he would find out why and use her fear. Subtly, of course, even sympathetically. There was no problem with her.

He was impatient for Clark Symons and Gus to arrive. They were the unknowns now. His impatience didn't show at all.

## TWENTY

WITH THE ENTRANCE of Gus and Clark, the office seemed to become very small. Helverson stood up and offered his hand; Clark apparently didn't see it, but went to the window and stood there, slightly behind Klugman, out of the line of sight of Dr. Grove. Gus shook Helverson's hand, nodded to the others in the room, and sat on the couch, next to Deena.

"You gentlemen all know each other," Helverson said. "Dr. Symons, I understand your wife might have used the *pa* factor on herself, and of course, that presents us with several problems. What I'd like is for you and Gus to consult with Dr. Grove, and Dr. Wells, of course, and answer any of his questions, explain exactly what has been happening in the animal division. Just a thorough briefing. Would you like to use the conference room?"

Helverson knew what he had to do. The decision had been there waiting for Clark's entrance to firm itself and make itself known to him; when he came to it, the plan was fully formed, ready to act upon. He trusted his decisions that came that way. They never had failed him in the past. The room had become small because of Clark Symons. Clark was radiating hostility and negativism. He would agree to nothing.

Right. Helverson stood up and the others did also. Bob Klugman looked anxious, puzzled; Grove also looked puzzled. This wasn't what they had talked about at all.

"Bob," Helverson said, "you can show them all into the conference room. Order coffee. That always seems to help. Take your time, gentlemen, and Dr. Wells. There must be innumerable questions to be answered, points to be explicated." Klugman bustled importantly now, led the way to the door. Helverson smiled at him.

"I have some rather pressing work to do," Clark said brusquely. "I'm sure there's nothing I can add to what Gus knows about the experiments."

Helverson held the door, motioned him through. "But only you know about your wife, Dr. Symons. You and Dr. Wells, that is."

Clark looked at Deena and his face tightened even more. She flinched and looked away.

As soon as they were gone, Helverson called Jack Newell and told him what he wanted done. "Bring me Anne Clewiston's file first, and then get to it. Very, very quietly, of course."

"Of course," Jack said.


"Where's Dr. Symons?" Emory Durand asked at the clerical-pool office door.

"A meeting," Mary Johnston said. "He and Dr. Weinbacher, Dr. Wells, Dr. Klugman, were all called to a meeting."

"DND meeting?"

"Yes, sir."

"Christ!" A "Do Not Disturb" meeting now! Damnation! He returned to Lola's cage and shrugged at the question on Jane's face. "She still out?"

"Yes, sir. No change."

Lola lay in a fetal position. The assistant had called Emory Durand when she went into convulsions, and within seconds that phase had passed and she had curled up and was staying curled up.

"No medication, nothing," Emory said. "But don't take your eyes off her. If there's a change, call me."

The image of the chimp in a tight ball stayed with him as he walked back toward his office and put in an emergency call for Clark, to be answered just as soon as the meeting ended.

"Why have you come here?" Anne demanded.

Edward Helverson was admiring the room. "Very, very nice," he said. "These old houses are still the best, aren't they? I have a modern plastic-and-chrome apartment. Makes me feel like an exhibit sometimes." He finished his survey and looked at Anne then. "And you, my dear, are looking very lovely." A mistake, he thought, the instant the words formed. He sat down opposite her at the small table covered with notebooks and charts. "And working, in spite of everything."

She continued to watch him. For a time there was silence as they regarded one another.

Arrogant, Helverson thought. Smart. Smarter than he was in many ways. And an idiot when it came to practical matters. How they detested him and his kind, and without him and his kind they'd all be blowing themselves up in basement labs. He had made a tactical error before; he wouldn't again.

"May I call you Anne?" he asked and waited for her nod before he went on. "Anne, I learned this morning there is a possibility you have tested your *pa* factor on yourself, and in view of the trouble that has developed at the laboratory, it seemed imperative to call on you."

She waited, suspicious and wary. Deena, she thought. Deena had done this. She didn't know why. She would have to think about the why later when she was alone, when there was time. She watched her tall elegant caller and waited for the rest of it.

Helverson wasn't perturbed by her silence. They were playing his game now, not hers; and in this game he was the expert. If she began to talk about experiments and *pa* levels and tests, he would take the back seat, but not now.

"If you used it, Anne, you have to submit to observation, testing procedures, you understand that. The only problem is where to do it. Not here, obviously. Competent people have to manage your case, and they are a scarcity. No one could ask them to abandon many patients to oversee the care of one, even if that one is as important as you to all of us."

"No!" she said. "You'd better leave now, Mr. Helverson. I am on a strict routine and it is time for my exercise."

"Yes, Anne. The IND has been approved, the next step is the human testing and teratology studies. I am already committed to having those results by next spring, so we must take that step this month or next. Nothing that has happened in the lab is enough in itself to force a postponement. We simply have contraindications that we will observe in our testing program. No fault there."

"I won't agree to go ahead until this problem is solved," Anne said. "I'll write to the FDA myself and outline what has happened."

"I considered that," Helverson said. "I understand your idealism. Understand and sympathize with it. Your elaborate plans for educating the test subjects, for being absolutely certain they understood what was being done, your personal involvement with that phase. Very commendable. And we had agreed to permit you to do it your way. That's how highly we regard you, my dear." He didn't reach over to pat her, but smiled gently and looked as if he might. Anne pulled back farther, hard against her chair. "We will go ahead, Anne," he said. "We have to. This is too important to everyone to let it sit while you start over. Five more years? Eight more years? You know it works, don't you? It worked for you. If you write that letter, you'll be discredited, my dear. I have a signed and notarized statement from Dr. Wells that your mental condition is such that no letter of yours could be taken seriously.

Hallucinations, delusions of persecution, sexual fantasies. You need treatment, my dear. If it is the *pa* causing your problems, it won't be a blemish on your future, don't you see? You sign the necessary papers, submit to treatment. You receive extraordinary care in a private room with the finest doctors available. If your illness isn't caused by the factor . . ." He spread his hands apart. "The same care, of course, but there it will be. And you must be treated, my dear. Two highly qualified doctors agree on that."

"Get out of here! Ronnie! RONNIE!"

Ronnie appeared so fast Anne suspected she had been standing at the door. Helverson stood up. "He's leaving," Anne said.

"We have scheduled a full committee meeting for 3 p.m. tomorrow," Helverson said. "I trust I'll hear from you before then." He bowed and left, Ronnie at his heels.

Dr. Grove had asked his last question. He closed his notebook and put it in his breast pocket. "I'll talk to Mr. Helverson," he said. "I'm sure we'll work out something that will be satisfactory to us all."

Deena rushed out, not looking at Clark. Bob Klugman looked about for something else to delay him, found nothing, and he too left. Only then did Clark stand up.

"By the way, Doctor," he said. "I meant to ask Deena, but forgot. What did she report?" He shuffled his notebooks and stuffed them back inside various pockets, and didn't look at the doctor.

"The usual thing. Your wife is feeling persecuted, there are sexual fantasies concerning Dr. Wells. Feeling very threatened. I understand she made some accusations about you." He patted his pocket, glanced at the table, and turned toward the door. "I'll see you tomorrow at the meeting, if not before."

Clark didn't move until Grove was out of the room. Then he sat down again hard. Gus went through the motions of pouring more coffee, which he didn't want, and sat down also, not looking at Clark.

"Deena's lying," Clark said. His voice was strained. "The filthy bitch! Why? Why would she?"

The phone rang. It was Emory Durand and he wanted Clark.

". . . might try electroshock," Durand said, and Clark couldn't remember what he had said before that, or after. Electroshock. Numbly, he turned to walk away from the cage where Lola lay barely breathing in catatonic withdrawal.

Durand started to call Clark back, and Gus's fingers hard on his arm stayed him. Gus shook his head and they turned to look at the chimp again.

Electroshock. Convulsions. Sometimes bone-breaking convulsions. Clark walked from the building and out through the parking lot to the street. He had not put his coat on, didn't feel the cold air. Presently he saw a taxi and hailed it and told the driver to take him home.

"Address, buddy?"

Clark told him and closed his eyes. He opened them again when the driver asked him a question. He hadn't heard the words, only the voice, the rising inflection.

"I said, I can't find that address. Isn't this Cherokee Drive?"

It was the wrong side of the park. Clark got out and started to walk through the winter park, desolate now, deserted, in shades of gray and brown and the deep holding greens of the firs and spruces. Mist blurred outlines and every depression was a pool. Now he was cold, the wind was starting to blow again. The sky was a rain sky; low, swollen clouds, shadows against the deeper shadows. He stopped to look down at a children's playground. The wind had started a swing in motion, and it squeaked, an eerie sound in the empty park.

*Not Anne!* he wanted to cry out, and there was no one to cry out to. Only naked trees, bare and black and uncaring. Somehow everything had got out of control.

With Deena's damning confirmation of what he believed, it had been taken from his hands and there was nothing he could do. They knew. They would demand this and that and he would walk alone in the park and accept his impotence. He felt shocked and numbed by Deena's acceptance that Anne had used the *pa*. As long as he alone believed it, there had been the possibility he was mistaken, and that possibility now was gone. He could have been convinced eventually that Anne's behavior was the result of confinement, the result of his actions and her reactions, that somehow he had had a need to think she had used the *pa,* and the need had made the link appear inescapable. But that possibility was gone now. Deena's observations, her conclusion, echoing his own, killed the possibility of mistake.

He rubbed his eyes to rid himself of the image of Lola in a fetal position, catatonic, dying. The image persisted. The swing squealed, sending goose bumps up and down his arms, and he began to walk fast, faster, until he was running. He stopped to rest against a very old, very large spruce tree. The branches swept down head high and shielded him from the wind for the moment. The bark was rough and he welcomed it against his cheek as he panted and waited for his breathing to return to normal. He was in a sweat and the wind freezing cold. His feet were soaked; his trousers, wet halfway to his knees, clung to his legs. He began to shiver and his shivering increased until he couldn't stop his teeth from chattering.

He knew he had to get inside, or get a coat. He started to walk. He'd get his coat and go somewhere, some place where he could think and not have to look at psychotic chimps, not hear Helverson's cool voice, not see the accusations in Anne's eyes. A bar, he thought. A dark, quiet bar where no one knew him.

He made a turn at the next intersecting path and left the park, walked two blocks to a business district, and found a bar. He ordered a double bourbon and before he touched it he called his apartment. He didn't ask to

speak to Anne, but said to Ronnie, "Can you stay until
I get there? It's important that she isn't left alone. And,
Ronnie, don't let anyone at all in except me. No one.
Do you understand?"

He hung up. There was nothing else he had to do,
he thought, except get drunk. Nothing else at all.

Somewhere, Anne thought, way back in her head, or
in her soul if it existed, she understood what Helverson
had been saying, demanding of her, but she couldn't
put it into words. She couldn't frame it in logical se-
quences so she could examine it and find its flaws. It
hung over her like some ghastly repression that was
responsible for flashes of terror that appeared inexpli-
cably, just came and went at will. She shuddered and
felt chilled and knew no cause for the mounting fear.

Ronnie brought lunch and Anne pushed it around on
her plate until Ronnie took it away again. Shortly after
that, Ronnie came back and said Gus was there, would
she see him, should Ronnie let him in?

Anne looked at Ronnie questioningly. Not see him?
It wouldn't have occurred to her not to see him. Gus
was brought in.

"Anne, is Clark here?"

"No."

"Goddamn it! Did he call, anything?"

"Edward Helverson came to see me," she said slowly. "He wants to put me in a hospital, doesn't he?"

Gus nodded. "Son of a bitch," he muttered. "That's
why he locked us up in the conference room."

"Can he do it, Gus?"

"I don't know. Do you have a lawyer?"

Anne swallowed hard. The flood of terror washed
over her again. She waited for it to subside, and said,
"You think he can, don't you?"

"Anne, I tell you I don't know. I'll write down a
couple of names, good men, both of them. One will be
able to see you today, I'm sure. Say it's an emergency,
that I sent you. Okay?"

She took the slip of notepaper and put it in her pocket without looking at it. "What did Deena say?"

"Nothing to me directly. I couldn't find her after our meeting. But I made Bob tell me. She said you, you accused her of an assault. A sexual assault. She said you were irrational, hysterical, completely out of control."

Anne felt tears scalding her eyes. Furiously she blinked them back. "And they believe her. The clincher. I didn't accuse her of anything, Gus. I didn't."

He sighed. "It's a real mess, Anne. Helverson hopes you took it, of course. You'd better call one of those lawyers." He stood up and walked jerkily to the window. "All this because Clark broke down one time and acted human!"

"It wasn't what he did," Anne said almost inaudibly. "It was what I had done. I wanted to be whole again, but on my terms. And that night . . . I hadn't realized until then that I blamed him for everything, and I hated him like I've never hated anyone in my life. Terrible thoughts came and went. Things like how much he had hurt me. I'm crippled, you know. He knows it. I'll have a limp the rest of my life. His mark. That's what I thought. And I thought of how much pain I owed him. How I wanted to see him hurt. I understood all at once how much I had been hiding from myself, and I felt like a child who screams and cries and says, 'I won't!' and all the while knows she is powerless."

She lighted a cigarette and watched the smoke. "After that kind of self-revelation, what can you do? You can yield, pretend it away, bury it again and be that child, forever hating, showing it in a thousand little ways every day. Or you can leave it. And if you've gone this far, you know burying it simply means it will ooze out when you least expect it. The hatred waits and strikes when the other is most vulnerable. It's a destroying kind of thing that will kill the hater and the hated."

Gus turned and yelled at her, "You can't hate him

for loving you! You need him now! Can't you see that?
He gave in to intolerable pressure. He couldn't keep up
a superman role. Because he's mad with love! How can
you hate him for that?"

She bowed her head. "You really don't understand,
do you? I don't hate him now. I can almost understand
him, I think. Gus, he would rather believe I used the
*pa,* that I am going crazy, that I'll become a psycho-
pathic killer, than face the truth. That isn't love. That's
the wail of a child who'd rather see the end of the
world than give up his grubby teddy bear."

"What goddamn fucking truth?"

"It doesn't matter. Let's leave it alone."

Gus pulled his chair close to hers and took her hand.
"Anne, maybe you and Clark have a real problem. I
don't know. I don't want to know. But put it aside
now, for God's sake! Anne, you need him now. You
need him to support you and hold them off! Let him
off the hook so he can get his head straightened out
again. He's in a daze, doesn't know his ass from a tea
kettle. And you need him, Anne. Take him back. Tell
him you don't want a separation. Let him help you."

She shook her head. "It would be a lie. He'd
know."

"He wouldn't know! You idiot! If you told him you
were the Queen of Sheba he'd believe it!"

Again she shook her head. "It isn't that simple. All
the strands come together here, don't they, Gus? The
human tests, what Clark believes, what Deena told
them. This is the spot marked X, isn't it?"

"Do you know what it will be to go in the hospital
with them thinking you've used the stuff? Daily blood
tests! Maybe two, three times a day. Tests of everything. Metabolism. Enzymes. Tubes down your stomach, up your ass. Hours with psychiatrists, perception
tests, eye tests. Drugs. The stuff you had to take before
to raise your blood pressure. Stress experiments. Your
own goddamn stress experiments! Twenty-four-hour
observation! Have you thought it through, Anne?"

When the color drained from her face, she could feel

it. Like drawing a blind, she thought. It was just like drawing a blind.

Gus was rubbing her hand and now his voice was low and hoarse. "Anne, listen to me. I didn't want to do that to you, but you have to understand. If you didn't take the stuff, there has to be a way to prove it. Let Clark say he was mistaken. Your notebooks. Something. There has to be a way. A diary?"

"I've thought," she said. "There isn't. During the really bad times I didn't write in the diary. Too dreary. Too repetitive. They can't start the human tests, Gus. You can't let them. Something's wrong with it and we all know it. Helverson must know it. Why does he say he'll go ahead?"

"Ambition. He thinks human testing will let us find the flaw in the coming months instead of having to wait years. And probably he's right about that. Besides, no one will ever know. The women will get the best of care, his conscience will be clear, and the rest of the world, when they get the stuff, will bless you and the company, and indirectly him. He'll get what he's after. It's a small enough risk for those gains."

"We don't even know if that percentage is right," Anne said. "Three out of twenty-three. Thirteen percent. That might mean sixty-five women, Gus! Sixty-five. What kind of facilities would they need to have the kind of care, the kind of observation you were talking about? What if that percentage isn't right? It could be twenty percent, or fifty. We don't know." She closed her eyes. "It could be all of them eventually."

"And even if it is all of them, if we find the cause or a way to control the effects, it would be a small price."

"You don't believe that."

"No, I don't believe it. We need time. You need Clark on your side, and between the three of us we might be able to get that time." He studied her for a moment, then took a deep breath. "I'd better get back. Maybe he's there now."

*     *     *

She hadn't been trained for success, Anne thought, after he had left, only for failure. Even her minor victories had been turned into failures. "Only second place? If you'd worked harder, it would have been first." "You made up your own bed? Look how lumpy it is! I'll have to do it over." "You won the scholarship? Tres has a new job! Nine thousand a year." "You're getting married? Tres has a baby son." "You got the job at Prather's? Your sister's husband won't let her work. They have a house-cleaning woman."

She knew how to handle failure. Work harder. But how would she have handled success? There was no way. It was inconceivable that anyone could be successful and cope with it.

She thought of her mother, only a housewife, she always said. Suspicious of Clark, of their work, of Anne's education. She believed the stones in the elephant were real. She still believed Anne was Clark's assistant at work. "He probably has a new girl to help him now. Have you seen her?" She could almost understand her mother, she thought. If Anne succeeded, it meant her mother had failed. At life. At everything. As if the two life styles were so incompatible that the one had to exclude the other.

And she could almost understand Clark. He hadn't been responsible for the accident; they both knew that. But he had welcomed it in some never acknowledged way. He had become more loving, more solicitous, more everything. He would love her more than ever if she were marred, he seemed to be saying, and she had rejected that because she had sensed under it another statement. He was safer now, that was what he felt. His mother knew, Anne thought. Intuitively she knew she had to handle him as the small boy, not the man, because he demanded it. He had needed it from Anne even more as success drew closer, and the accident had provided him the added assurance of her need for him. And then she had rejected him that night. He had said she was in shock, but that was wrong. He had been in shock. And he hadn't been able to face it but had leaped at the chance she had used the *pa*. If she was mentally unstable, her rejection was meaningless, not real, not a threat. He had no choice but to believe she had used the *pa*. And once more he was safe. Damned but safe.

*Crying in the dark won't turn on the sun.* Her grandmother had said that, she remembered. All right, Clark had to believe. Helverson had to believe. Deena, for God alone knew what reason, had to believe. And between them they would put her in a hospital. She held the arms of her chair hard to prevent her hands from shaking.

"No!" she said aloud. "I won't let them!"

## TWENTY-ONE

AT SEVEN, Clark woke up with a hangover. He was on his bed, still dressed as he had been the day before. He had dim, disconnected memories of the afternoon and night. The bar, a movie, because he had been so cold, another bar, a girl. Her room sometime after that. She had thrown him out with two dollars clenched in his fist. She had also called him a cab. "Good girl," he had said, over and over to the driver. "Heart of gold." His watch was missing. Heart of gold, watch of gold. Good girl.

Anne's door was closed and locked. If his head didn't ache so goddamn much, he'd kick it in, Clark thought. He made coffee, tried the door again, and sat down in the dining room. "You know the trouble with my wife?" he had said to the girl last night. "Yeah, she doesn't understand you."—"Wrong. She understands me too fucking much." He winced. He didn't think they had made it. He hadn't been able to get his clothes off. "You know what I'm going to do to her?" he had said.—"Walk out."—"Wrong. I'm going home and show her who's boss. That's what she needs. Uppi-

ty. She's uppity. She wants it, but she pretends."—
"Some women are like that."—"Wants to be domi-
nated, that's it. What she wants, to be dominated.
Overwhelmed."

Clark groaned and stood up. "Keerist!" he muttered.

Another memory: "Tell you about my wife?"—
"Yes, you did."—"Smart. She's smart. Smarter'n
me."— "You told me."—"Smart as hell."—"But you're
still boss. Right?"—"Right. That's exactly right. Exactly
right."

Anne heard Clark at her door that morning. She had
heard him come home, and after he had fallen across
his bed, she had gone into his room to see if he was all
right. She should stick a note to his pillow with a
dagger, she had thought, and resisted the impulse. "Kil-
roy was here!" affixed with a dagger. She had smiled
and returned to her room and locked the door behind
her.

After she was certain he was out of the apartment
she got up, and using her crutches awkwardly, but
better than the day before, she walked to the kitchen
and poured coffee. She looked at the crutches with a
gleam of triumph in her eyes. She had coffee and toast
and then went back to her room. She timed herself
going back. Five minutes. The triumph faded and she
regarded the crutches with loathing.

There was a typewriter on the small table now, and
many pages of typescript. She had worked on notes for
hours, had written letters, more work notes. She wasn't
finished, but she knew she would be in another hour at
the most. When Ronnie arrived at nine, Anne was at
work.

"Still?" Ronnie asked at the doorway. Her face
reflected deep concern as she looked at Anne. Yesterday she had called Dr. Radimer only to learn he was
due at the apartment that morning at nine. The news
had not lessened her concern.

"More coffee," Anne said, then looked up and
smiled. "Morning, Ronnie. Raining?"

"What else does it ever do around here?" She glanced at the other door, Clark's door, but he was gone. "Be back in a minute with coffee."

"Oh, Ronnie, no swimming this morning. Dr. Radimer's coming over."

"Anne, is there something wrong?" Ronnie asked then, entering the room, her umbrella dripping on the floor.

"Yes. You know it. After I talk to the doctor, I'll tell you, Ronnie." She turned again to the typewriter and began to type.

When Dr. Radimer arrived, Anne had Ronnie bring him coffee, and starting very slowly, speaking faster as she went, she told him everything. "I can't prove I didn't take it," she said. "But I'm afraid of the state institution. Mr. Helverson is right in saying I must be under observation, however, until there is no longer any doubt one way or the other."

"Bullshit!" Radimer said, explosively. "The biggest crock I've seen in a long time. Of course you can't go to one of the state hospitals! If you weren't crazy when you went in, you would be within a month!"

"You'll find some place for me?" Anne asked. "Get the papers for me to sign?"

"Yes! Take an hour, no more. Bloody Jesus! Goddamn chickenshit executives! You know what's ruining this country? Those goddamn chickenshit company men! *Ronnie!*"

Ronnie hurried in, examined Anne anxiously, and waited.

"Anne's going to a hospital. Mount Holly. Can you go, be with her?"

"Hospital? Anne?" Again Ronnie's eyes made a swift appraisal and she looked mystified. "I can go," she said.

"I'm leaving, be back in an hour. Ronnie, don't let anyone in here. No one, you hear? If you do, I'll skin you." Muttering obscenities, he left.

Ronnie went with him to lock the door and returned

to stand with hands on hips before Anne. "Now," she said. "Now, you just unload. Mount Holly!"

Clark had haunted the hallway outside Helverson's office all morning, but Helverson didn't show up. His secretary said repeatedly he would be late; if Clark would return to his office, she'd call . . . The son of a bitch used the private outside door, but sooner or later he would show, and Clark would be there. Gus found him and pulled him back to the lab.

"You're acting like an adolescent waiting for your girl's new boyfriend to show so you can punch him in the nose," he said.

Clark yanked free of his hand. "They can't have her! They can't have her!" He could think of nothing else.

Gus jerked him into his office and closed the door behind them. "Sit down! Time for melodrama is over, Clark. They've got the votes in the committee to do whatever they want. The best we can hope for is to get Anne into a private hospital somewhere."

"Sold out, Gus? What was the price?" Clark's voice was savage with hatred.

"I'm being realistic. If she used it, she belongs in a hospital. You want her to roll around on the floor in convulsions like Lola?"

"You son of a bitch! Company policy?"

Gus slapped him hard, then slapped him again. For a moment Clark swayed.

"You want to pull yourself together, or go out and hang on another one so you won't have to know what's happening?"

Clark shut his eyes, his fists slowly relaxed, and he sat down. Dully he said, "I owe you for that, Gus. What do you want me to do?"

"You have to tell them you're putting Anne in a private hospital, and make it stick, no matter what they say. Can you?"

"I'll keep her home. Hire a special nurse. Stay with her myself."

"That won't satisfy anyone. It has to be a hospital. Damn it, Clark! It has to be a hospital! You have to do it!"

"I can't."

"If you don't, you're turning her over to Grove and his gang. It's that simple, Clark. You do it or they will."

Clark's face was gray, eyes red-rimmed. Gus remembered what Anne had said. She had wanted to see him hurt. He turned to look out the window.

"You remember what Deena said about her fear of hospitals, Gus? It's true. A pathological fear of hospitals. She thought they took her grandmother to the hospital to kill her. Even knowing she thought that once, knowing why she's afraid, she has that kind of fear. They had to send her home too soon because she was making such a bad recovery there. And they'll hurt her. Every needle, each time they take blood, everything. How can I send her back, Gus? How?"

"You pick the lesser evil. It's all you can do."

Clark shook his head. "But I can't do it," he whispered. "She'd never forgive me. I'd lose her completely."

"And I'm telling you if you don't, you'll deserve whatever hell you find yourself frying in!"


Anne waited for Edward Helverson and wished her hands would not perspire so much. She wiped them again and lighted a cigarette and stubbed it out. Her mouth felt parched from smoking so much. Dr. Radimer paced, not talking now, not even cursing under his breath. Finally Ronnie came to say Helverson was there.

"I'll wait in the other room," Dr. Radimer said. "Call me when you want me." He left and Ronnie went to bring Helverson in.

"My dear, you didn't have to see me personally," Helverson said. "A phone call would have done. I can't stay more than a minute. A luncheon appointment, I'm afraid."

"I am ready to tell you my plans," Anne said, and her voice was crisp and steady. "I have signed myself in as a patient in Mount Holly Hospital, under the care of my physicians, Dr. Horace Radimer, and Dr. Samuel Erikson. It is already done. I have only to report in person for treatment to begin."

Helverson sat down and smiled gently at her. "I'm afraid that won't do, my dear. We discussed this, you see. We feel we must have some control over the treatment, not possible in a private hospital, you understand. And the sympathies of the doctors? Altogether different, you see."

"You don't understand, Mr. Helverson," Anne said. "I am not asking permission. I am telling you what I have done." Her hands were steady as she lighted a cigarette. "I have made out a statement for you in which I swear I am doing this of my own free will, that I understand there is a possibility I might have used the *pa* factor, and that I have no memory of having taken it. I believe it is sufficient. Also, I have given permission for certain experiments to be carried out, with the consent of my attending physician, and with the consent of Clark and Gus. If there is any dissent about the experiments or tests, Gus is to be the arbiter, the final choice his. My doctor has agreed this is necessary under the circumstances."

Helverson had stood up and now he sat down once more, a watchful, wary look on his lean face. Like a silver fox, she thought, watching a rabbit.

"I must say," Helverson said softly, "this is most reasonable. I believe we can all live with this agreement."

"The rest of it," Anne said, "is that you will not proceed with any human tests until a brain specialist, to be selected by Gus, is brought in and given time to assess our work and make his recommendations. However long he takes, you'll agree to wait. And if his report is negative, you will then withdraw the approved IND and wait for the solution of this problem before we submit it again."

Helverson leaned back and studied her. He didn't reply for several minutes, then he shook his head. "I don't think so, Anne. Legally we are free to take that next step. No fault could be found, because we do have the approved IND. No, I think you have stepped too far."

"If you don't agree," Anne said, and she could hear a new tightness in her voice, and didn't care: his renewed wariness meant he heard it too, "I'll go public with the work. I have written a dozen letters with sufficient details to permit anyone in this line to pick it up and carry on with it. The letters will be mailed to newspapers, to other companies, to universities, to journals, and to the FDA, if you go ahead without the explicit recommendation of the brain specialist Gus brings in." She could feel a pulse in her throat now, and she knew her hands were wet again. She didn't dry them.

Helverson got up and walked to the wall, where he studied the hanging from Venezuela. He touched the telescope. He went to the window and looked out over the wisteria tree to the park. "You're threatening me with blackmail," he said. "That's a crime, you know."

"So have me arrested."

"It's also a breach of contract. You'd be blackballed. You'd never work again, or teach. Back to the kitchen scrubbing pots and pans, my dear. And your husband, I'm afraid, would be tarred with the same brush."

"And that isn't a threat, I guess."

"No. That's the reality."

"Mr. Helverson, I didn't ask you here to bargain with you, or discuss this or anything else. I asked you here so I could tell you what I plan to do, what I have already done. Now you may leave."

For a moment his face became rigid, then he turned away. Presently he asked, "Have you discussed this with your husband, or Gus, anyone?"

"No. Only my doctor, and the attorney who is holding the letters." She paused, then added, "And I never will unless you force it."

"I see." Again he was silent, and when he turned to her again, he was smiling. "My dear Anne, I confess I've been absolutely wrong about you from the beginning. I didn't believe you thought the problem was so serious. Of course, it is your work and if you feel this strongly there is a flaw in it, the company wouldn't condone exposing others to such danger. Naturally we will take no chances on premature testing. My dear, you have my word, my solemn word, that we will not go into the next phase until a brain specialist agrees it is safe to do so. I rely on the expertise of others in these highly specialized areas, as you know, and I was made to understand by Dr. Klugman that we were ready to go to the next step."

There was fire in his eyes, and pools of ice, and admiration and hatred, Anne thought, and in his voice there was honey, and the ring of Carborundum on Carborundum. She watched him as he buttoned his coat.

"Now I really must leave. I'm afraid I shall be late, but I am glad we had this talk. You will enter the hospital when?"

"This evening."

"I see. Mount Holly. And you will be ready to commence the tests tonight? In the morning?"

"Whenever it is convenient."

"Good. At our committee meeting this afternoon I shall explain your decision and authorize Gus to bring in as many specialists as he feels necessary to expedite this research. And now may I wish you a speedy recovery, my dear." He paused a moment as if considering if he should approach her, decided against it, bowed and left the room.

Anne sat without moving until Ronnie and Dr. Radimer joined her. She was afraid she would start shaking if she moved.

"That silver-plated bastard!" Ronnie said. "He wanted to know if we were alone here. I think he meant to send a goon squad here to snatch you or something. I introduced him to Dr. Radimer and said he was staying with you this afternoon. Should have seen his face. Looked like a kid who swallowed castor oil thinking it was honey."

Anne laughed and couldn't stop. Finally she gasped, "He wouldn't have tried anything like that."

Dr. Radimer scowled and muttered, "Goddamn chickenshit company men think they own the country, do what they want to with the people in it . . ." He looked at his watch. "Shit, I'll have patients sitting on patients. Clark coming in at noon?"

Anne nodded. "I asked Gus to bring him over. I'll tell them then."

"Okay. Helverson won't try anything. He'll find out he can't have you legally committed since you've already signed yourself in Mount Holly. Nothing he can do but bear down and take it. I'll see you every day or so at Mount Holly. I'll keep in close touch with Sam Erikson. What a crock of shit!" He stamped out angrily.

## TWENTY-TWO

GUS AND CLARK arrived before twelve. Clark glanced at the bed, covered with folded clothes, an open suitcase. Ronnie had been packing.

"It can't be true! I don't believe it. What did he say to make you do this?"

"'Sit down, Clark. You look awful. He didn't do anything. I did it. I want to tell you about a dream I had last night. Or maybe the night before. I don't remember when.

"I was walking on a street in a city none of us has ever seen. Trees everywhere, blooming flowers, bushes, each building white, like the Parthenon, set in its own green frame. Beautiful. There were women everywhere, all pregnant. They crowded around me, smiling, happy, pressing bouquets on me, so many bunches of flowers I couldn't hold them all and they began to slip through my fingers. When they hit the sidewalk, they shattered, like wineglasses, into tiny, colored shards. I was afraid and started to run, dripping flowers as I went, cutting my feet on the pieces. There was a trail of blood behind me, and the women were running after me. I couldn't lose them or gain ground, and they couldn't catch me. And we all cut up our feet on those pieces of flowers." She was shaking. Gus pulled a chair close to her and took her hand.

"Finally I came to the edge of the city and there was a high wall, so high it went out of sight. I turned and ran along the wall, trailing my hand along it, searching for a gate, a doorway, any way out. There wasn't any way out. Not for me. Not for them. I gave up. I just stopped and waited for them to catch me and I became more frightened than ever, more than I could bear. So I woke up."

"For Christ's sake, Anne! A dream! A lousy dream and you come around to this?" Clark yelled.

"I have to. There's no choice left now. I'm fighting to protect my work with everything I can use! That's all! It's good work and they shall not ruin it! If this is the only way I can save it, this is the way it has to be done."

"You don't have to go into any goddamn hospital! You're not crazy! They can't force you into a hospital!"

"Will you tell them and make them believe I didn't use the *pa?* Can you make them believe it? Do you believe it?"

The room became preternaturally quiet, as if they were in the void Anne had imagined so often. Accept it, she thought at him. Accept that there can be no guarantees, that we have problems, that we might not want each other when and if we ever face those problems. You can't bind me down, she cried silently. You can't tuck me on a shelf and lock the door and know I'll be there later.

Clark couldn't sort out the images that raced through his mind. The dead kitten, the baby chimps, Anne's stranger's eyes that examined him as if they never had seen him before. All he could coherently think was that he was losing her, and he didn't know why. Because he loved her, had forced love on her. Even as he thought that, he knew it was false, and there was no truth he could insert instead. "Anne," he cried, "the accident was my fault. A better driver might have avoided it. God knows I'll live with that the rest of my life!"

She was shaking her head impatiently. And he knew this was another falsehood. And again there was no truth to replace it. "I'll take you away!" he yelled. "You don't have to do it this way. I'll take you some place where we can get a good doctor for you. Where we can relax and rest and you can be treated . . ."

Gus held Anne's hand, and when it started to tremble again, he said, "Clark, why don't you get us all a drink. I think we can all use one about now."

Clark hurried from the room, relieved to be doing something. Give her a chance to reconsider, understand what he was offering. He would devote the rest of his life to caring for her, protecting her, loving her . . .

"There isn't any other way, is there, Gus?" Anne asked, almost pleading with him.

He squeezed her hand and stood up, slouched across the room to the hallway door and closed it. "No," he said. "What nails did you use to drive it into Helverson's hide?"

She shook her head. "He has his test subject, we have what we need—time. You'll see me each week, and if he goes ahead with the human tests, you'll tell me, won't you?"

He nodded. Then he nodded again and the questioning look left his face. "Honey, if I didn't have a perfectly good, usable wife, I'd propose right now."

She smiled, a fleeting expression that was replaced

by a look of haunting fear. In a whisper she said, "Gus, I'm so afraid."

"Yeah," he said. "I know." He kissed her forehead, crossed the room, and opened the door again. "I'll take you and Ronnie over there. What time?"

"Four."

He nodded. Clark returned with a tray of drinks, and after sipping hers, Anne said, "Clark, don't come to see me. It . . . it would be painful for both of us."

Clark put his glass down and looked at her bitterly for a moment, then turned and left. They heard the front door close hard.

"It's a hell of a life," Gus said and finished his own drink. He stood up. "Be back before four." He waved carelessly and ambled out after Clark.

Ronnie had gone on ahead, in order to have her own car available. The county road Gus was driving on now was winding through gentle hills and small farms. The road followed a stream, swollen with flood rains, brown with silt. The water lapped the edge of the road in many spots.

"You'll be all right," Gus said. "Of course, if you had taken the stuff it would be a different story. Not a nice one."

"How long have you known?"

"I don't know. I didn't think so, then thought maybe, then definitely no. Put myself in your place," he said, turning to grin slightly at her. "Easy enough to do, actually. That's funny, you know. You and me. I'd have done the same thing. It'll be painful, humiliating, offensive, disgusting . . . You know all that. But it will end."

"I know that, too," she said. She was looking straight ahead. "He'll probably get another job. Maybe teaching. He said once he'd like that. He'd be good."

"Yeah."

"We turn here."

He turned and very soon they turned again to a

small private road that ended at a gate with a guard-house. A uniformed man came to the side of the car.

"Dr. Clewiston?" he asked, looking at a notebook.

"I'm Anne Clewiston."

"And this gentleman?" He closed his notebook.

"Dr. Weinbacher," Gus said.

"I'll have to call for permission to let you enter, sir," the guard said. He looked again at Anne. "Your nurse is here already. She didn't mention someone else would be bringing you."

He started for the guardhouse and Anne opened the door. "I'll walk," she said. "Don't call."

"Anne, we'll wait," Gus said. "How far is the place?"

"Couple hundred yards," the guard said. "Can't see it from here, through that next gate, around those trees there. That gate isn't locked or anything. Just around the trees."

"I need the exercise," Anne said. "I haven't prac-ticed yet today."

Gus got out and helped her out, handed her the crutches.

"How long will your brain specialist take, Gus?" she asked then.

"He'll get here in ten days to two weeks, another two or three weeks after that, give or take a week."

She nodded. Six weeks. In six weeks she would be walking without the crutches. "See you, Gus," she said, and began to walk toward the gate. She didn't look back when the gate clanged behind her, but maintained her slow, deliberate progress. Gus watched as she opened the second gate and passed through it, closed it behind herself, and then continued toward the trees.

And in six weeks, he thought, he'd come back and take her away from here, back to the world. Eventually she'd go back to work, down at the bottom of the heap now. Maybe in ten years, or fifteen, or maybe never, they'd have answers, prove her right or wrong, and until then . . . No husband, a dream turned into nightmare, and still, he thought watching her halting walk, still, he'd say to her, "You've won, Anne. You've won." And they'd both know it was true.

She had reached the trees now. She didn't look back at him, didn't pause, and she turned the corner and vanished behind the mist-softened trees already swollen with the promise of spring.

# Keep Up With The BESTSELLERS!